In the sky, there is no distinct. ___ ____ ___ west; people create distinctions out of their own minds and then believe them to be true.

Siddhãrtha Gautama

YVETTE WEISS

A PASSAGE THROUGH TIME

Matador
9 De Montfort Mews
Leicester LE1 7FW, UK
Tel: (+44) 116 255 9311 / 9312
Email: books@troubador.co.uk
Web: www.troubador.co.uk/matador

ISBN 978-1906510-114

A Cataloguing-in-Publication (CIP) catalogue record for this book
is available from the British Library.

Mixed Sources
Product group from well-managed
forests and other controlled sources
www.fsc.org Cert no. TT-COC-2082
FSC © 1996 Forest Stewardship Council

Typeset in 10.5pt Palatino by Troubador Publishing Ltd, Leicester, UK
Printed in the UK by The Cromwell Press Ltd, Trowbridge, Wilts, UK

Matador is an imprint of Troubador Publishing Ltd

For my dearest Jay, Lesley and Noreen,
without your support and trust
this would still be a dormant dream.

PART I
THE ENCOUNTER

CHAPTER 1

Not even the comfort of a first class seat made it possible for Chris to sleep during the long overseas flight to Madrid. After the second round of the shops at Barajas airport, she felt exhausted. Chris checked her watch. Still three hours to go before the departure of the BA connecting flight to London. She was looking forward to seeing her friends again. She was also happy to be in her grandfather's country and felt safe knowing that she could stay there as long as she needed in order to begin the new life she planned for herself. Escaping from reality wasn't necessarily the solution to her problems, but her recent time at home had not helped to lift her spirits. She convinced herself that running away from everything had, after all, been the best decision and she was to be proved right. The memories that flooded her mind would soon cease to torment her.

She settled into a seat near to the gate for the London flight, hoping to sleep a little. On the seat someone had left a copy of one of the many trendy 'jet set' magazines. She flicked through the pages without interest except when she came across a good picture. Photography, which started as a hobby, had become the passion of her life and her profession; no good image ever passed unnoticed for she could immediately envisage the photographer choosing which camera to use, selecting the appropriate lens, the perfect angle and precise moment to take a shot to capture the perfect image. Just before laying the magazine down, her eyes caught the headline of an interview with a famous psychiatrist who specialised in paranormal phenomena. 'Over the last ten years,' the interviewee was saying, 'through my work with hundreds of patients, I have become convinced that we have not one, but many lives.'

"Uh no, thank you, I have more than enough trouble with the one that I have!" She closed her eyes trying to get some sleep despite the uncomfortable seats. The rest would do her good because she was certain that Anne and Patrick had planned a welcome celebration that night, which meant being out until late.

She was right. As soon as her friends had met her at Heathrow and Anne had lectured her on how terribly thin and worn out she looked, they announced that in order to celebrate her arrival they had reserved a table in a well known restaurant.

"Right, let's go," she said. "It won't do me any harm to start enjoying myself will it?"

Around two o'clock in the morning exhaustion overcame her and she could not hide her desire to go home.

It had taken them a good couple of hours to catch up on everything that had happened since they'd last met: Anne was still doing her eternal linguistic studies dedicating this year to oriental languages and was still working as an interpreter at Patrick's publishing company; he had become Director following his father's death almost a year ago, and just as they continued to work together, they also continued to share the same large four-floored old house in North London. Chris was aware of the renovations they had been doing to the house and what she saw when they arrived was to her taste. The rooms had been decorated with elegant simplicity and each had a welcoming feel; the only place still needing a great deal of work was the garden.

"If you fancy the idea and if the wonderful weather that we have in this city allows," Anne said with an ironic smile, "your help would be much appreciated."

The moment she entered her room she decided that the unpacking could wait, as she could hardly keep her eyes open. She got under the covers and soon slept soundly.

When the ringing of the telephone woke her with a start she looked at the clock and was shocked to see that it was past midday. No one answered the call, so she assumed that Anne had accompanied Patrick to the airport. His family, owners of an important vineyard situated a few kilometres from Strasbourg where he was born, had planned a big celebration for his sister's wedding and he had to be there for her.

Chris made herself a coffee, enjoyed a long shower, dressed in jeans and a T-shirt and, after leaving a note for Anne, went out.

It was almost sixteen years since she had first visited London with her grandfather. She was overcome with emotion remembering the day when he had come looking for her at school and, after giving her a hug, had put into her hands the envelope containing two tickets.

"It's time for you to learn more about the world, love. I promised your grandmother that I would take you to England and that's exactly what we are doing. I know she will be with us," he had said.

The news of the trip had caused tension at home as Chris's parents had absolutely refused to accept that a man of almost seventy years of age could travel alone with a girl of fifteen. Chris had never witnessed such serious words between her grandfather and her parents yet her mother's father had always known how to defend his right to spend time with his granddaughter. From the day she was born, she had been the light of her grandparents' lives.

It was only months after they returned from their trip that Chris found out why her parents had finally allowed her to go. The fabulously expensive house where her parents lived belonged to the old man; they were not prepared to give it up and so they caved in with their objections. Chris's disillusionment with their behaviour caused her to distance herself from them and naturally drew her even closer to her grandfather.

Whilst her parents criticized her ideas and opinions, her grandfather knew how to find the words that Chris needed. Without spoiling her, simply by helping her to see the various alternatives which life offered, the old man became her friend, confidante and guide. Even during the terrible time of her separation from her boyfriend Steve, when she felt unable to bear the pain, her grandfather had offered her support and eased her agony with his wise words.

One night, scarcely three weeks ago, her grandfather had called her to his room. He had given her a delicate but strong gold chain from which hung her grandparents' wedding rings.

"Wear these as a symbol of our oneness. I remember the day I met your grandmother. An old woman came up to us in the park and said that perhaps we were all part of a great soul. In that moment your grandmother and I felt that we had not just met but had rediscovered each other. Her death never really separated us and I am certain that very soon I will meet her again. You will also meet someone special before long Chris. Accept your feelings, knowing that life's paths are strange, unpredictable and surprising. Things happen for a reason, even if that reason is not shown to us at the time. Never forget that I'll always be with you. We'll always be together. And now sweetheart, give me a goodnight kiss and a hug and go in search of your dreams. Don't let anyone take them away from you, promise me!"

"I promise grandfather...I love you."

The following day when she woke, she went to see him knowing that she would find he had passed away. His face had a look of indescribable peace. It was then that Chris decided to leave her job, her family and her city to start a new life in England. London was her grandparents' home and the place where she would go.

Chapter 2

*I*n London, Chris walked aimlessly, trying to keep her mind blank. Finding herself on a main road she immediately felt the energy of thousands of people rushing this way and that with too many cars and the risk of crossing the road without being sure of looking in the right direction. This was not how she remembered London. When she had been here with her grandfather she hadn't felt that the city was stifling her and began to wonder whether a tranquil Caribbean island might not have been a better idea for her period of mourning, but then remembered the pleasure of seeing Anne and Patrick again. Anyway, she was here now and wouldn't allow herself to become discouraged. She stopped a cab and asked to be taken to St. James' Park where she admired the beautiful gardens and the pretty lake and walked for quite some time, thinking of everything and nothing, until she reached the Pergola in the Park. She ordered a coffee. Her earlier feelings of suffocation had been replaced by an immense peace; it was as if this place had reached out to welcome her, like when one returns home after a long time away. She was so mentally exhausted that she had no desire to question the sensation; she just wanted to enjoy it. She didn't notice how quickly time passed until she heard someone mention how late it was. It would be better to go back, because Anne would have returned a long time ago and would be waiting.

The famous London cabs and the double-deckers danced in and out of the narrow streets and the wider avenues. Some of the buses had their top deck open to the sky, the preserve of more adventurous tourists, ready to defy the autumn clouds which at any moment might open to release a downpour. And here also were the numerous London pubs, on every corner around the city. Some were resistant to the passage of time and indeed of centuries, others more modern but still keeping their character and all prepared to offer their customers a drink to drown their sorrows or liven up their celebrations.

Without a doubt, what most fascinated Chris was the mix of architectural styles. She had a definite preference for the Victorian era. From childhood she had enjoyed films which transported their audience back to that particular time. In solitary moments she sometimes imagined living back then and she felt a strange melancholy which she could not fully understand. She remembered the magazine that she had glanced at in Barajas. 'Could it be true?' she thought. 'And if I have had a previous life...might it have been in that time? No, it's completely crazy.' She brushed aside her confused thoughts.

When Chris arrived back, Anne was waiting for her, ready to take her to a mystery restaurant that she was sure Chris would love.

"At least you always said that you adored this food, so I hope I haven't made a mistake in the choice of eating place." And she hadn't. If there was an exotic food that Chris really loved, it was Thai.

Most of the evening was spent talking over old times, but towards the end Anne brought up the subject of Steve.

"Chris, you told me all about the death of your grandfather, but you still haven't said anything about Steve. What happened sweetie?"

Chris had been expecting the question. She knew it would do her good to unburden herself.

"Are you sure you want to know?"

"Of course I want to know."

"Well, it all started almost three years ago, during the celebration of our anniversary." Chris began to tell her friend.

"Happy anniversary, sweetheart," Steve said smiling and holding his glass of champagne, "I hope we'll have many more moments like this. Thank you for being in my life and for making me the happiest man on earth."

"Happy anniversary, my love, it's very easy to make you happy being so happy myself." Steve took an envelope from his pocket and handed it to Chris.

"What's this?" she asked taken by surprise. She wasn't expecting any presents.

"Open it and you'll see." She did and found two airline tickets inside.

"Miami? Next week?"

"Well... not exactly Miami, baby, although I need to be there for a business meeting next Thursday. I thought we could use the opportunity and spend a week in the Bahamas."

Later that night, lying next to each other after making love, Steve said: "Remember that guy I told you about, the one who asked me to be his exclusive representative?"

"Uh-huh?" Chris muffled.

"Well... I decided to accept."

"Well done! Oh sweetheart, I'm so proud of you!"

The following years the business did extraordinarily well. One day she decided to bring forward her return from one of her trips. Chris thought she could surprise him. She little knew she was the one to be surprised.

Once in their flat, she could hardly move around. There were boxes everywhere. She managed to get to the bedroom to leave her suitcase. The room was chaos but she was sure Steve had a good reason for leaving it like that. After all, he didn't use to store work stuff in the flat. She went to the kitchen for a drink and wandered between the huge boxes, dipping in here and there, curious. Each contained generic-looking DVDs. Chris picked one at random, popped it into the machine, and crouched in front of the TV. And if it hadn't been for her curiosity, she would never have discovered what she did. The first few minutes were about new computer developments and guidelines to use different programmes but the next minute she was shocked. She got up and picked another DVD. Exactly the same, the first minutes of guidelines and then it changed. Every single DVD in the boxes contained child porn. She looked around and saw the door to the study shut. They never shut it. She walked towards it and opened it almost afraid of whatever she would find. There were a few more boxes and on top of the desk, Steve's briefcase. She moved slowly towards it and laid her hands on it. It was open. She saw a newspaper and underneath, to her amazement, the bag with the white powder. She felt sick. Please, let him have a good explanation for this, aware she was being too naive. The main door was opened and two people came in, laughing. One of them was Steve, the other a woman.

"Baby, you shouldn't have left it on, you know what happens to me when I watch it..." he said, groping the woman like an animal avid for sex. Chris just stood there, frozen and pale, until he turned and saw her and froze for a second but then he jumped towards her.

"Oh my God, Chris! What... what are you doing here? Baby... let me explain..."

Chris pushed him away, grabbed her keys and her bag and run out, towards the stairs and the parking.

"Chris!" she heard him calling.

She drove for hours around the city without a destination, too horrified to cry, too disturbed to think. She could hear her mobile phone calling and receiving messages, but she didn't have the strength to talk to anybody. She spent the night in a hotel. The next day when she went back to the apartment to pick up her stuff, Steve was there.

"Baby, please let me explain..." he was in a state which Chris had never seen before, unshaved, his hair ruffled, his shirt crumpled up and he was smoking.

"I couldn't say no, when I got the first shipment of boxes... I regretted so much... I tried to get out of the business but I... I promise baby, I will get rid of..." Chris didn't let him go on.

"When did you start lying to me, Steve?"

"Sweetheart, I'm so sorry, please let me explain..." he tried to hold her hand but she moved it away with a sickening look.

"Don't Steve, don't. Don't touch me and don't humiliate yourself like this. Whatever you say is worthless. I'm here just to get my clothes."

"Oh baby, please don't leave me." Steve was begging her with tearful eyes.

"It's too late. You should have known better before getting involved in this, before betraying my love, my trust, before betraying yourself... and you should leave too..." it was hard for Chris to speak, words didn't come easy. "You should leave too because I won't lie if somebody asks me. I won't lie like you did to me," Chris said while throwing her clothes into another big suitcase. Her heart was beating so loud that she thought he could hear it too.

"Please Chris; for God's sake, please forgive me!"

"I loved you, Steve. I loved you so much! I never thought you could stoop so low," she said with tears in her eyes and closed the door behind her.

Anne was holding her friend's hand.

"I left him there, a human wreck. I went to my grandfather and told him everything. He hugged me and I felt... oh Anne, I felt that somehow he knew my relationship to Steve would end badly. He comforted me as he always did. Not like my parents." Anne made a dismissive gesture. It was no secret that she didn't like them.

"When they found out, you can't imagine the scene they and my dear sister made. God had punished me, my mother said. I'd been asking for it, my father added. He told me I was a fallen woman and my sister said that I got what I deserved. And yet for me they were irrelevant. The only opinion I cared about was my granddad's." Chris thought for a moment. "You know, I could never understand, and I still can't, how my parents have the gall to preach so much about God and love. My granddad took me away from there and we went to the beach house. He told me he would no longer tolerate the way his daughter treated me and that he would change his Will and leave everything to me. He knew that would really shock them, give them what they deserved. But I asked him not to do it."

"What? After the way they treated you? As if you were nobody? For God's sake Chris, you are their daughter!" replied Anne, incensed.

"What does it all matter Anne? You know I loved my granddad

and that the only thing I ever wanted was the beach house, the house where I spent so many happy times with my grandparents."

"What happened to Steve?"

"Some days later we heard that the police had raided both the office and his apartment and that he'd flown the country. During the weeks that followed he bombarded me with telephone calls, begging me to please give him a second chance, that he couldn't live without me, that he loved me, that he was sorry and, more than once, I felt like surrendering to his words and promises, longing for his love. I had to force myself to remember all his lies and him caressing that woman and finally I stopped taking his calls. Then he started calling my friends until they got really bored and told him there was nothing he could do, that he should forget me. Then... my granddad passed away and a few days after his death his lawyer called us for the reading of the Will. We found out that he had left everything to me. My parents and my sister went ballistic, you should have seen them. But I told them not to worry, that I wouldn't throw them onto the street, that they could keep the house." Chris smiled.

"It wasn't enough for them! They accused me of having influenced my granddad against his own daughter and warned me not to expect any thanks from them. At that point I got up and told the lawyer that I would be in contact and I told them that I had long ago stopped expecting anything from them. So, here I am!"

"Yes, here you are," said Anne, "but how are you?"

"I just am, I guess. I breathe, I move around, but I feel empty. You know how much I loved Steve. Luckily my granddad was there for me, but when he died, Anne, call it cowardice or whatever you like but I couldn't stay there. I knew it wouldn't matter where I went in the city; memories of the two of them followed me everywhere. I resigned from my job, sorted everything out and, like I said, here I am. I shall see how things go here, I might go back, but I am not sure right now. I feel a bit more relaxed here and I hope the unhappy memories of Steve will fade and I will eventually get over him. But my granddad... oh Anne, I miss him so much!"

"Sweetie, I don't know what to say to ease your pain."

"Don't worry, there is nothing to say. I suppose it's just a question of time."

"Right," Anne said a few seconds later, grasping her hands together, "perhaps it will cheer you up to know Patrick and I have decided to take the holiday which we have been putting off for so long. That will give us more time to be with you, we can hang out, meet people and, who knows, find things to do to help you forget."

"I really appreciate that. I'm looking forward to re-discovering London and I could do with some decent company."

CHAPTER 3

*T*he following day, they decided to go out early. Their intention was to go for a stroll, do a bit of shopping and find a place to sit and chat over a coffee. When they reached Upper Street, Anne was delighted to see a friend coming towards them. Chris gently refused the idea of being introduced.

"Maybe another time, you take your time to have a chat if you want to. I'll wait for you in Heggarty's." Anne protested but finally agreed and went.

Chris had discovered the bookshop the day before and was keen to browse around it. She found herself on the pedestrian crossing, waiting for the light to change, looking back in the direction Anne had gone to greet her friend. To her right she noticed The Mall, a small antiques market which she would doubtless visit on another day. It was then that it happened.

She didn't know where all the mist had come from. She felt a shiver run down her back and briefly regretted having trusted the blue sky. In less than a minute the mist had become so thick that she was unable to see the other side of the road. There was no sound, absolutely nothing, only a sepulchral silence.

What had happened to all the noise? How was it possible that a sudden mist could obscure everything? Chris desperately wanted to feel the sun breaking through in order to continue her walk, but her wish went unheard. Some minutes passed in this illusory, white death and she began to worry. This was not normal, her shivers were not normal, the silence was not normal. Suddenly she heard a faint noise in the distance which seemed familiar to her but she couldn't place it. Chris strained to see something but there was nothing. A few seconds later the noise became louder and more distinct. She had seen them and heard them before, but that was not the rhythmic clip-clop of the mounted police. It was the sound of mad horsemen charging about. Her body trembled, wanting to move but incapable of doing so. How could she know where to go to be safe?

Suddenly something hit her and knocked her off her feet. She felt she was falling apart. She fell to the ground, hitting her head. Everything started to go dark around her and the mist disappeared only to be replaced by the blackness which dragged her slowly into unconsciousness. There was nothing there, only an enormous void.

Chris strained her eyes one final time but the weight of her eyelids defeated her. It was as if an immense curtain was falling in front of her, putting an end to the theatrical drama in which she was the lead. Her thoughts drifted away and shadows closed in. In her last conscious moment she lifted her hand and held tight to the chain around her neck.

"Granddad..." she murmured, before she fainted.

The throbbing in her head brought her back to consciousness. What had happened? Where was she? She felt the burning heat of the sun's rays on her face and body. And then she remembered, remembered the cold, thick mist and realized that this was not a dream. The pain that she felt all over her body was proof of it. Now there was no mist. She lay there until she realized with surprise that there was no pavement. She found herself lying on a verge, in long, fresh and sweet-smelling grass. She lifted herself up to look around.

"What...?" Chris could not believe what she was seeing, only emptiness. There was nothing but countryside, bushes and treetops dancing in the wind, birds swirling in the air above and the sound of water, a river flowing nearby. Where on earth had the city gone? What had happened? Much as she wanted to believe that she was dreaming, she could not: this was real.

She turned around and saw there was someone lying next to her. A body covered by a dark brown cape, at one end some strange shoes and at the other a hat, a mix of tricorne and turban. She tentatively touched the body to reassure herself that it was breathing. She found a pulse, albeit a weak one and her spirits rose. At least she was not entirely alone in this place. She uncovered the face and was shocked to see it completely covered in blood and dirt. Instinctively she pulled herself up and searched for the river. She carefully dragged the body the short distance to the bank, tore off a piece of the cape to soak it in the water and started cleaning away the blood. Removing the strange headgear, Chris gave a cry of surprise. It was a woman laying there, a young black woman, who for a few seconds opened her eyes, stared fixedly at Chris, tried to say something but then slipped back into unconsciousness. Chris wondered who she could be; she remembered the noise of the horses and frantically tried to understand what was going on. Maybe the woman would be able to answer her questions, but she would have to wait until she was in a fit state to speak. Chris finished cleansing her wounds and sat down beside her to try to bring some sort of order to the situation.

The only logical explanation was that someone was playing a preposterous joke on her, perhaps to distract her from her recent troubles. Some joke! She was sure Anne and Patrick were involved, but why go to so much trouble for this? She couldn't imagine a good reason, but there was no other explanation. Most probably when that mist came down she tripped over and hit her head. Somebody must have given her something, and then they had taken her in a car to the outskirts of the city. Yes, something like that must have happened. She had heard of this type of incident somewhere. Chris despaired even more. Her story appeared to her extremely absurd and completely unconvincing but what else was she supposed to think? Better not to think at all until she could speak to her unknown companion.

She lifted her hand to her neck, searching for the strength of the rings. She wanted to believe that she'd be home soon – or at least in some restaurant or a pub, telling Anne off for her bad taste and most of all for the bump she received. That hadn't been strictly necessary. To calm herself down she thought of her grandfather and his advice to never stop being positive even in the bleakest of moments. The image of the old man was so vivid that she became peaceful. Her head no longer ached, only a nagging pain in her leg remained.

Chris had never been extremely keen on tricks or practical jokes but she was fine and that was the most important thing. She looked at the young woman beside her and wondered if her presence was helping her to relax. She lent her back against a tree and looked at the time. Her watch had stopped. "What are you looking at?" she heard the woman asking.

"The time, but this thing is broken. I probably knocked it when I fell. How do you feel?"

The young woman ignored her question and instead said, "You speak very strangely, who are you?"

"I speak strangely? Maybe it's because I'm not from around here, how is your head?"

"Where are you from? Why are you dressed like that?" The interrogation went on.

"Listen, I asked you how you were, you could at least answer, couldn't you? You gave yourself a real crack on the head."

"My head is well, even if it hurts a little. Are you going to tell me what you are doing here?"

"You know that better than me, don't you? It's your joke, after all." Chris responded harshly, running out of patience with the conversation.

"Why should I know what you are doing here? What is a joke? I don't understand you, you are strange."

"Great, thank you. You don't look very normal to me either, dressed in these things. But I guess everyone dresses as they like, don't they?"

"Are you going to tell me who you are?" the young woman repeated.

"Who I am? But didn't they tell you when you were all planning this madness?" Chris lowered her eyes shaking her head. "Look," she said, "I think there's a limit to any joke. Where are the others?"

"The others? Who are the others?"

"Oh please, stop the nonsense, will you?" she yelled, "How do I get home?"

"Where is your home?" The woman asked gazing fixedly at Chris.

"Where's my...?" The question disconcerted Chris and made her think she didn't have a home anymore. "I don't live in London, I live on the other side of the world, but...forget it. It really doesn't matter. Just tell me how to get back to the city."

"You live over the sea?" The young woman looked astonished. "And you want to go back to the city, have you been to London before?"

"Have I been to London? Look, it's really none of my business if you are high or drunk or whatever, I just need to go back."

"Go back? Go back where?"

"To London, damn it! Where else could I go?" Chris thought she was very close to losing her mind and stood up.

"I am going to London, if you want to come with me, but it will be dangerous if they see you with me. They will think you are helping me," she said with conviction.

"What do you mean by helping you and why should it be dangerous?"

"Well, even though you did not help me it will still be dangerous if they see you with me and your being white..."

"Hey, wait a minute. Being white?" Chris was puzzled. "Look, if you've got a problem with my being white, that's your business, but I don't think that in the 21st century – and even less in London – your racial prejudices are very up to date! I don't mind if anybody sees me with you. And finally, if it upsets you I have no problem at all going by myself, just tell me how to get to the city, ok?" The woman looked shocked.

"What's wrong? Did I say something to offend you?" Chris asked ironically. The last thing Chris wanted was to be friends with this strange woman.

"You said...21st century?"

"Oh please," Chris grimaced and thought for a few seconds. "Don't tell me that part of this charade is to make me believe that we're in another century? And let me see..." she put her fingers to her temple as if in thought, "you are a slave, fleeing from your

English masters. Let me tell you something, as soon as I get back, Anne is going to regret this stupid joke. I'm going to pack up my stuff and move to a hotel!"

"I don't understand what you are saying, Stranger, and I do not know your friends. But I *am* a slave and I *am* fleeing, and I do not intend to return. I will go to London and I will purchase my passage on the boat. I can pay!" The woman got up, pulled a bag from under her clothes and showed it to Chris. "Look, I have the means!" Chris's mouth fell open. She was no expert when it came to jewels, but she was perfectly capable of recognising real gold when she saw it. She picked up a few pieces and realised she was looking at a fortune in gold rings, diamonds, bracelets and broaches.

"What...what's going on here? What is all this?" Certainly no joke could go this far.

The women fell silent: both heard the same noise. There it was again, the sound of galloping horses. Only this time the hooves were hitting not road, but earth.

"It is them, we must hide!" the young black woman murmured and hid the jewels quickly.

"No way," said Chris, "this time I'm not falling for it." But just as she was about to get up and meet those whom she thought were her friends, she was pulled to the ground and then into the thickets. The woman held her down and covered her and herself with branches and dry leaves.

The men stopped their horses just a few metres away. Chris heard them shout things she did not understand and their voices didn't sound familiar. She tried to get a better look at them but only managed to make out the back of one of them. He was wearing a hat and had long, untidy and dirty hair. He also wore a cape, fastened with a belt from which hung a rope, chains and an enormous dagger, and across his back, a musket with a bayonet. The woman covered Chris's mouth with her hand to avoid them being heard. The men kicked their horses and left. Once they had disappeared from view, the girl muttered:

"More slaves must have escaped, for they wouldn't send so many hunters just for me." Chris realised this wasn't a game.

"Hunters?" she asked, while her face turned pale.

"Yes, slave hunters."

"But... slavery was abolished centuries ago, around here during the eighteenth century!"

"You are very strange, you know? This is the eighteenth century, in the year 1780! Now will you tell me who you are?" she demanded.

CHAPTER 4

"My name is Chris," she responded like a robot obeying a master's voice.

"I am called Sarah."

Chris was not listening. She was in shock and staring into space. 1780? How was that possible?

"You said that you live on the other side of the world, how did you come here?" the young woman interrupted her thoughts.

"Hum? You...you wouldn't believe it if I told you," Chris looked away and whispered, "Surely it's not possible...what did you say your name was?"

"Sarah," she repeated smiling with a puzzled frown, "What is wrong, Stranger?"

"If this isn't a joke, you're not going to believe it."

"What will I not believe?"

"Something that is just impossible."

Sarah took something out of a bag she was carrying and started eating. "Would you like some?" she offered.

Chris shook her head. How could anyone think of eating at a time like this?

"What is this impossible thing?" Sarah persisted.

"All this, the things that happened to me, how I got here..."

Sarah drank from some sort of bottle made from animal skin and began to talk. "When I was a child," she paused to chew another piece of whatever she was eating and put the rest back in her bag, "my grandfather used to talk to me about other worlds far beyond the horizon, where slaves were treated like human beings. I did not believe in those worlds. But it made him happy to tell me these stories and if he was happy, I was happy. Later it occurred to me that he told me about them to teach me to dream and to fight for my dreams." She sighed deeply before continuing.

"When the slave traders arrived at my village in Africa, we were captured and put in chains and brought to England to serve men who called themselves our masters. And as time passed, I realized that it was my grandfather's dream which kept us alive. I also learned from our masters that there is another land beyond the horizon, south of the place they called the West Indies." Sarah's eyes looked sad.

16

"On his deathbed I promised him I would not rest until I reached that new world and he promised me his spirit would always be with me, protecting me. Now you tell me that you came to England from beyond the ocean. That means the stories my grandfather told me were true and it is not impossible for me to fulfil my dream and reach these lands!"

The young woman fell silent and Chris decided she had nothing to lose in telling Sarah about the *impossible* thing she had referred to. She had bigger problems and one more would make no difference. And so what if Sarah thought she was mad? Anyway if in the end the whole thing was a joke, certainly this would put an end to it. Playing the fool was worth the laugh if it meant going back to normality.

"You told me that this is the year of 1780."

"Yes."

Chris was gazing down when she said, "Sarah, until a few hours ago, I was living in the future, more than two hundred years in the future." There were no hoots of laughter, not even a chuckle, there was just silence. Chris looked up, surprised by the lack of reaction. Their eyes met and stayed locked for what seemed to Chris like an eternity. A sudden and unexpected shiver ran down her body and ended up as a stabbing pain in her stomach. Chris blushed, almost ashamed and feeling uneasy with Sarah's piercing look. It seemed to her that this woman could read from her eyes her most hidden secrets. Chris glanced down at her watch and unfastened the strap. She passed it to Sarah, who only then looked down. Then Chris opened her bag and emptied out the contents: her passport; credit cards; loose change; a few pictures and lastly her little pocket calculator.

"Do any of these objects mean anything to you?" Sarah picked them up one by one and studied them carefully, looking obliquely at Chris.

"They are all very strange," she said and handed them back after rolling them in her hands, keeping only the pictures.

"In my world these are everyday objects." Only after a long silence, Sarah spoke quietly.

"It is true, you come from another world, from another time." Her statement showed that Sarah was absorbing this fascinating fact. Chris was amazed with Sarah's calm reaction and her words.

"Many times at night before going to sleep, I have thought about what lies beyond those stars and whether we really are capable of seeing everything that exists." After another long pause she added, "I don't know why, but I believe you, Stranger."

"I thought you'd say I was mad." Chris could not deny she felt pleased and she smiled, relaxed.

"No, I don't believe you're mad. What I do believe is that if they find you and you repeat what you've just told me, many people will want to condemn you. The slave-hunters will not hesitate in killing you, even more than killing me!"

"That means..."

"That means that we should stay together and if possible, I will help you to return to your home."

"Oh, right!" Chris burst out with a hoot of false laughter, "First we're going to meet a mad scientist who has discovered the time machine. Then we'll ask him to set it for two hundred years into the future and then I'll suddenly appear in the middle of Upper Street and..." she fell silent.

"What's wrong?" Sarah wanted to know.

"My friends! Oh my God. And there I was, thinking they were playing a trick on me. What will Anne think when she can't find me anywhere?"

"You must not think about that now, we must concentrate on getting to London and, if you want, with these jewels I can pay for you too."

"Pay for me? Pay for what?"

"You may come on the ship that I will..." Chris didn't let her finish the sentence. "Look, I'm not coming on any ship, Sarah. Where would a ship take me in the middle of the 18th century? No, I must stay here, I have to, I have to...heaven knows what I have to do!"

"You must have faith, Chris. You will see, by the time the ship sails in winter..."

"Winter? Winter? But that's two months away!"

"The sun will set soon and then we can start out without being found," Sarah ignored her last outburst.

Chris didn't know what to say, what to think or do. She kept quiet, shut her eyes and immediately found herself praying to her grandfather like never before in her life. She tried to think clearly. What options did she have? Stay here on her own, waiting for the mist to appear and carry her back or go with Sarah? If she stayed, how long would she survive? And if she went with Sarah to London, what would she find in an 18th century city which she knew in the 21st century?

Hiding her face in her arms, she tried to control her fear. Tears rolled down her cheeks.

"You must have faith," Sarah repeated, stroking her hair as if she wanted to calm her. Chris stood up and walked towards the riverbank where she flung herself down, inconsolable.

Did she have any options? Terrified of the idea of staying there on her own, she had to follow this woman and listen to her. She had to try and feel the faith about which Sarah spoke. Suddenly her grandfather's last words came to her mind, *"Things happen for a reason...."* Things had happened indeed, she thought. She had no idea what the reason could be, but she could only hope the answer would come. In the meantime, despite her fear and her desperate need for answers, until everything returned to normal she had to try to get used to surviving in this past into which she had been precipitated.

Sensing the fear in her new friend, Sarah came over and sat beside her. "Sometimes it helps to talk to calm the heart," she said in a whisper and looked at Chris hoping to inspire confidence in her.

"I was thinking," Chris's voice was scarcely audible, "about how this could possibly happen; how an unknown past could become the present and a familiar present could become simultaneously your past and your future..."

"You know?" said Sarah, "When you first told me that you came from the future and I looked into your eyes," she paused briefly, "It's very strange but I felt I knew you. You are here for a very good reason though I fear your time here may be brief."

"I know you are trying to make me feel better, Sarah, but..."

"No, no, listen. I'm not saying it to make you feel better, I'm telling you because I feel that it is true. I cannot explain it. I've felt this only once before and it was about my grandfather."

"Your grandfather?" Chris looked at her questioningly.

"A few days before he became ill, I started to feel distant from him. Each time I looked into his eyes, I saw in them a strange light and I felt inside that he wouldn't be with me for much longer. He asked me what troubled me, why I was sad. I told him and smiling he said he would never abandon me, he said he would always be with me." Chris thought with surprise that the same had happened with her grandfather.

Sarah continued: "A few days later he fell ill and I knew this time he wouldn't recover as he had several times before. Just as I felt that he would go soon, so I feel now that you will go as well."

Even more worried than before, she remembered the morning when she, herself, had woken and gone to her grandfather's room, knowing she would find him dead. Sarah's account with respect to the death of her grandfather had been true, just like her own experience.

"Are you saying...I'm going to die?"

"No, absolutely not!" Sarah hastened to explain. "I do feel that you will go but not that you will die. It is as if I knew that you will return to your right place and time."

"Oh, good, thank you. That makes me feel better!" She tried to make light of it, although she could not manage a smile.

"Chris, those portraits that you showed to me, one of them, the one of the young man, it made you sad. Don't worry, you will go back, I know you will return to your people, to him."

"Listen Sarah, I will try not to lose faith in my return. But it isn't for him that I want to go back. He was already in my past when I arrived here and he will stay there even if I do go back," she assured Sarah. Not even two hundred years would make her go back to Steve.

"Your heart is sad for him?"

Chris really did not want to explain to an escaped eighteenth century slave, the reasons she had to leave him so she said:

"It was sad, yes, because he was someone important in my life, but not anymore. His memory, as well the dreams we had together, have been shattered. The truth is...the truth is, I don't want to talk about it," she added, feeling she had said enough.

"Our dreams cannot be broken," Sarah said, "if they are it means they were only illusions. Real dreams are eternal." She paused then went on, "I will succeed in making mine reality and you will too, Stranger. You will return to your home."

Chris wondered if that was her dream now, or if she had any dreams at all. She wished she could have as much confidence as Sarah. If believing firmly in them could help, it must be worth a try.

A long silence fell between them and it was Sarah who eventually broke it.

"Tell me about your world."

"What would you like to know?"

"What is it like?"

"Do you really believe me Sarah? Do you really believe that until a few hours ago I was living in another time?"

"Why do you ask me? Did you lie to me?"

"No, I didn't lie. I have no reason to lie to you."

"Well then, tell me. How is your world?"

Chris began to describe the world from which she had come and Sarah listened intently to every word.

CHAPTER 5

As sunset fell they started off on their journey to London, thinking the best idea was to travel during the hours of darkness and hide from the hunters in the daylight. They would follow the course of the river so as not to lose their way. The problems would start when they reached the city, where they would need to find old Isaac, about whom Sarah's grandfather had often spoken. He was the only one who knew how to contact the captain of the ship which, in exchange for some of the jewels, could carry her to freedom. For this, they would need to go south. They walked for some hours through wild country, crossing dense woodland and wading through streams before they decided to rest for a while. Chris did not really care how long it took to get there. After all, what attraction was there in reaching a city which was two hundred years behind the one she had known? Who could she possibly meet there? She only knew one person and she was next to her.

Chris picked up Sarah's leather flask and staggered to the river bank, losing sight of her companion. Having quenched her thirst and refilled the flask with fresh water, she realized how easy it was to get lost and headed back to where Sarah was resting. She had only taken a few steps when she heard the noise of a branch breaking and seconds later Sarah's muffled scream. Chris froze for a moment but then immediately pulled herself together, instinctively grabbing a log. She was not sure if it would be of any use but at least she'd have something to defend herself with.

She ran back, following the sound of the noises and saw the man struggling to subdue Sarah, who was defending herself like a wildcat. Chris crept up behind him and without hesitation she landed a blow on his back. Unfortunately, this had no effect at all. Furious and growling, the man pushed Sarah away and turned to see what or who had attacked him. Chris was rooted to the spot with the useless weapon still in her hands. She trembled at the sight of his contorted, inhuman face. It was the face of a beast defending its prey. His drunken eyes were full of hatred; she was horrified by that look, but rather than dropping the log in fear, she desperately tightened her grip. The man turned his back on Sarah who, now recovered from her fall, launched herself at his feet knocking him off balance. Chris saw him falling towards her with his arms outstretched in a repugnant travesty of an embrace. Instinctively she moved to one side, raised the piece of wood a second time and, as his body passed beside her, she brought it down hard on his neck. His body bounced on the ground. To their surprise he began to rise up again. Not understanding how a head could withstand such a blow, and not wanting to give him a chance to straighten up, Chris hit him again with all the force of her fear. The man finally fell unconscious. Despite the fading light they could see blood spouting from the wound. Chris had split open the poor wretch's head. Her body unclenched and she let the wood fall. She realized that she had just killed someone.

That shock evaporated as she remembered Sarah, who was still on her knees on the ground behind her. After checking Sarah was all right, she hauled her up by the arm and forced her to run, almost dragging her. They ran as if the devil were after them until both fell, exhausted. After getting her breath back she looked around and said, "Now I really think we are lost, Sarah." But Sarah didn't seem to hear, she just stared at Chris.

"What's the matter?" Chris asked, aware of the fixed stare.

"Why did you save me?" Sarah whispered.

"Why did I...what are you talking about? I don't understand what kind of question is that?"

"Why did you save me?" Chris noted anger in her voice, mixed with sadness. She was disconcerted.

"Well, perhaps you'd have preferred me to leave you there with that animal without even try to help you? Would you have liked me to run away? I don't even want to think what he'd have done to you, for heaven's sake, Sarah!"

"You should have escaped while you had the chance, Chris. The hunter would just have taken me! Now...now my liberty is no longer mine...now it's not the most important thing."

"Wait, wait just a minute," Chris got up, moving to stand in front of Sarah, hands on hips, defiant, "Look, my head is spinning and I'm trying to understand why you're reacting like this. What harm was there in helping you? Or perhaps I should ask what you'd have done in my place? I really don't want to think that you'd have run off! Or would you just have stood there, watching? And anyway, what's all this about your freedom not being yours anymore?" She paused for breath and waited for Sarah to say something, but she remained silent and Chris continued speaking, more to herself this time, "If someone had said to me I would cross the time barrier and that just a few hours later I'd be questioned and criticized for doing something which I instinctively thought was the right thing to do..." She sat down again, rooted around in her bag and grabbed a cigarette. "So much for trying to quit," she said.

Sarah said nothing for a moment, but then she insisted: "Can't you understand it would have been simpler?"

"*What* would have been simpler?" Chris raised her eyebrows. "For whom? And what does this have to do with your freedom? I thought we had agreed to stick together."

"It is tradition among my people; if you face danger for defending someone and you overcome the danger, you have the right over the life you defended."

"Sarah, that's ridiculous, it seems to me just another form of slavery."

"My people do not consider it slavery. You offer your life to that person as a sign of gratitude until..."

"Until nothing, Sarah." She could not believe she was in the middle of the eighteenth century having this argument. "Heavens! Do you mean... are you telling me that your life belongs to me now, just because I helped you?"

"You saved my life, Chris. And now I shall follow you."

"That's enough now. This is absurd." Chris was very upset. She had just killed a man and now this? "I am not going to listen to you anymore."

"But my people believe..."

"I don't care what your people believe!" Chris shouted at her, staring fixedly into Sarah's eyes, emphasizing each word: "Let's make it clear; I didn't save your life so that you could give it to me. Helping you was a natural reaction. Your customs belong to your people, not to me, ok? And what's more, as you said yourself, you and me, we are unlikely to be together for long. We are helping each other. I will come with you until you find this ship of yours which will take you to freedom."

"It's because my skin is not like yours, isn't it?" Sarah hung her head miserably.

"What are you saying? You are totally wrong! Your being black has nothing to do with it. If you go to help someone, you don't first think about the colour of their skin. Will you please stop talking rubbish? I'm sure you'd have done the same for me." Chris sat down on a fallen tree.

"It's getting late, Sarah. We are lost, it's dark and we need to rest." As she spoke, she felt the weight of the last few hours on her shoulders. She didn't have the strength to go on. A twinge in her stomach reminded her that they had had no food at all. She tried not to think about it; at least they had water.

Noticing Sarah's silence, Chris began to gather as many dry leaves as she could, to cushion her from the hard ground. She lay down, looking at the stars.

'This is just a night's camping,' she thought, 'just one night in the open air, sleeping peacefully under the stars."

Her eyes began to close and she yielded to sleep. She hardly noticed when Sarah curled up and covered them both with her cloak.

Chris would most probably never admit it to anybody, but she was happy not to be living this adventure through time all alone.

CHAPTER 6

Chris woke up with the warm sun rays stroking her face gently and immediately thought of the weird dream she had had. She regretted deeply that she could not write it down straight after waking up. This dream had been incredibly real. Chris turned round and the hardness of the ground shocked her. She was definitely not in her bed, which meant that her dream was not a dream but a scary reality. Sarah was nowhere to be found. Sarah had said that because Chris had saved her life, she would have to follow Chris. She should be there then, but she was not. Sarah was gone and Chris was on her own in a place and time that did not belong to her. Her fear made her burst into tears like a lost child. "Granddad," she voiced in a moan, "I wish you were here!" It was difficult to breath and her vision became blurred. Chris grasped her grandparents' rings on the chain around her neck and closing her eyes, she lifted them to her lips.

She did not know how long she sat there, feeling hopeless and afraid. In desperation, she rummaged in her bag until she touched cool metal. Whilst her fingers unfolded the penknife, fragments of memories flashed through her mind. She put the sharp blade against a vein, imagining the redness of the blood that was soon to flow from it.

Chris thought of some of the many movies she had seen. Everything seemed so simple on the screen, to switch from past to future and from the future back to the past. She remembered herself enjoying every scene, imagining herself being part of the adventure. Later she would leave the cinema thinking how wonderful it would be, if what she had seen were true. And here she was now, in the middle of the worst nightmare! What if she was already dead? But what if death did not really exist? Where was God if there was one?

She was momentarily distracted by the reflection of a bright object next to her on the grass. It looked very much like the charm Sarah wore on a thin leather cord around her neck. Made of gold, its design was simple but eye-catching; a double circle containing a cross, its arms stretching as if reaching towards a meeting point. The pendant was not complete, though. Half of it had been twisted off. She stared at it. Why was it here? She was so tired of questions and adventures.

In recent days she might have gained some knowledge; whilst she now knew that crossing the gates of time was possible and that the spirit might endure, knowing these things did not help her ease the fear of remaining displaced forever.

The bright blade of her penknife shone again, as if calling her, challenging her, tempting her to take the easy way out. Was she brave enough to press it on her skin though? What if all this was a test? What if she found the courage to kill herself and in doing so wasted the opportunity to find an answer? Her grandfather's words came to her mind, 'Carry these rings as a symbol of our unity,' he had said. Chris relaxed her grip and put the knife away, closing her eyes and sighing deeply. She had to face her fate if she wanted answers. She had to surrender to whatever life decided to present to her. She had to try to understand what she could understand and accept what she could not change. Miraculously, as soon as she realized this, she started to feel different, stronger, as if a river of calmness was flooding her senses.

This new experience of peace and well-being was proof enough that she had taken the right decision.

Her only responsibility now was to survive, knowing that what had to happen would happen, whether she wanted it to or not. She had often wondered how strong and brave she was. Undoubtedly, the time had come to answer that question.

She thought of Sarah speaking about her grandfather, telling her he would never leave her, that he would always be with her, protecting her. Her grandfather had used similar words. And all of a sudden, the message was clear. By leaving the symbol behind, Sarah was telling her that fate would bring them together again. She needed to strengthen her faith now and stop wasting time wondering how this was to happen. The first step was to find food. There was plenty of firewood and water nearby.

She found some sweets in her bag and even if they were not much, they would stop her feeling hungry. The tiny first aid kit she had thought a good idea to bring was also still in her bag. Chris could not help smiling at the thought of Steve making fun of the amount of stuff she always took when she went away, even if it was for a few days. It was her turn to smile now. Meticulously she put everything back, picked up the cloak Sarah had left and decided to set off, following her instinct towards the highest hill she could see from there.

She walked almost all day, trying not to think of anything that would sadden or discourage her. She just had to learn how to enjoy and prolong this sense of well-being, no matter where she was. By the time Chris reached the top of the hill she was almost overcome with fatigue but the scene from the top was of such indescribable beauty, that she immediately forgot her tiredness and sat down to admire the view. The valley that lay before her was breathtaking: trees of every shape and size and wide swathes of green dotted with patches of wild flowers whilst the river wound through the countryside like a silver serpent. She stood there in astonishment enjoying the view, until she fixed upon something that looked like a cabin. She headed towards it.

Keeping to the trees, she approached the cabin but halted when she heard noise and hid again. A man appeared and walked out, staggering towards a pile of firewood. Even though his face was covered and she could not see him, for some unknown reason Chris quivered. The man, covered with a long filthy cape, struggled to bend down to pick up some logs and when he got up, his head became visible. Chris saw his bloodstained face. It was the same human beast she thought she had killed the day before. Here he was, still alive and standing very close by. Chris wanted to run but felt paralysed. She would wait long enough for him to go back in and then run away as quickly as she could. There was absolutely no need to face him again. The man's body was swaying from side to side, the firewood slipping from his arms. He was not only still alive, but still drunk, and on this occasion she was pleased to see someone so blind drunk that he could hardly stand. Even a toddler could easily run away from such a human wretch. Unfortunately, Chris realized her assessment was premature. As the man bent to pick up a log, another one fell from his grasp, and it was then that Chris saw, to her amazement, Sarah coming out of the cabin. Sarah had probably thought she could flee towards the trees, but he saw her, and he dropped his load except for one lump of wood which he hurled towards the young woman. His scream terrified Chris, and Sarah, hit by the missile, was knocked to the ground. He lurched towards her, grunted and kicked Sarah with such force that Chris could feel the blow.

Sarah lay motionless on the ground. He took hold of her arms and, as if carrying a dead animal, dragged her into the cabin. Brimming with anger but dazed with fear, Chris did not move. When he shut the door, she crawled towards the cabin and saw him through one of the side windows. Even in his drunken state he knew exactly what he was doing. He pushed Sarah's unconscious body into a corner and sat down at the table. He picked up the flask in both hands and drank from it, letting the liquid spill from his mouth. Chris felt nauseous as she watched him. There was no question about it, she had to get Sarah out somehow. She searched her bag again for the penknife and, although it was laughable as a weapon against that man, it was her only defence. She wanted to believe that while Sarah was unconscious, provided he had not killed her with that log, he would not bother her again. At some stage, whatever he was drinking had to take its toll and put him to sleep. That would be her only chance.

It seemed an endless wait. The man was sitting there, holding the flask with the clear intention of draining its contents. Finally he emptied it, and by then he could no longer keep his head up. The flask fell to the ground and smashed to pieces. Chris waited a moment to be sure he was not moving. Then, shaking from head to foot, she moved towards the door but failed to see the pitchfork lying on the ground. She trod on it and it hit the door. Chris almost collapsed with fear. She heard a groan, then silence. She took a deep breath, put the penknife back and picked up the pitchfork. She quietly opened the door. The air in the cabin hit her. It stank of alcohol and excrement. She was glad her stomach was empty. Surely even a slaughterhouse would be preferable to this.

Once in front of the man's body, everything happened too fast. Chris could not believe this was a human. He opened his eyes and, recognizing the intruder, he tried to stand up. Cursing and shouting words Chris didn't understand, he started to get up, but she gripped the pitchfork with all her might and before he could reach his feet, she launched herself at him. The prongs of the fork pierced his neck just as their eyes met. His face started to twitch and redden but he still found the strength to grasp the handle of the fork with both hands and wrench it out. Blood spurted everywhere, soaking everything. He took a couple of steps towards Chris but she dodged out of the way and he fell against the table, crushing it, spread-eagled on the ground. He made one last attempt to get up, but fell dead at Chris's feet.

Chris vomited in shuddering spasms. It took her a few minutes to recover and to realize that Sarah was still lying in a heap in the corner of the cabin. Chris prayed she was still alive but, frightened that she might be wrong, she approached slowly. She took Sarah gently in her arms and carried her out of the cabin. Struggling with the weight she walked slowly so as not to fall, until she finally reached the river, away from the horror of what had happened.

After laying Sarah's body on the grass, Chris sat motionless, staring at her, not daring to feel for a pulse again. This woman was no longer a stranger. She willed her to be alive. Carefully she cleaned Sarah's scratches and bruises, thinking how weak and defenceless she seemed. How many blows had she received, how many scars marked her body; all reminiscent of her life in slavery. Chris thought of their first encounter and silently promised she would do anything she could to help Sarah make her dream of freedom come true. If this was the reason why she was here, if this was her mission, she was determined to achieve it. She was lifting Sarah's head and shoulders to lay them on her lap when she heard her moan with pain. Chris stroked her face tenderly, tracing with her fingers the lines of her features. She had captured so many faces with her photographic shots, all different, all unique in their happiness or sadness, that she couldn't remember the last face which had drawn her attention. This woman had one of the most beautiful faces she had ever seen. Staring at her closed eyes she whispered: "You'll be fine, you'll see. I'll take care of you and we'll make your dream come true." And it seemed that from her unconsciousness Sarah had heard her words. Sarah's body relaxed in her arms, accepting her friend's protection.

CHAPTER 7

*A*gain the warm rays of the sun woke her, but the pleasure of its caress did not last, as lack of food made her stomach growl. At her side, Sarah tried to raise herself up but fell back down again, whining.

"It hurts," she moaned again, lifting one hand to her neck. Chris helped her to put her head on the cloak as a cushion.

"Try not to move Sarah; you received one hell of a blow."

"What...what happened with...?"

"Shush, don't speak; I'll tell you later, now you must rest."

"I didn't want you to..." Sarah insisted but Chris touched her fingers on her lips.

"Later," she said, "we can talk later when you feel better, ok? Now it's important that you recover, there is nothing to worry about right now." Well, at least that man would not bother them again, but Chris did not know what they might face later. "Listen Sarah, I need to go back to the cabin. Maybe I can find something to eat. Will you *please* promise not to move?" Sarah murmured assent.

She took the path back to the cabin, walking as quickly as her strength allowed. She could not take too much time. She should not leave Sarah on her own for too long.

The scene she found made her sick. The body was still there, but not as she had left it. Some wild animal had smelt the blood and decided to have a feast. Before she started vomiting again, Chris took his dagger and then covered what remained of the body with a cloak. She picked up a worn leather bag and put in it whatever she thought she could use: there were some knives; a couple of small bowls to eat from; a pot to boil water, a few bags with some sort of sun-dried meat preserved in salt. In the next room she found clean clothes inside a drawer.

It was unlikely that this man had ever worried too much about his looks. The cabin was probably not even his. She grabbed a couple of shirts not caring about the size which they could check later and two clean cloaks that would suit them very well and protect them from the cold at night. Not seeing any other useful things to take with her, she went out, happy to breathe fresh air. As she walked back, she picked some wild berries. Sarah welcomed her with a smile, happy to see her.

"The hunter?"

"You can forget about him." Chris explained what she had seen.

Looking up at her friend, Sarah said, "I owe you much more than my life, Stranger." Chris smiled at the sound of her nickname.

After having some of the dried meat and berries for breakfast Chris looked at Sarah and asked, "Why did you run away Sarah? Why did you leave the charm?"

"It was my grandfather's legacy," she began, "handed down from generation to generation. My people believe the symbol represents the individual souls that together form the unity of the spirit. For many years, my grandfather carried it believing that one day he'd find his twin soul. And so he did, when he was still very young. Since the first moment he saw my grandmother, he felt she was the one with whom to share the symbol, and he gave her part of it. Then, war was declared between my grandparents' village and another African village. After a long time of fighting, finally there was peace again and they were able to share their lives until she died. The rest of my family had died too, some killed in the war and some killed by a plague brought by outsiders. Before he died he gave the symbol to me and told me I would know when to share it with someone. My ancestors believed that if the charm was divided, both souls would feel the void of their twin and they would look for each other until they could meet again."

"It's a beautiful story, Sarah, but why did you leave it with me? I'm not your twin soul!"

"How do you know?"

"Well, I don't, but it's unlikely, it's just not possible. You're a woman and so am I and I...forget it, ok? And please don't run away again because you think it's less dangerous for me. I really think we should stay together." Chris had no idea why Sarah's words and actions made her so uneasy. She handed the pendant back to Sarah.

"Stranger, I don't know how life is lived in your world, but my grandfather always taught me that things happen for a reason even if those reasons are not immediately clear. My actions are led by my heart, please keep it."

"And what does your heart tell you Sarah?" Chris was not sure she really wanted to hear the answer to that question. She accepted the symbol back.

"That you're someone special. That there is a powerful force behind our meeting, mysterious though it is. Besides, I feel..." she went silent and Chris noticed she was slightly nervous.

"You feel *what*?" Why was she insisting on hearing something she wouldn't know how to deal with?

"I feel that you and I, that your soul and my soul have met for a second time. This was my reason for leaving you, Chris. I don't want you to be harmed for my sake."

Chris did not know what to say. She re-played the moment that she had felt the sharp pain in her stomach. Was it because she had somehow recognized Sarah as well? How could it be? She only knew that had this happened under normal circumstances, they could have been good friends.

"Why is your look so sad Chris?" Sarah tried to move, to take her hand, but felt immediately drowsy and her limbs seemed so heavy. Chris bent down to her.

"Please Sarah, try not to move, you need to stay still!"

"Tell me."

"Tell you what?" Chris tried to laugh off the question. She did not want to open up to anybody again.

"Why is there so much sadness in your eyes?" Sarah persisted.

"My grandfather also died Sarah. Not long ago and," she hesitated, "I really don't want to talk about it. What matters now is your recovery so that we can go after that ship. I promised I would help you and it's exactly what I'll do." Chris knew it was not the only reason for her sadness, but she felt too vulnerable to offer more.

"What are you afraid of Chris?"

"Afraid? I don't understand what you mean."

"Can I help you with your secret?"

"I don't have any secret, Sarah." She said defensively. "But if you insist, I can tell you. I don't easily make friends and having met someone like you..."

"Someone like me?" Sarah interrupted.

"Well, yes. You are a good person and under different circumstances we could have been good friends, but I guess when things return to normal it won't be possible to see each other again and..." It was time to shut up. Sarah didn't say anything either. Chris got up and walked to the river, while Sarah followed her with her eyes. Chris was disappointed with herself, at her lack of self-control. She could not disguise her emotions with this woman. Sarah's presence made her extremely nervous but at the same time she felt so good with her! She felt like protecting her, taking care of her. Chris realized she was losing the inner peace she had gained the previous day and she could not let it happen. She sat down watching the running crystal clear water and let the river take her unsettling feelings away in its stream.

The rest of the day went by slowly, too slowly, but there was nothing to be done about it. Whilst Sarah slept, Chris needed to stay alert to possible dangers. By the time Sarah awoke the sun had gone down and with it the temperature. Chris began to gather firewood.

"Do you know where we are?" She asked later watching the shape of the flames. Sarah, who had been silent until now answered,

"No, I only know that we are to follow the river. My grandfather told me."

"How did he know?"

"He was a very calm and reserved man. Lord Wesley liked him for that, and he always chose him as his servant whenever he had to go to London. Once there, my grandfather had often the chance to walk around on his own. Lord Wesley knew he would never do anything silly and would always go back to him, as long I was left at home, watched by his men with the other slaves. On his return he used to tell me about the places he had seen and that all the rivers in the vicinity lead to the Thames." Her voice sounded muffled and, although she looked much better, Chris could see that every word still sapped her of energy and that she was shaking. She rested her cool hand on the sick woman's forehead.

"You're burning with fever!" She tucked her up with the cloaks and searched in her first aid kit. She was pleased to find some pills that could help bring down the temperature. Sarah took them obediently. Chris stoked the fire and lay beside her praying for help, praying that nothing happened to Sarah who, half asleep, snuggled down unconsciously looking for warmth and protection. Chris however, stayed awake until very late.

CHAPTER 8

When Chris woke the next morning, Sarah was not there. Disappointed, she thought that her companion had run away again, but she was wrong. Sarah's voice floated up from the river in a gospel song. Following the notes, Chris found her sitting on a rock, cross-legged. Sarah was holding the pendant in one of her hands. Her song and her smooth movements were like a tribute to the river. Instinctively Chris got hold of her symbol. She wanted to share with Sarah the dream she had had but it seemed that would have to wait. Sarah sensed her presence and stopped singing.

"I was worshiping Obatalá, our love Goddess. If you ask her, she will protect you too, with her wisdom and enlightenment. I was also singing to my grandfather, thanking him for looking after us during the night," she said without turning around.

Chris was shocked. In her dream it was her grandfather who had been there, sitting close to them watching their sleep. Chris went back quickly, to check the fire. It was still burning, as if someone had fed it during the night. How could that be? It was hard to believe, but she knew it was as hard to believe as jumping from the future into the past as she had done. She sank to her knees. Sarah came up behind her and rested her hands upon her shoulders.

"He's with us Chris and he'll accompany us on our journey." Still looking at the flames Chris nodded.

"Yes, Sarah. I know." She didn't mention though that in her dream it had been her grandfather who was protecting them.

"Open your heart Chris," Sarah whispered gently in her ear. "Let me know what is inside."

"What for Sarah? Why do you want to know?"

"Because I want to understand: I want to know who you really are; why you showed up here, all of a sudden, in my time; why my grandfather was smiling in my dream; why I felt that I had to share the symbol with you."

"All I know is that we dreamt similar things, Sarah. I dreamt of my grandfather and he too was smiling."

"That must mean something."

Chris did not mention either, her grandfather's previous words, about finding someone special soon, about her not going against her feelings and about paths of life being unpredictable and surprising. Now Chris wondered if Sarah could be this special one. Did her grandfather know that all this would happen? How? She fearfully let her next thoughts take shape and astonishingly, words emerged, in a whisper,

"I had never before thought about how small we human beings are." She looked around and up to the sky, "There seems to be so much knowledge in the stars, in the universe, in nature, everywhere! Is it possible that we are not open to it? I wonder how many people have gone through this experience that you and I are living." Her eyes met Sarah's. "When I go back to my world, do you think anybody will believe me? It's very likely they will think I've gone mad." Chris smiled a faint smile, still staring at Sarah.

"I know you're not mad." Chris was touched and grateful for her answer and a sudden impulse made her lean over and kiss Sarah's cheek.

"It's very kind of you to say so," Chris added, "but you believe it because you are here with me!"

"Do you care very much what your people think?" Sarah questioned taking Chris by surprise.

"I admit I did sometimes care. But my family taught me not to and eventually I learned."

"In your world Chris, white people and people like me, how do they live?"

"Well Sarah, people like *you* and people like *me* learned how to live together long ago, but differences still attract fear and injustice."

"What do they do to those who are *different*?"

"It doesn't happen everywhere and to everybody, but when it happens they isolate them, criticise them, condemn them."

"And you?"

"Me? What about me?"

"Why aren't you like them?"

"Well, I really don't know, I'm not sure I can say I'm completely free from prejudice. I admit there are things I neither like nor accept, but skin colour isn't one of them."

"And what is it that you don't accept?" Her question unsettled her and she didn't know why.

Chris thought of Steve. "Well, I just think sometimes people act in a way or do things that I consider unacceptable." Sarah noticed Chris' discomfort and changed the subject.

"I don't understand why some people can be free and others cannot. You do understand why I escaped Chris, don't you?" Chris nodded. "I just want to know the freedom my grandfather told me so much about, the freedom that I used to have when I was a child but I hardly remember anymore. Will you come with me, Stranger?"

"I promised, remember? I promised that I would help you find your ship."

"Yes, I remember. What I mean is will you come with me, beyond the seas?"

"Sarah, you know I can't do that, I can't leave."

"But why can't you? This is not your homeland, you have no one here. What will you do?" Sarah got up and poked the fire. It was sunny, but a chilly wind was blowing.

She knelt on the ground and started playing carelessly with a stick.

"You don't want to go, or is it that you don't want to go with me?" she asked timidly.

"*That's* absurd, Sarah," Chris said defensively. "You know that I could be taken back again at any moment, and if I leave this country that might never happen! We already went over this, remember?" She shivered and covered herself with one of the cloaks. "If I got here, I guess this is where I'll leave from, not from across the seas!"

"And what if you don't go back? What if you never go back?"

"If I never...well, you said yesterday..." She had not really considered that option. What would happen to her if she didn't go back? Could she just disappear from her world? What would happen with her life? She suddenly thought about the people who went missing. Some of them showed up again, that was true, but many had never been seen again. Why? Had they been victims of a kidnapping or some other crime or had they also been taken by some mysterious force into another world, into another time?

"If I don't go back...I guess I will try to find others like me," she tried to look strong and determined. Sarah grabbed her symbol and lifted it to her lips as she lay back by the fire.

"Are you ok?" Chris asked.

"If you don't mind, I would like to stay here and rest for a little longer and then we can go." Sarah said with a gloomy voice.

"Of course I don't mind, there's no hurry, is there?"

CHAPTER 9

The sun was at its height when they set off heading south, following the river.

From time to time Sarah had to stop to rest for the high fever had weakened her considerably. Chris on the other hand kept scanning the horizon, looking for the city. Somehow she had assumed they were close to London, but how could she be sure where they were and where she'd *landed* from her time?

"Are you sure we're going in the right direction?" Sarah nodded. "You're very quiet, Sarah. What's wrong?"

"Nothing, I was just thinking."

"Would you like to tell me?"

"I don't know." Sarah hesitated.

"Come on, tell me." Chris was intrigued now.

"Since my grandfather passed away, I've begun to dream of achieving my freedom and leaving my life as a slave behind."

"Sounds like a reasonable dream to me."

"Yes, I know being free is a good reason, but..." she stopped.

"But?"

"I know we've only just met, but after what we've been through, I'm not sure anymore."

"What do you mean? Do you regret having escaped from Lord Wesley?"

"Not at all, it's not that."

"What is it, then?" Chris looked at her, waiting for her to continue.

"I'm not sure that I want to find the ship anymore. Haven't you ever felt that suddenly something changes in your life and you lose interest in what you had wanted so badly?"

"Oh yes, I have, but talking about something as important as your freedom, Sarah?"

"Oh, don't get me wrong, I do want to be free, I already feel free."

"Then, I don't understand."

"I want to be free, I like being free. I'm just not sure I want to go away, Chris."

"But Sarah, you can't stay here, in a country where *black* still means *slave*." Chris thought of the ship's eventual destination. What if she was taken to a place where slavery was even worse? They were, after all, in the 18th century and slaves existed in too many countries. What could she do if that happened? But she had no right to destroy Sarah's dream. "This place is not for you, Sarah. Not after escaping and stealing those jewels from Lord Wesley."

"How would it be in your world, Chris?" she asked with little confidence, as if considering one of many choices. Chris was speechless. She felt Sarah's glance but didn't return it. She couldn't help being confused, feeling her head spinning and getting lost in the eeriness of the events. Everything was happening too fast and she easily lost control of herself.

"In my world? You mean the 21st century?"

"I want to go with you."

"Oh no, that's not possible, I don't know why I'm here, Sarah. I don't even know how I got here in the first place! I don't know for how long I'll be around, is it going to be forever or just long enough to learn something from this? I haven't the faintest clue of how I could go back, even less of how *you* could go back with me. I might think that you don't belong here, because of how you talk or think or whatever; I might think that you, too, come from my time, that you and I have something in common... but go back with me? No way, that's not up to me Sarah, sorry..."

"I owe you so much Chris, more than you can imagine. You saved me twice, you looked after me when I was ill, my life is bonded to yours, Stranger."

"We don't know that, Sarah. Besides, it was because you were here that I didn't kill myself two days ago, I was so afraid! And that means you saved me too. The problem is that we might separate at any moment. I can disappear like a soap bubble. What's the point in thinking of the future if we don't know what will happen in the next minute? Please Sarah, I already told you, you don't owe me anything. I didn't help you to make you feel eternally grateful. I just did it, ok?"

Chris thought, 'This is madness.'

"You are the only person apart from my grandfather who has shown any interest in me, Chris."

"Oh, I get it...you're right, but that's because I'm the only one around! As soon as you're safe somewhere, there will be others and you won't need me."

"I don't want to lose you."

"Lose me? You talk as if we'd spent our lives together!" Chris felt distraught which made her raise her voice. She got up and moved away a few metres. Sarah made her feel trapped. And that feeling was really very hard to control. That's exactly why Chris had chosen the profession she had. That's why she'd fallen in love with Steve. That's why she loved her grandfather with all her heart. There were no demands at all. There was freedom in their love. On the other hand, maybe this excess of freedom was what destroyed everything she had with Steve. She had to consider that possibility. What about her friends? She knew lots of people whom she called friends but her only real friend was Anne. And now, this woman from the 18th century had become, after only a couple of days, closer than many other people. She started to realize how she'd lived her life; she saw lots of her grandfather, she was a workaholic and even when she and Steve were together, they rarely mixed with other people. Did she have any *normal* relationships at all? How was it supposed to be? She thought of her friendship with Anne. She never felt overwhelmed or trapped, on the contrary, she felt extremely comfortable. Theirs was a very affectionate relationship. They kissed, held hands and hugged each other and that was okay. She never felt unnerved by Anne like she did with Sarah. But she wanted to believe that it wasn't Sarah who made her nervous. She had enough other reasons to feel out of sorts. She was in an unreal world, she had crossed the line of time as if passing through a door, she had found a slave from the 18th century escaping from her masters, pursuing her dream of freedom, and she had fought like a movie heroine against a human beast, killing him with a pitchfork. It was fine if all this happened in a book that you could put away anytime, but she couldn't put away her present.

"I'm sorry Sarah. I didn't mean to raise my voice to you. It's just that this still seems so unreal, so crazy..."

"Maybe if you don't despair and just accept it, Chris." She said calmly.

"Don't despair? Sure, that's so easy to say because, slave or not, you're still living in a familiar place. I don't find it easy and it's hard just to sit and wait until something happens. Maybe that's what I should do! Just wait here for that mad scientist to show up, or a taxi driver, with a huge beer-belly and a long moustache. He'll stop right here and he'll ask in a deep voice: *Where ya' goin' luv?* And I'll say: *Please be so kind as to take me to Heathrow airport? My plane to the 21st century's about to leave!* ... yeah, that's very, very likely to happen any minute..."

"Maybe what you have been looking for is here."

"What I've been looking for? Here, in the middle of the 18th century? And what would that be, Sarah? What do you think might be here for me?" Chris felt like running away.

"Me...?" Chris raised her eyebrows in response.

"Maybe I'm part of your dream."

"Of my dream?"

"Don't you have a dream?" Sarah asked with surprise.

"Yes, I used to but..."

"Well, maybe it's me." Chris didn't let her go on. She didn't feel at ease with the conversation.

"Let's stop it now, please. I don't know what you really mean and I'm not sure I want to know, but let me tell you something. I never dreamt of finding someone two hundred years in the past and even less did I want that someone to be a woman."

"I'd love to tell you about the rituals in my village."

That was an unexpected change of subject indeed and Chris was pleased with it. "Every time the moon completed its perfect circle..." Brusquely Chris lifted her hand to her lips beckoning her to be quiet.

"I think I heard... come Sarah, move!" And they ran to hide in the wood. Sarah couldn't hear a thing and when she was about to ask something, Chris pressed her hand over Sarah's mouth.

From the same path which they had been following, a man appeared, riding a horse whilst pulling another without a rider. A second man came close behind him, driving a two-horse carriage. The strangers stopped a few metres from their hiding place, precisely where they had been talking. The men exchanged some words and the first one walked away to urinate. Meanwhile his companion checked the load on the carriage and took out a sack. Minutes later both riders galloped off, abandoning the wagon.

"Now, *that's* strange," Chris murmured, "why would they do that?"

They stayed hidden and quiet in case the men decided to come back. They didn't. After a while, Sarah said, "I don't think they're coming back."

"Probably they were brigands leaving the carriage to travel faster." Chris could only guess. They left their hiding place.

"We were lucky this time," Sarah said.

"Yes, we were, but I'm afraid the closer we come to the city, the more dangerous it will become, Sarah."

"Are the cities in your world dangerous, Chris?"

"Yes...and no. You can be sure you wouldn't find this sort of danger, like being chased and attacked by drunk slave hunters wanting to kill you, or bandits riding horses...but yes, there are too many criminals around, in some places more than in others. Wait! Did you hear that noise?" Chris strained her ears.

"No, I didn't." Another silence and then she heard it too. Some muffled moaning, coming from the carriage.

CHAPTER 10

*P*erhaps she was getting used to it, or maybe she was just following her instincts, but Chris lowered her hand down to grab the dagger she had taken from the dead man in the cabin. They both looked at the load and saw something moving beneath the covers. As Chris was about to take it off, Sarah grasped a rock, prepared to hit whatever might attack them. They glanced at each other, nodded and Chris pulled back the blankets, revealing a woman and a man, gagged and hands bound. Between them lay a little boy, also gagged and his arms tied behind his back, his fearful eyes swollen with crying.

"My God," Chris exclaimed when she saw the blood covering the man's shirt, "Let's untie them, Sarah." They lifted the boy out first. He started crying again as soon as he felt his mouth free. Then they helped the woman, who immediately held the child to her, begging them to help the man. They released him and struggled to lay his unconscious body down on the grass. Chris inspected his wound.

"It doesn't look good at all, we need to clean it before it gets infected," she said, looking at the woman who was still in shock. With Sarah's help she made a fire to heat the dagger and then tore his shirt. As the blade became red Chris plucked up the courage to cauterise the wound. She almost fainted at the smell of burned flesh, she held her breath. Another experience she never thought she would need to go through. She strode purposefully to the carriage and returned, pleased, with a bottle of Scotch. She had no idea if it would be of any use, but she poured some of the alcohol on the wound and applied an improvised bandage.

"I hope this will be enough. I suggest we put him back on the wagon and look for a safer place to hide, what do you think?" Sarah and the woman followed her in silence.

Contrary to what she thought, it was extremely difficult to manoeuvre the wagon. The horses weren't keen on moving and this amused Sarah, who was openly laughing at her.

"I'd love to see you driving a car for the first time in a traffic jam, dear," Chris defended herself from Sarah's mockery, "I'm sure you wouldn't find it that funny!" It was good to see her happy though. And have a nice laugh herself.

"That might be a good place," Sarah suggested, still giggling, pointing to a place next to the river but protected by high rocks and thickets, "at least until he recovers." Chris agreed, though she didn't hold out much hope for his recovery.

They took him down again and laid him comfortably on the ground. The woman placed the now sleeping boy between the blankets and Sarah helped Chris to release the horses and set up a new campsite. By this time the sun had already set and the temperature had dropped abruptly.

"It's going to be a very cold night," she said to Sarah. "I just hope there won't be a problem lighting a fire behind these rocks."

The woman didn't speak and remained next to the man, whom Chris assumed to be her husband. She moved closer and looked for his pulse.

"He looks better, madam, he's breathing more easily and his colour is returning to normal. He will be fine, don't worry." They all needed to have faith to help him heal.

She left the woman there and went back to Sarah, who was gathering firewood. "Let me help you, Sarah." She put some dry leaves under the wood and lit them with her lighter.

"What is that?" Sarah hadn't seen anything similar.

"This? Oh, just a lighter," she handed it over, showing her how to use it.

"There must be so many fascinating things in your world." She smiled.

"So many, in fact, that you wouldn't go to sleep for days, maybe weeks, trying to find out about everything."

They were having a long, relaxed chat by the fire, until the woman approached them with a bag. She took out a metal pot and provisions.

"I can cook something," she whispered, shyly.

"That would be really, really nice, madam," Chris smiled at her, "let me get some water."

"No need, we have a large barrel on the carriage. Before we left home we filled it up with fresh water, in case we had to divert from the river during our journey to London." Chris and Sarah looked at each other.

"You are going to London?" asked Sarah with a big smile.

"Yes we are." That was really good news.

"Madam, if I might ask, what happened? Why did those men...?"

Before telling their story, the woman introduced herself and her family.

"Please call me Elizabeth. That's my husband Joseph Priestley and our son Jonathan."

"I'm Chris, Elizabeth, and this is..." she was interrupted by Sarah.

"And my name is Sarah, Lady Priestley, and I'm her slave." She looked at Chris and went on, "We too are heading for London, to find my lady's relatives." Chris looked at her, amazed by this spontaneous invention. She played along with the charade, though neither noticed Elizabeth's smile.

"Well, yes," she added, "Sarah's coming with me but not really as my slave, I'd rather say she's keeping me company. I don't like to travel alone, you see." She looked at Sarah teasingly.

"I hope you find them all very well." Elizabeth wished.

"Thank you, I hope so too."

"Well, I'll fetch the water."

"Please let me do that!" Sarah urged and got up quickly, taking the pot from Elizabeth's hands.

Chris went back to check Joseph's wound. Surprisingly, the injury looked much better – as did Joseph himself.

Whilst Elizabeth was busy preparing the meal, Chris asked about their story.

"Will you tell us what happened with those men?"

"Well, we left our home some days ago and when we got back the cabin had been burned down. The terrible thing was that amongst the ashes and debris we found human remains. Joseph thought it was the slave hunters getting their revenge."

"Revenge?" Chris was surprised.

"Yes. We have had problems with them in the past, for defending some slaves. So we packed the few belongings that survived the fire and we decided to move to the city." Sarah and Chris exchanged glances. Chris immediately thought that the other slave hunters would blame Elizabeth and Joseph for the death of that man.

Sarah's thoughts were elsewhere. "You...you have helped slaves?"

"Yes, dear. Slavery is an abhorrence. We do what we can. We don't believe that the colour of the skin makes a person inferior."

"Well, I'm very pleased to hear that, Elizabeth, because Sarah is not my slave." Chris was happy to confess.

"I know, dear."

"You *know*?"

"A slave would *never* dare to speak in front of her mistress and without her consent, Chris," she smiled.

"I feel really silly," she blushed. Sarah herself was speechless.

"Don't worry, I understand."

"The truth is that we're going to London to find a man who will help Sarah escape from England, Elizabeth. From there we'll probably need to continue south to find the ship. I promised I would help her." Chris felt she could trust this woman.

"I'm sure you'll be able to help her. As long as everybody thinks that she's your slave, you won't have any problems in London. And we will help you too. It's the least we can do after you saved our lives.

"Why were you tied up in the carriage?" Chris asked, with a feeling of relief.

"We met the two outlaws on our way and they forced us to go with them and deceive their persecutors. They threatened to kill our son if we didn't do as they said. When we finally met the guards, they didn't question whether these men were travelling with us. Later on, my husband attempted to escape but they stabbed him and gagged and bound us. They kept us as hostages to release later. That was when you found us."

'I wonder if I will have the chance to tell this story to my people,' Chris thought.

When the food was ready, Sarah and Chris satisfied their hunger silently. Elizabeth fed the boy and they lay down beside her husband.

"What are you thinking, Chris?" Sarah asked when they were laying by the fire. Chris answered looking at the stars. It seemed that their previous conversation had been forgotten.

"I was just remembering the different experiences that we've been through," there was a pause, "and thinking that after this my life will never be the same again."

"And you regret it?"

"I'm not sure if I regret it. The truth is I don't really know how I feel, Sarah. I have told you, all this is very confusing. There are moments like now, when I feel so placid but all of a sudden everything becomes messed up in my mind again and I feel lost and just want to run away. It scares me, because it makes me feel I lose control. It's like living two lives at once; it's like leaving one familiar road in life to step on an unknown one..." she hesitated, "don't listen to me, Sarah. It's not easy to explain."

"But I do understand, Chris. I understand because something similar is happening to me. I feel as if my past is fading away. I've never been alone physically, you know? I was always surrounded by people in my village, then during the slavery years I was always busy, doing things I was ordered to do. Nevertheless, I always felt lonely. My grandfather was the only one who really mattered to me. And my strength comes only from my faith and my dream of freedom. But this dream vanishes as well when I think that you are my friend now and I'll have to leave you for it to happen."

"Don't say that Sarah. You mustn't speak like that. It was you who said to me that you would fulfil your dream. As soon as you do it you'll see how your life changes, everything will be different. You will have left your life of slavery, you will be free and you will meet other people. I've been thinking that maybe if there's something I do have to do here, that is definitely my task."

"What?" Sarah asked.

"To help you is my task; what I have to do."

"Maybe, I don't know." Sarah added. "Your presence gives me peace, Chris. I know you have been upset with some of the things I have said; I didn't mean to upset you. You are a good friend," she said with a sad voice. Chris was quiet, staring at the flames.

"I know I don't belong here," Sarah added after a while, "and I will be in danger if I stay, but I have also thought that maybe there is no place for me beyond the seas... that's why I said what I did about going with you, Chris. I'm really sorry it upset you." Chris thought Sarah's worries made sense and she deeply regretted her reaction during that earlier conversation, though she didn't say anything. Sarah spoke again.

"My grandfather used to tell me stories when I was young and couldn't sleep, and there is a special one I always remember." Chris listened with interest. "It's a story that has passed on for many generations, a story that our ancestors wanted us to keep as a lesson not to be forgotten. It's about the spiritual leader of an ancient nation who lived by the Nile, not far away from the great pyramids. The old man was very ill and almost blind, and the people, noticing his weakness, started to lose their faith and to fight amongst themselves. One day, almost unable to stand on his own feet, the old man went off, walking slowly, towards the pyramids. Many days passed without anybody seeing him again. Some thought he'd left to die alone, some said he'd been devoured by wild desert animals, others thought the sands had swallowed and buried him. One day though, the old man came back, and he was no longer ill or blind." As Sarah spoke, Chris imagined the scenes. "The old man called them together and everyone obeyed, silent and fearful of the miracle before them. He said he'd left because he didn't know how to help them anymore. When he got to the pyramids, he fell to his knees in front of Khafre and he prayed to Obatalá. It was then he saw the big white bright light descend from the sky and hover above him. Then, smaller multicoloured lights cascaded from that white light and began to dance around him until they came to rest on his ill body which started to tremble, but not in pain. Sometime later the lights faded away. He explained that Obatalá had sent her light messengers to heal him so that his people could keep the faith: faith was the only way to stop war from happening."

"It's a beautiful story, Sarah."

"Maybe you come from there." Sarah gestured to the sky.

"For heaven's sake," Chris smiled. "It's weird enough to accept being here, but believe me, that's not where I come from."

"Do you think there's life out there?"

"I don't know, maybe. I've never thought about it." Her thoughts went back to the interview she read about in the magazine at the Spanish airport.

"I have," Sarah continued. "I want to believe that one day our souls will be able to travel through the universe, and maybe we'll do it too."

Chris looked at her and said, "What amazes me the most, besides the fact that I'm here and that I've met you, is the way you express yourself. I've already told you, I never thought someone from your time would talk like you do, about souls travelling around and that sort of stuff. I can't say I believe that's possible, but after experiencing this time travelling, who am I, to talk about possible and impossible things? At least I can tell you that man has been to the moon! I mean he will get there in two hundred years..."

"What? Is it possible to go to the moon in your time?" Sarah was astonished.

"Some have been there, yes. These people are called astronauts. There are spaceships as well, sorry, there *will* be. And a space station, built by a group of countries. I guess man seeks tirelessly to find out what's beyond..."

"Your world of the future must be very beautiful."

"What makes you say that?"

"If you say that in two hundred years man has gone so far, it can only mean peace has been achieved and illnesses probably don't exist anymore."

Chris didn't want to disappoint Sarah, but what was the point in telling her the truth? What would happen if she told her that man had learned very little from the many big or smaller wars? What if she said that the world in the 21st century was a great place to live? That finally everybody, every single person had learned to live in harmony because there's enough for everybody? But making up things had never been one of her skills and she decided to go with the truth.

"Well...yes and no. Unfortunately it's not going to be easy. Over the next two hundred years the word *war* will still be part of the daily vocabulary. Among too many others, there will be two world wars with horrendous results in many countries. In one of them, millions of innocent people will be cruelly slaughtered. Every war, small or big, will seem to bring a peaceful time, but it won't last.

People will continue to kill each other for their beliefs, for their land, for their wealth, for whatever reason. There will still be people living in palaces surrounded by servants called employees; whilst very close you'll be able to find starving people, poverty, and illness. Still in the 21st century, Sarah, too much evil exists, too much meanness finds its way. It seems to me that man's fate is never to feel satisfied, always wanting more: more wealth, more power. For some people, who call themselves politicians, war is too good business. Too many people forget that we're killing the only planet we've got to live on. I'm sure every planet dies naturally after so many thousands or millions of years, but I'm afraid I also believe man's speeding its death with greed, selfishness, and a huge lack of responsibility."

"I don't understand." Sarah was sad.

"There are millions who don't understand, millions." It was the first time in her life Chris had voiced her feelings about the world she lived in. It was like discovering herself.

"Can I ask you something, Chris?"

"Of course you can, but I don't promise an answer, and even less a happy answer," she tried to smile.

"Do you think we'll know one day why we met?" It wasn't the question Chris had expected.

"Aren't you forgetting what your grandfather told you? About things always happening for a reason? I, myself, am starting to believe that now, that we forget too quickly and I also believe that your grandfather and mine had lots in common."

"No, I don't forget, it's only that sometimes I doubt I'll get the answers at all and that makes me sad."

"Well, I do understand your sadness, because I've felt it myself."

"And what do you think?"

"I don't know. Maybe we just need to learn how to feel satisfied, happy with what we have here and now. Maybe it all depends on how strong our faith is, because feelings aren't easy to prove," she smiled.

"Why are you smiling?"

"Out of anxiety I guess. Look, a week ago I would have never imagined myself speaking about these things. Actually, I never needed to, before. My world was so busy; I didn't have any spare time to think about things that wouldn't have a clear and straight answer. Every minute I get more and more convinced that this strange journey happened to teach me something, even if I'm still not aware of what it is that I have to learn. If he were here now, my grandfather would probably say if I hadn't been ready, nothing like this would have happened to me, because... it very well might be that we can only learn when we are ready to, don't you think? And we despair when we don't understand, like a child despairs when he wants to run without being able to walk. That child trips over and over again and every fall hurts. He stops trying and then he tries again, until one day, when he's ready, he can run! Don't we go through life doing the same? Take faith, for example. I never needed it, but I never experienced anything that I couldn't get over without faith. I guess I wasn't ready to know what faith was. Maybe now I'm ready to start learning about it," she looked up to the stars and went on, "Maybe now that I'm going through the worst moment of my life, when the meaning of life itself seems so dim, maybe faith is the only thing which will take me through it."

"So now you have faith?"

"Well, I'm getting there, I guess, by accepting that something inside me could be changing. Too many things have happened, things that hurt me and no matter how deep the wounds are, they always heal. Yes, Sarah, I do think that someday we'll know why our lives crossed each other as they did."

"Thank you, Chris."

"What for?"

"For being with me and helping me."

"In that case, thank you too, Sarah."

"I find peace in your words, Chris," she knew Sarah was sincere and that made her feel good. "I'd love to tell you about the rituals that used to be held among my people."

"And I'd love to hear about them, but can you tell me tomorrow, please?"

Chapter 11

When Chris woke up next morning, two big eyes were staring at her. The boy was obviously very attracted by these two strangers and determined to catch their attention, but as soon as Chris returned the look with a big smile, he ran back to his mother. Sarah went off to the river as soon as she saw the kid staring at her too, full of curiosity. 'Maybe she doesn't like children,' Chris thought.

Joseph had recovered very well from his injury and, although still very weak from the loss of blood, he was in an extremely good mood.

They all seemed to enjoy having breakfast together. Chris was deeply touched by the interaction of this small family. Joseph was such a nice man and so sincerely grateful for the women's help that a close bond built up between them very soon. He showered a lot of attention and love on his wife and son and for Chris that was a natural and immediate reason to both like and respect him. Elizabeth was lovely too and it seemed that love for her family poured out of her with every movement, with every look. She had taken such good care to ensure that nothing was missing for her family. Chris was next to tears when she thought of her own family.

Later during the conversation, Joseph explained they would have to travel all day and part of the next to reach the outskirts of London.

"My wife told me why you are going to London," he mentioned with interest and noticed Chris's silence. "What's the matter? You look worried."

"All of a sudden I've got a bad feeling, Joseph. It doesn't seem sensible that Sarah is seen there." Her knowledge about the history of London was not something she would show off about, but she knew enough to know that in those days the city was far from being a quiet place, especially those areas that they would need to explore looking for old Isaac. As a black man he would never be allowed to live close to the white, not even if he had obtained his freedom.

"She doesn't need to worry, and neither do you, as long as we're with her," he smiled, understanding.

"What I don't understand Sarah, is why did you escape?"

Elizabeth interrupted them. "We've always heard that Lord Wesley treats his people very well, including his slaves. Why did you choose to risk your life in such a long journey, for a future potentially full of difficulties? At least with Lord Wesley you had people who cared about you, didn't you?"

Listening to Elizabeth, Chris realized the important information she was missing about Sarah's life at Lord Wesley's. How did she get those jewels? Was there any other reason why the hunters were after her? Had she been wrong about her? No, that was hard to believe. Chris noticed Sarah's silence and thought this could be the right time to give Elizabeth and Joseph an explanation about the events in their cabin.

"There's something you must know," she started and then told them the whole story from the moment she met Sarah some days ago. Of course, she did not mention her real origin. "I was only trying to help, Joseph. I couldn't let him hurt Sarah," she justified her actions. "He had attacked us before and wouldn't let us go just like that."

"I believe you, Chris, I believe you. These men, the slave hunters, they don't show any mercy when they find a black slave, woman or man, who has escaped. They chase them; they harass them and beat them to death. They show even less mercy when it comes to young and beautiful women like Sarah."

Sarah remained silent. It was obvious that this conversation was upsetting her immensely and that she could not listen anymore; she got up hastily and walked off to the river.

What had she experienced? Chris felt furious at the thought that Sarah might have been abused, just because they considered her a living *thing* at the service of white people. If she was right, then that man had deserved the death he got.

"You better go and talk to her, Chris. In the meantime my wife and I will get everything ready to set off," said Joseph, holding his wife's hand.

Sarah was on her knees, crying. Chris took hold of her gently by the shoulders and hugged her firmly.

"It's fine, it's fine, you're not alone anymore," she was trying to avoid the tears herself, almost feeling Sarah's sadness.

"I couldn't stay there any longer, I just couldn't!" she sobbed. "When my grandfather died I lost the only person who would talk to me nicely and treat me with respect and..."

"And?"

"I lied to you, Chris. My grandfather didn't die because he was sick."

"Why don't you tell me what happened?"

"Wesley's not a good man, Chris! He beat us when we didn't do what he wanted us to." Sarah took her shirt off and turned around silently. Chris was horrified at the sight of the scars covering Sarah's back. How many lashes had she received! She wished she could rub off these marks but maybe not even time could do it. Time...if only she knew how long she'd have to be with her. She helped Sarah to get dressed again, hugged her and dried her tears, trying to give her a little comfort.

Sarah clung to her and whispered, "Don't leave me, Chris, please don't leave me." She was begging her and Chris heard her own words, slipping from her lips, unstoppable.

"I won't leave you Sarah. I'll stay with you as long as I am allowed to stay, I promise." She felt suspended between her past and an uncertain future and she did not want to think what their future might hold.

Once she calmed down, Sarah lifted her face and held Chris's to kiss her on the cheek. Inadvertently her lips brushed past the corner of Chris's mouth. Her whole body was shaken by Sarah's proximity. Chris panicked. She moved her face away and said, trying hard to look calm, "Everything will be fine, Sarah. We should go back now; Joseph and Elizabeth are waiting for us." Chris stood up thinking, 'What the hell is happening to me?' By the time they reached the campsite, everything was ready as Joseph had said. Chris and Sarah got on the back of the wagon and they made themselves comfortable.

After some hours the sun was just overhead; Joseph stopped the horses so they could rest and drink some water.

"It would be good for you to rest too, dear," Elizabeth suggested to her husband. He lay down obediently while his wife played with her child.

"Do you know when the ship will be leaving?" Chris asked Sarah.

"I remember my grandfather saying something about Christmas, but I'm not sure. We need to find old Isaac to know."

It was October when she came here and suddenly she wondered if the dates were still the same.

"Still two months to go," Sarah said as if reading her mind.

"That means we'll have to find a place to stay and wait until we board the ship," Chris added and noticed Sarah smiling. "What, what's funny about it?"

"You said until *we* board the ship..."

"Sorry, I didn't realize..." Actually Chris hadn't. "I... I need to check on Joseph..." That was a good excuse to change the subject, "I'm not sure those long hours and the banging of the wagon on the hard road was good for his wound."

She was right. The wound had opened again, which meant Joseph had to travel lying in the back, exerting no effort at all.

They let him rest for a couple of hours before continuing their journey. Chris was driving the horses, but she did not do it for long. Shortly after setting off, they heard a loud crack under the carriage. They jumped off to check what had happened and looked at each other, silently. One of the wheels was wrecked.

"Could we fix it, Joseph?" Chris asked.

"We could try but without proper tools I doubt it will hold for a mile."

"Then I guess the best we can do is make a sort of stretcher for you, because riding a horse won't do your wound any good."

They built a stretcher with two long planks and a big blanket and tied it to one of the horses. They loaded both animals with the contents of the carriage, leaving the water barrel behind. They would not need it if they followed the river.

"This will slow us down, girls. I'm sorry I can't go faster." Joseph apologized.

"I don't think a few days will make such a difference."

"Sarah's right, Joseph, and don't apologize please, you must get well." Elizabeth added.

Chris was silent, her mind again full of thoughts she wasn't used to having. For example, had the power of the mind, something that lots of people talked about, anything to do with her time travelling? Could it be possible, that whatever the human mind was able to imagine, becomes true? And if she was solely responsible for bringing herself here did she have the power to send her back? 'Granddad...you've got no idea how much I need your advice,' she mused.

Jonathan's innocent and spontaneous laughter brought her back to reality and she was grateful. The boy took her hand and walked beside her, until he found out it was much better and less tiring to be carried.

That night was very special for Chris. She felt extremely relaxed having dinner by the fire. Although the meal consisted only of some potatoes and soup, it tasted like a celestial meal to her. And their company gave her the feeling of having a family. If only her grandparents could be here, *that* would make her really happy. They chatted and laughed, celebrating Jonathan's attempts to repeat the difficult words his father was trying to teach him. Both younger women heard how lucky Elizabeth and Joseph thought they were, to have the opportunity of enjoying their small family. They also learned that Elizabeth had almost died when she gave birth.

Sarah looked very relaxed too. The relief of letting go of some of her memories as a slave seemed to have given her new strength.

Chris couldn't help looking at her when she laughed, thinking how hard it must be to get over any physical abuse. The scars on her body were probably as difficult to erase as those in her mind, if not impossible. Just thinking about the cowardly and brutal behaviour of some men made her sick. It was tremendously discouraging to realize that abuse and mistreatment were part of history and it was also ironic to believe the future might be considered 'civilized'. If, on the one hand, the coming times were full of promises of major material development, on the other hand too many events were related to what she'd already said to Sarah: the insatiable thirst for power of some; lack of interest for others; a general spiritual stagnation.

Her thoughts were suddenly interrupted by the brightness of Sarah's glance and when their eyes met, it was as if her mind became translucent, allowing Sarah to read from it. Chris thought of Anne. She missed her friend and remembered when they had had those moments too. A special glance and there was no need of words to communicate. They knew each other so well that they knew what the other was thinking. Anne had always been more of a friend and more of a sister than her own one. Then she thought of Patrick and tried hard to imagine what they were doing. Surely he'd already returned from Strasbourg. Were they looking for her? What were they thinking about her disappearance?

When little Jonathan started to show clear signs of tiredness, his parents decided it was time to go to sleep.

Once left alone, Sarah asked, "Are you thinking of your world?"

"It's really spooky how you read my mind sometimes! Yes, I was thinking of my friends." Then she asked Sarah to tell her about her people.

CHAPTER 12

"The memories I have about the rituals are still so real," she started. "I remember the bonfire and the women dancing, following the rhythm of the men and their drums. It was always the same, the dance ended and my grandfather took me away. When I was older, though, they expected me to be there until the ceremony was finished. As soon as that happened, some of the women sat down, others were taken by some men to the different huts. My grandfather explained to me that the remaining women stayed there because they were either not *ready* to be taken by a man or because of some divine decision they were not suitable or not worthy to be mothers." Sarah sighed deeply. "The day came when I was ready too. I was expected to worship the Goddess, demonstrating my fertility. Men started drumming and for the first time I was invited to dance with the other women. The sound of the drums calmed down and the dancing ceased. By the time one of the men approached me, I was terrified. He lifted me and took me to his hut. Until that very moment, Chris, I didn't know anything, I didn't know what was going to happen, my grandfather had never explained to me what happened in the huts and it was not allowed for the women to talk to each other about the rituals. The man who had chosen me poured out all his brutality and strength on me. I rejected him. I wanted to run away but he was drunk. First he got furious and then he started hitting me. I felt him over and over again in me..." Chris could see the pain in Sarah's expression. "I woke up the next morning and my grandfather was beside me. I told him that I didn't want to participate in the rituals anymore. I was used to his kindness as a man and thought that other men had to be the same. I don't know if the other women were treated like I was but anyway, he told me I had been rejected by our people. I was not allowed to go back and dance. The women felt ashamed of me and men averted their gaze. But I didn't care, Chris. On the contrary, I felt so relieved!" Chris didn't say a word, but she did dry some tears rolling down Sarah's cheeks.

"I was a disgrace to my people, they used to say, but I didn't really care. My grandfather had always taught me to act listening to my heart and without hurting anybody, and that's exactly what I did. I was sad for him though, because he stood by me and he was dishonoured too for protecting me." While Sarah spoke, her eyes followed the smooth dancing of the flames.

"Time passed and one day the slave traders arrived in my village and whoever was healthy was given the opportunity to come to England to work for the rich landlords. They promised we would be looked after and that we would get paid for our work. Once here, when the only pay we would get turned out to be food, some clothes and a place to sleep, we realized the slave traders had lied to us so they wouldn't have any resistance. Some fought back, resisted, but they were killed. The rest had no choice; either we worked or we would get killed as well. We couldn't run away, where to? We had no idea where we were. My grandfather and I were allowed to stay together...this was something I always thank God for, still today. At the beginning, slavery was for me more or less the same as living in my village rejected by everyone. And somehow I thought that was life, until life changed. Lord Wesley started looking at me in a different way and one day I told my grandfather. I still remember his words... *'My child, you must get used to people looking at you, anyone who can see, will be fascinated by you. You have been blessed with beauty. I don't think Lord Wesley will hurt you.'*

'Your grandfather was right, Sarah, you're beautiful.' Chris almost said, but she held back her thoughts. She had said it many times to Anne, when she'd got a new dress or a new hair-do, or for whatever reason, but this was different.

"But my grandfather was wrong about him. For Wesley it wasn't enough to just look at me. One day he approached me and wanted to kiss me, but I pushed him away." Chris could imagine what followed.

"He threatened to punish my grandfather if I didn't do what he wanted, so I had to obey him but I didn't have to like him. He noticed my look of hatred and he started beating me up, to *tame* me, as he said. My grandfather noticed the bruises and... I couldn't stop him. For the first time in my life I saw him lose control. I never knew what he said to Wesley, but that night, his white employees whipped my grandfather in front of me until he fainted. I tried to cure his wounds but he only recovered to say his last words about the new world. That's when he made me promise I would go for my dream and he promised his spirit would always protect me. After his death, all I could do was plan my escape. I made Wesley believe that he had subdued me and I faked every single minute I was with him. When I found out where he hid the jewels, I waited until he left for London, knowing he wouldn't come back for a couple of days. That night I took the jewels and I ran away. Unfortunately his foreman noticed and set off after me." Sarah looked at Chris and said, "Two days later you and I met."

"So we don't know what Wesley is really doing to find you..."

"No, we don't. That's why I told you it was dangerous for you to be found with me."

"I don't know what to say... I wish I could do something to help you forget..."

"You're already helping me, Stranger." Chris smiled back, gently.

"I don't think that man – and I refuse to call him lord, he doesn't deserve it I don't think he'll stop until he finds you, we need to be extremely careful."

"He won't find us, Chris. Why should he guess that I...that we're heading to London? The only person who knew about this ship was my grandfather. He heard it from old Isaac and he never told anybody else."

"But if Wesley's constantly coming down to London, he might get information about people who help slaves."

"I've chosen to take that risk, Chris, rather than staying there and putting up with it."

"I can understand Sarah, I can understand very well."

"Then you also understand how dangerous London will be and if you prefer not to be seen with me... "

"I don't prefer anything, Sarah, okay? I won't change my mind and besides, I've got the feeling that your grandfather and mine are really helping us." Out of the corner of her eye, she looked at the family they had encountered *by chance.*

"I know what you mean; I don't think we met them fortuitously, I think there was a reason to meet them."

"Chris?" Sarah spoke again after a long silence.

"Hum?"

"What would you have done?"

"About what, Wesley?"

"Yes, about him and about the rituals."

"I want to believe I'd have had the courage to do the same, escape, run very far away and try to start a new life, leaving the past behind. I'm also sure it would have been extremely difficult to think that there was any good in men, not that I've had better luck but yes, I would have done exactly what you did, Sarah."

"Wasn't it what you did when you came to this country?"

"I thought we were talking about you," Chris feigned a smile. She knew Sarah was right.

"Yes, we were, but... Chris, you've told me things about your world, I've seen the kindness in your acts, you have cared about me, you put your life in danger to help me...you have listened to me silently, letting me know that I can count on you and I...I'd like to do the same! I'd like to listen to you. I can see your soul through your eyes and I'd like to go beyond, I'd like to know other things about your life. But also I can see how you build up a sort of a wall to protect yourself and I can't break through it. Why don't you want me to take that wall down?"

Of course Sarah was right. Chris's distressing and disappointing separation from Steve had ended up erecting these walls around her. She knew it. She also knew she wasn't the most experienced woman in life in matters of the heart, but the only people she'd ever loved were not part of her life anymore and that hurt a lot. Her family did not care about her, her beloved grandparents were dead and the only guy she had fallen in love with had betrayed her. Unconsciously or not, she built up these walls to protect herself; she didn't want to become vulnerable again, and she didn't want to suffer again. The irony was that she didn't know how to take the walls down, either.

"Why are you so interested in knowing me, Sarah?"

"Because of all you've done for me. And because you've been, apart from my grandfather, the only one who's treated me like a human being."

"You know what? You definitely can't be from this century!" Sarah jumped as if something had frightened her. "What? What happened?"

"I remembered something that my grandfather told me once, many years ago, when we were still in Africa. He said that I didn't belong to that world and I also remember him saying that one day I'd understand..." she felt silent for a moment and then she added, "Maybe..."

"Maybe what?"

"Couldn't it be that I'm a product of your imagination?"

"Sarah, you're nuts and I need a cigarette."

Later on, after a long silence, they both heard the same, '*Don't lose your faith...*'

They looked at each other, obviously their thoughts being the same, 'Grandfather.'

Chris put the cigarette out and she lay down, covered herself with the cloak and tried hard to go to sleep. At least for a few hours she wanted to forget about everything and just sleep. Forget about ceremonies worshipping a Goddess whom she'd never heard mentioned before, forget about slave hunters, rapists and voices looming up from the void.

There was blood everywhere and a body lying on the ground

just beside her. She was running, trying to escape. She was running towards the figure in front of her, but before she could get there, the figure vanished in a heavy fog. Chris woke with a start and immediately she could hear Sarah, who was wriggling next to her.

"It's moving... it's moving too much... the screams... people are so afraid..." What was she dreaming about, people screaming? Chris was about to wake her when Sarah fell into a deep sleep again. She went back to her own nightmare. Could it be a premonition? No, no way. Why would she believe that? She'd never had these sorts of dreams before. Why should she start having them now? But the fog...she couldn't get it out of her mind. And what if it was a premonition? That could only mean that she'd go back to her time. But on the other hand, it could also be a trick of her mind, replaying images of the fog and Joseph's wound.

"Are you awake?" Sarah asked softly.

"I thought *you* were sleeping."

"No... I had a very strange dream."

"I know, you were saying something about people screaming. Do you want to tell me about it?"

"It was so real! At first I was in a dark room and though I couldn't see anything, I knew someone was there, with me. Everything was shaking and I could hear the desperate screams. Then... suddenly it wasn't dark anymore, there was plenty of light everywhere and I saw myself walking, at night. Everything was very confusing and oh yes, it was very hot... and you were there. I mean, I couldn't see you, but I could feel you... I had a warm feeling about the place, as if it was home... I can't remember anything else." After a pause she asked, "Do you remember what you said, about me not being from this century? And remember my grandfather's words?"

"I do, why?"

"Do you think it's possible to go away while you're dreaming?"

"Go away? You mean... travel while you're asleep?" Sarah nodded. "People call that astral travel, and if you'd asked me a week ago I'd have said you were mad. Now I don't know, maybe, but I really don't know."

"If time travel is possible, astral travel might be possible as well."

"Are you telling me that you just came back from a short journey?"

"It's possible, isn't it? Or maybe you are a product of my imagination too and maybe there are many other people who have had this same experience and maybe at some point we'll just remember it as a bad dream, or..."

"Yes, yes, and maybe there are gates between dimensions and

we've crossed them and maybe... there are too many *maybes*, Sarah. One thing we know, though. This is not a dream. A dream doesn't last *days*."

For some minutes they were silent. And then Sarah took her friend's hand and lifted it to her own cheek. Chris stared at her and blushed. She definitely didn't feel like this when Anne touched her. Sarah's question made her even more nervous.

"What do you feel when our skins touch?"

"I...it's a normal sign of affection, isn't it?"

"Yes, but what do you *feel*?" Chris was not going to tell her how she really felt. She wouldn't tell her that it was an unknown sensation that unsettled her, that made her anxious. And of course she wouldn't tell her that she felt like running away but at the same time she longed to stay there, very still, waiting for this not-so-unknown-woman-anymore, to hug her.

"Well...it's... nice..." and very quickly she added, "And you? What do you feel?"

"I feel the same I felt when we first met, that it's like knowing you from long ago. I also feel that our skins would recognize each other, as if they were one."

'Perhaps we are all part of a great soul.' Chris was startled at the sound of these words in her mind. And she was really shocked when she realized that Sarah had heard them as well.

"This is crazy, absolute madness." It was all she could say.

"Maybe it's just that our souls must be together for some reason, because we're alike?"

"We haven't got anything in common! You're from the 18th century, I'm from the 21st and besides, you're a woman and so am I!"

"If our Gods live eternally, why can't we, their creation, live through time?"

"Because we are born, we grow up, we get old and we die. That's why. We die, do you understand?" Chris felt torn apart. Her heart was begging her to have faith but her mind refused.

"And the soul, what happens to the soul? What happens to what we learn? My grandfather used to say that we were born to learn..."

"Whatever we experience, we share it with our friends and families, and we pass our knowledge to our children."

"And our feelings, what happens to our feelings?"

"Oh Sarah...I don't know!" Chris wished she was as calm, relaxed and peaceful about everything as Sarah was. But no, she felt a hurricane building up in her. Hadn't she learnt anything from her grandfather? What was the matter with her? 'Life's paths are strange, unpredictable and surprising.' There they were again, her grandfather's words.

"Why can't I just believe?" She realized she had voiced the question only when Sarah spoke, smiling.

"You must be patient and not despair."

"And you find that funny?"

"Have you realized that we are helping each other?"

"Of course, you're helping me by being here; I'm helping you to get to the ship."

"That's not what I mean. What I mean is that when I've been weak, you've been strong and when faith seems to abandon you, I feel I can help you to get it back."

Sarah's words had a magic effect. She felt a wave of tranquillity overcome her, as if her mind and her heart were in unison. Hopefully this serenity would last.

Without a word she leaned on her side, looking at the flames they had been feeding during their conversation, and when she felt Sarah leaning towards her and covering them up, she stayed very quiet. And she didn't feel uncomfortable either when Sarah rested her head on the curve of her neck, touching her face. To her surprise, Chris felt welcomed and protected and for once she forgot about her pride in always being strong. It *could not* be wrong for one woman to embrace another in the way Sarah was embracing her now. They were protecting each other.

A few minutes later, whilst watching the changing shapes of the flames, Sarah whispered in her ear, "What do you miss the most?"

"That changes all the time, depending on how I feel. When I first arrived, I mean in England, I could only think of my grandfather and of someone I spent many, many years with. I know I will never forget my grandfather, but Steve? His image is vanishing, although not completely. The same is happening with the rest of the people that I left behind, in the city where I used to live. Now, everything's so confusing, you've noticed. I lose control over my thoughts and over my memories. I do know that I miss things like having a drink in front of the fire in a fireplace, a nice long hot shower, the..." Sarah interrupted her. She wanted to know how a shower worked and after hearing about it, she laughed.

"I've only had cold baths in my life!" Another silence invaded their space and Sarah broke it when Chris was almost falling asleep.

"The man in one of the portraits you showed me, is he the one you called Steve?"

"Yes."

"Did you love him very much?"

"I was crazy about him, for many years."

"Are you going back to him when you go back?" Sarah was

interrogating her again but this time she seemed not to mind. She felt drugged, absent.

"*If* I go back, you'd better say, and no, I won't see him again."

"Why?"

"Because he belongs in the past."

"I also will be past if you go back..."

"It's not the same, it's not the same!"

"What's the difference between one past and the other?"

"The difference is huge; the things that happened are different. There were lies and actions which destroyed the confidence and the respect that once existed. When that happens, nothing can be the same again."

"Haven't you ever lied?"

"I might have, but only about silly things. I don't remember lying about feelings or important matters. I believe the truth always comes to light."

"Do you remember when we first met?"

"How could somebody forget such a meeting?"

"When you told me that you came from the future and you thought I wouldn't believe you...and when I told you I felt I had known you before...I had this dream, about someone coming into my life. I didn't tell you about it."

"That's not lying; you just didn't tell me something." Sarah ignored her comment.

"There was somebody coming into my life but I couldn't see a face or body, it was very blurred. What I did know in my dream was that this person would come in a very strange way and I wouldn't understand very well why. I also knew that this person would be very special and important in my life."

"Sarah..."

"No, Chris, please let me go on. When we met, I felt you were that person. I was afraid and I didn't understand why you were a woman, that's the real reason why I ran away that night. Now, it doesn't really matter anymore. If it is possible to cross the time line, come and go many times and if you and I are going to separate, we will separate, because it is meant to be. But I promise you, I will look for you, Chris, my soul will be looking for you until we meet again."

Chris felt her heart pounding as she had never experienced before. She didn't say anything because there was nothing to say: she could only feel Sarah hugging her. She also remembered her grandfather's words, 'You will also meet someone special before long Chris.'

'Is it her, granddad? Why?'

CHAPTER 13

A strange sound woke Sarah the next morning.

"Saada... Kiss... Saada... Kiss..."

"What, what is it?" She saw the boy's big eyes looking at them.

"Saada... Kiss." This time Chris woke up too.

"Sadakis? What is it, Jonathan? What is Sadakis?" She looked at Sarah.

"Don't look at me; I don't understand what he's saying."

"Saada, Kiss, eet!" The boy insisted. They glanced at each other again, smiling and shrugging their shoulders.

"He's calling you to wake up and have breakfast," Elizabeth explained the child's language with a giggle.

"Sarah, Chris, eat!"

"What's that, son?" Joseph pulled the boy up and looked with interest at the object he was holding. "Where did you get that?"

Chris saw her key-holder, with Anne's coloured house keys. It seemed that Jonathan had been sticking his nose in her bag. She searched for an acceptable explanation for them, but there was no need. Joseph told his son how rude it was to look into someone's bag and he handed the keys over to Chris.

"Thank you," he said with a giggle.

After a quiet and very nice breakfast, they got ready for the last stage of their journey. Chris and Sarah looked both happy and relaxed. Sarah had a special look in her eyes, different to the usual one.

To their delight, the sun was shining again and the temperature was lovely. It seemed they would have a great journey.

While Elizabeth hummed a quiet song to Jonathan, Joseph asked Sarah about the location of the lodging where they were supposed to find old Isaac. The descriptions of the place that she could remember from what her grandfather had told her, sounded somehow familiar to Joseph. He thought they might have been in that place before. In their conversation they also mentioned a place in the suburbs, a hill called Hampstead. When Chris heard that name, she felt eager to know where they were but she restrained herself from asking. She also thought that she had to find out where she was when she met Sarah, because if the gate to this time had opened there, shouldn't she be there to find her way back?

Then she remembered her promise to go with Sarah. Her thoughts became confused again but Joseph cut across them. He was walking slowly next to her.

"What Jonathan took from your bag, Chris." She knew it. She knew the coloured keys had attracted his attention.

"They are keys, I know, but the material and the colours they are made of, it's very strange, I haven't seen anything like that before."

Little Jonathan helped her out this time, by asking his father to carry him and by chatting to him.

When the sun's position indicated it was around midday, they stopped to rest and have something to eat.

"We'll need to hunt for our dinner," warned Joseph who, to Chris's relief, seemed to have forgotten about the subject, at least so far.

They went on until sunset, when they set up the last campsite they would have before reaching the city. It was Sarah who offered to help Joseph with the hunting, which was perfect for Chris since she much preferred to stay and make the fire. Jonathan was happy to help her pile up firewood.

A while later, the hunters of the group returned with their catch. Two little hares and a bird like a peacock hung from Joseph's shoulder. Chris looked away. If she had not done so, she knew the view of these poor creatures hanging lifeless would definitely destroy her appetite.

Their last night in the open air passed quietly. As usual Joseph and his family went away to sleep while Sarah spent her time asking about Chris's world. A couple of hours later, they too fell asleep.

The next morning, shortly after setting off on the last part of the journey, they saw more and more travellers, coming and going.

"We're here," Joseph said and pointed to one of the hills ahead. "This is Hampstead."

"Hampstead..." Chris felt suddenly happy. "If this is Hampstead, Camden should be over there and Islington there..." She saw Joseph's look and knew immediately she'd said too much. She had no idea at all if these boroughs already existed, at least with the same names. Elizabeth, who walked beside her husband, looking everywhere with interest, seemed not to have noticed what had just happened.

"I can see you know the city better than we do, Chris." Joseph said.

"Well..." she didn't know what to say and the first thing that came to her mind was, "I've been visiting my family a lot." Feeling really stupid she looked at him but Joseph did not look back. He just lowered his head.

'Why do I have the feeling that if I tell you where I really come from you won't be surprised, Joseph?' she thought.

PART II
THE RETURN

CHAPTER 14

Chris was astonished. She could not believe her eyes. Could this be the same city she had walked around only a few days ago? It could not be true and yet it was so real. She felt nauseous. There was dirt and extreme poverty, sick faces that looked into your eyes without any hope, lifeless people everywhere. Some of the children playing looked fine but too many of them would probably not reach their adolescence.

"Chris, are you alright?" Sarah was looking at her, worried, while Joseph and Elizabeth walked ahead of them carrying little Jonathan, who slept.

"What?"

"Are you alright? You look really pale."

"Yes, I'm fine. It's just that this looks really different, I don't know why I thought it was going to be really nice to reach the city, but this..."

"What were you expecting?" How could Sarah imagine a city two hundred years more developed? What was it that she had really expected to find? She realized she had been fooling herself for the whole journey. How did she manage to convince herself that once there everything would be fine? Maybe she had had a silly, subconscious idea that she was returning to the reality she missed so much? That she was going back to her friends? This was far from anything she knew; it was more like a horrible nightmare that made her sick and sad and frightened and from which she desperately wanted to wake.

Somehow Sarah understood what was going through Chris's mind and in a sympathetic gesture she took Chris' hand and squeezed her slightly, as if to give her courage.

"Joseph, what are we going to do here, do you know where we are?" Chris asked anxiously.

"We need to cross the city first, to reach the river. Once there we won't be far from the lodging where we've stayed before with Elizabeth, during previous trips."

"Lodging?" She tried hard to imagine the kind of place Joseph was talking about.

"Of course, you don't think we'll sleep on the streets, do you?"

"No of course not." Anywhere would be better than staying around here.

"Why do you look so surprised? I thought you had been in the city before." Joseph frowned.

"I just... don't recognize this part, I must have entered another part." She knew she would need to tell them the truth at some point. It was worth the risk. What could she lose if they thought she was insane? Even in the worst scenario, they would go their own way.

They walked for another couple of hours along the cobbled streets before they reached their destination. To her relief, the area which they reached was not too depressing. Chris was reminded of those paintings from London in the 18th century that she had seen. The lodging did not look bad either; it certainly was not a five star hotel but, although basic, it was surprisingly big and very clean and, to her amazement, cosy and welcoming. On entering the main hall, her spirits lifted and Chris was reminded of some saloon in a Wild West movie. The decoration was sparse, consisting of a few paintings faded by years; the lighting emanated from oil lamps, some hanging from the walls and some were attached to the main beams. To the right, a wide wooden staircase led to the rooms on the first floor.

Madame Juliette, the owner of the place, was all smiles when she greeted them. She lifted little Jonathan into her chubby, strong arms and squeezed him against her huge breasts.

"God bless you, child! You look healthy and so strong. You definitely are a sight for sore eyes." Jonathan was scared by such effusiveness and almost losing his breath, tried to defend himself, stretching his arms out to his mother. But before Elizabeth could react, Madame Juliette had already put him down and within a few seconds she was squeezing the life out of Elizabeth, shouting happily,

"My dear, it is so lovely to see you again, welcome to my house!"

"Thank you Madame Juliette." Her words were muffled by Madame's immensity.

Chris and Sarah giggled and exchanged a childish look.

Joseph whispered in their ears, "Believe me, she's a sweet, great and trustworthy woman and she cooks wonderfully!"

"Have you known her for long?" asked Chris.

"For a few years now, when Jonathan was born. She brought him into this world." As he spoke, Madame Juliette rushed towards him with open arms and after squeezing him too, she turned her eyes on the young women.

"And who do we have here?" She gently pushed him out of the way and moved towards them. Chris expected some effusiveness too, but luckily it did not come. Madame Juliette stopped in front of them, reaching out her hands for theirs, in a warm gesture of welcome. She held them for a moment while looking from one to the other.

"It certainly will not be easy to keep the rest of my guests away from such beauties." Chris blushed, feeling embarrassed by the unexpected compliment. "You will stay in the room next to mine, to protect you from any night intruders!" She laughed loudly.

"But come, come with me, it will be my pleasure to look after such esteemed visitors." She put two tables and enough chairs together and sat them down.

They learned very quickly that time vanished when Madame Juliette started to tell her stories. Firstly she told them about Samuel and Joshua, her two loyal employees.

"They are brothers, you know? They were brought by slave traders to this country many years ago. Unfortunately for their owner but luckily for me, they got sick and were abandoned because some stupid lord thought they were useless. Imagine! I found them, gave them food, clean clothes and a bed to sleep and rest like any human being. To my amazement, they are so strong that they recovered very soon and when they did, they refused to leave me. They said the only family they had, had been killed by the slave traders and that I had saved them, so their lives were mine."

Chris and Sarah exchanged a deep look. Madame Juliette continued,

"I told them I didn't want their lives, but I could use their strength and kindness to help me out here. It was hard to convince them that I would pay for their work, but in the end I succeeded, and here they are. I don't call them by those names though, even if other people do. I think we should always honour our names so I keep their original ones, *Babatunde* and *Oluwaseyi*."

Darkness had already fallen by the time she finished her second story, the anecdotal account that Joseph and Elizabeth knew so well, of her life in Paris, where she used to own a busy brothel. She was so drunk that she could hardly perch on the chair, so *Babatunde* and *Oluwaseyi* helped her up the stairs to her room. Later they came back to dismiss the few remaining guests of the inn; lock the main door and retire to their own room.

Not feeling tired enough to go to bed, the newly arrived travellers decided to stay up a little longer to enjoy the sudden quietness and the cosiness of the place.

Joseph looked at Chris and in a very calm way he asked the question she was dreading, "Where do you really come from, Chris?"

Chris wondered if they knew how to deal with the truth? She could only hope they would and so she simply said, "From here."

"Would you mind explaining that?" He would not give up.

"I mean I come from London but from another time." She waited for the reaction her statement would provoke.

"I knew it!" Joseph was beside himself.

"What are you saying, dear? What is it, what did you know?" Elizabeth was eager to know why her husband was so happy. Sarah remained silent. Chris was still astounded by Joseph's reaction.

"He knew that I come from the future, Elizabeth."

"You come from the future?" She turned pale and smiled nervously.

"Yes, I do. I don't know how, but I just arrived here from the 21st century."

"But..."

"Let her speak, woman, let her speak." Joseph couldn't hold back his enthusiasm.

"For some unknown reason I was transported through time and showed up just when Sarah was escaping."

"Somehow I knew it had to be true!" Joseph added, but his wife was still trying to make sense out of this bizarre conversation.

"What are you talking about, Joseph?"

"I never told you dear, but a couple of years ago I met a man here in the city. After a few glasses of ale he started talking about travelling in time and flying machines."

"Flying machines? Are you mad?"

"That's why I didn't tell you anything, I knew you'd say that." Elizabeth was not sure whether to laugh or cry.

"He's not mad, Elizabeth," Chris intervened, "What happened to that man, Joseph?"

"I never saw him again and I was told he never went back to the hostelry where he was living either."

"Well, I'm happy to hear that because it would prove, at least to me, that I'm not the only one which is definitely very reassuring to know. Talking of flying machines though Joseph, that's not how I got here. It just happened. At one moment I was in my time about to cross a street and the next I was in the middle of nowhere in the English countryside, in 1780."

"Marvellous!" Joseph looked like a child mesmerised by an incredible invention.

"Can you prove what you're saying?" Elizabeth was much more sceptical. "We have already had that incident with the hunter and the burning of our house. If the guards question us and hear you talking about the future, be sure nobody will hesitate to execute us." Joseph took her hand.

"I don't intend to go around telling everybody what I have just told you, Elizabeth. I only did it because I don't want to lie to you. Besides, if it happens again, I'll just disappear and you'll never really understand what happened." Chris said.

"It is too unbelievable for me, dear." Elizabeth added.

"I don't blame you, Elizabeth. I wish I was knowledgeable enough to tell you about things that are about to happen in this city these days, but unfortunately the history of England was not my strongest subject at school."

"I believe, you." Joseph said.

"And I do too." Sarah added with a big and supportive smile.

"The future, can you tell us about it, please? It must be so different and fascinating." Joseph spoke again, determined to be informed. Chris smiled and had a sip from her glass.

"It is very different, Joseph, it is." He was so eager that Chris could hardly answer one question before he had already asked the next.

"Half a day to cross to the Americas?" Joseph was astonished. Chris laughed and started drawing, with Sarah, next to her, mocking her artistic attempts. Elizabeth's distrustful expression was slowly changing.

"This is more or less how a *flying machine* looks. They're called airplanes."

"And what is this?" They wanted to know.

"This should be a mobile phone."

"What is that for?"

"We can speak to each other over it when miles apart. It doesn't matter where you are, whether in the same country or another country."

They went on like this for a long time, Chris drawing all sorts of things unknown at that time and her friends watching, delighted.

Finally Elizabeth said, "Is it true then? How can it be?"

"Every single word is true. Unfortunately, I can't explain how it happened."

"I'm not sure I'd like your world." Elizabeth said.

"There's not much choice if you happen to live in it."

"After all that you've told us, people shouldn't be still fighting! They do execute people here, which is horrible and often unjust, but it's hard to believe that there will still be so much killing in two hundred years time." Chris felt she had betrayed her own world.

"It's not that bad." Chris said unconvinced.

"Maybe," Joseph said, "but why invent so many machines and good things if it seems that people are never satisfied?"

"Well, that usually happens in the big cities; people are in a rush, they collect more and more things and for some people it's hard to step back from their jobs and be satisfied." She was thinking of herself. How often had she worked non-stop for days, to get a special contract or because she just liked it?

"I don't know, Chris." Joseph said, "What about the wars you've told us about? They will still go on in two hundred years which isn't right, and the weapons; more and more powerful weapons that they will invent!"

"There are lots of people all over the world doing good things and it's not so bad if you learn to enjoy what you have and stop being carried away by uncontrolled greed. Besides, you can't spend your life thinking that the world is a mess and that everything's wrong. That attitude would only drive you mad. Too many people criticize what's wrong, thinking that they know what's right! At the end, it's a fact that every age has had good and bad times. This city for example, it's going to be so many times bigger! It will be so densely populated, with people running to and fro all over the place but there will also be people sitting in the parks having a good time. People won't die in the streets as they do now and life expectancy will be three times higher! For good or bad, the world will go on and on, until every natural resource that supports life is used up. We might be coming closer and closer to the stage of not having a planet anymore. Considering that man has long ago landed on the moon and..." she couldn't go on. That was very hard for the couple to take in, and they shouted at once,

"On the moon?"

"Oh yes, that will happen in 1969. For the first time man will step on the moon and then the exploration will continue and encompass other planets in our universe and beyond. Doubtless, in maybe three hundred years from now or less, space will be colonized, the same as England established its colonies beyond the seas." She told them about the space station already being built and then about the increasing problem with global warming and natural disasters all over the world. Joseph changed the subject.

"What do you do in your world? How do you live, where do you live?" Without exhaustive details she told them about the city and her family, about her grandparents' death and about her decision to start a new life in England.

"Do you work, too, as everybody else seems to?"

"Yes, I do... I did. I took pictures."

"Pictures?" That was her subject for sure. She took the ones she had in her bag; the ones that Sarah had already seen. Joseph took one of them and studied it thoroughly.

"This is more perfect than a painting!" Elizabeth was amazed.

"Yes it is, but it will be invented in about forty years and the first ones won't be like this one. It won't be coloured, only black and white. First they will have problems fixing the images and only some years later, around 1839, a French man called Daguerre will make it better through a chemical reaction. Please don't ask me to explain how exactly." She giggled. "Towards the end of next century there will be some experimenting with coloured pictures, but they will really work only in the 20th century."

"What pictures do you take?" Joseph was interested to know.

"Well, depends on the subject. I used to work for a magazine and my team and I were sent to different places. My colleagues wrote the article about that place and I was in charge of taking the pictures, hundreds of them. Then we sent all the information through the computer for app..."

"Through the what?" Joseph's eagerness interrupted her and Chris tried during the next half hour to explain what a computer was and how one could send messages and pictures through it.

"I would love to see that."

In the early morning hours, tiredness overcame them and they went to sleep. Once in their room, Chris smiled pleased to see the bed. It was small but it would be much more comfortable than the bare ground. Next to it she saw, on a simple night table, a candle that gave the room a faint light. In the corner there was one of those wash basins that she had seen so many times in antique markets. Next to it was a jug full of water.

"I could really use a shower now," she whispered to herself, sighing.

Almost asleep, Sarah said, "Do you think the world will end?"

Chris was taken by surprise and thought she had misheard. "Pardon me?"

"Do you think the world will end?"

"Sarah, I'm so tired that if it ends now I wouldn't notice."

"You are making fun of me, Stranger."

"I'm not, Sarah, aren't you sleepy?"

"I'm afraid."

"Afraid? What are you afraid of, the world ending?" Chris lay on her side and watched Sarah's delicate profile highlighted by the reflection of the moonlight bathing the room.

"Yes."

"I can promise you it won't happen during the next two hundred years at least, don't worry."

"But..."

"Do you remember your grandfather?"

"Of course, always."

"What did he think of death?"

"That it didn't exist at all, that we only transform."

"Doesn't it help you to think about that? We'll all die one day, Sarah but that's no good reason to go around thinking about it, don't you agree?"

"It's not death really that scares me."

"What is it, then?"

"Not knowing what's beyond." Chris thought about it for a minute or two and then she said, "I came here and I found you. Maybe that's what happens when we die, we go somewhere else."

"If you go back to your world and I stay here, am I going to see you again?"

How could she know that? Sarah's question made her sad but she knew she had to be strong. She gave her an affectionate look and smiled.

"Why don't we think that, if it happens, you and I will communicate as our grandfathers do?" Sarah did not answer. She just snuggled up to Chris, as if looking for shelter, and she found it. Chris hugged her understandingly and they fell asleep to the sound of the steps of the man outside who walked the cobbled streets with his lantern each hour, proclaiming all was well.

CHAPTER 15

When they came downstairs the next morning, *Babatunde* and *Oluwaseyi* were playing with little Jonathan who had already discovered that calling them *Baba* and *Olu* was much easier. The two brothers were pleased with their new nicknames and they were also happy to entertain the boy. His parents and Madame Juliette were chatting. Chris and Sarah approached them and heard Madame mention Old Isaac. Chris and Sarah exchanged a glance. Sarah asked,

"Do you know him? Do you know Old Isaac?"

"I do know him. What's your business with him?" Madame seemed uncharacteristically secretive about the fact she knew the old man.

"Don't worry. If Madame Juliette knows Old Isaac, everything's just fine, we're in good hands." Joseph assured them and Chris and Sarah told her why they were looking for the old man.

"Hum..." The big woman leaned back in her chair, crossed her arms over her bulky stomach and half closed her eyes and nodded.

"Madame Juliette," Chris said as she moved to the chair next to hers, "Do you know where we could find him?"

"No, nobody knows that, dear." Madame Juliette said. Chris looked back at Sarah and noticed how her happy expression had turned to disappointment.

"Although... maybe, only maybe, there might be something I could do to send him a message." She smiled. Sarah's expression changed again.

Chris intuitively felt that Madame Juliette knew very well where the old man could be found and that his whereabouts were safe with her. She liked that, she trusted her. She was also very pleased to see how respectfully she treated her two black employees and how grateful they were to be considered equals, irrespective of the colour of their skin.

Madame Juliette got up and left the room, taking *Baba* with her. She came back alone a few minutes later and returned to her seat.

Chris admired the strength that this woman radiated. From listening to her stories last night, she found out she was a rare person: she was a fighter, with a strong character and determined to get what she wanted; she had lost her whole family back in France when she was still very young and, as she said, under tragic circumstances that she would not explain to anybody. Being left alone in the world had not beaten her; she managed to remain optimistic and keep her will power. Something told Chris that Madame Juliette would be incredibly supportive; the best ally they could have found.

"Don't worry. In a couple of days, maybe a couple of weeks, we'll hear from the old man. Until then I suggest you're very patient, very cautious and try to enjoy your stay. Nobody will bother you here."

Over the next days they accepted gratefully any suggestion Madame Juliette made. Joseph told her about the events in their house, and she advised them to stay away from those places where the guards might be. Money did not present a problem either. Sarah had given her one of the many jewels and Madame Juliette arranged for them to have everything they needed. They bought adequate clothes and food and they could move around in Madame Juliette's old wagon. The woman was clearly happy to look after them, showing them the city and spoiling little Jonathan, whom she loved dearly.

Every day that the group spent in that London of the 18th century was a new adventure and a new opportunity to learn more. They experienced the extreme degradation of the city: its filthy streets full of festering rubbish creating an intolerable stench; the fog and the smoke of burning coal which made them fear they would never see the sun again; the cold nights when they would endure the highly disagreeable smell of the coal; the daily burglaries, robberies and endless other crimes and the subsequent hangings and arbitrary justice.

But they also had the opportunity to enjoy the beautiful gardens that had been declared open to the public for a fee; roads as beautiful as the road to Kensington crossing Hyde Park and the many aristocratic mansions, contrasting with the countless urban developments for the poor, that were of such poor quality that they would often collapse, sometimes killing whole families as they slept.

On their trips, they would also talk about the reigning Monarch, George III, and Elizabeth and Joseph would be shocked when Chris told them later in his reign he would suffer a permanent mental illness. During the 20th century it would be thought that he actually suffered an inherited blood disease.

Joseph was relentless. Every time he noticed her surprise about something she had seen he would start his interrogation about how things would evolve or what would disappear during the following two hundred years. Everything was worth a comment. Joseph tried hard to imagine Tower Bridge, the gigantic statues that would be built years hence, Big Ben, the embankment along the river, the fast roads that would cross the city and the place which many years later would be one of the world's major airports. There was so much to explain and for Chris to draw. She was happy with it. Her memory comforted her. She very quickly got used to the lack of comfort. She accepted the absence of electronics, TV, mobile phones, lap top, cars and even the showers or appliances so well known and naturally accepted in a daily life in the 21st century. She did think of her friends and she missed them. She did not understand why, but she knew that Sarah's presence was significantly influential to her happiness. They spent long hours walking, talking, laughing and even losing themselves in each other eyes, in a complicity that only they seemed to understand. She stopped feeling unsettled if Sarah suddenly hugged her or took her hands in a clear and open demonstration of how much she cared about her. Chris did the same. Sarah was her 18th century friend, like Anne was her 21st century one.

Weeks after their arrival in London and returning one afternoon from the common, where Jonathan had been playing and running after birds, they found Madame Juliette talking and drinking with Joseph, Elizabeth and a man they had not seen before. Little Jonathan ran to his mother's arms and started babbling impatiently about the many new things he had seen on their walk.

"You were right, Juliette, when you described the beauty of these young women," the man said, getting up and approaching them. They stared at him.

"Ladies, may I introduce you to Old Isaac," Madame Juliette said and they smiled, pleased.

"You are beautiful, child." He hugged Sarah and added, "Your grandfather did not do you justice." Sarah blushed. Then, looking at Chris, he said, "Bless you, child. I've already heard about how helpful you've been." Chris felt inhibited by his comment and could barely respond to his greeting.

After a couple of hours with each other, everyone felt very comfortable. Old Isaac told them everything he knew about the next ship, how to find the captain and the date it was supposed to set sail from Eastbourne on the south coast. They still had a couple of weeks before the date came.

The following day, they decided to spend a day in the fields to the west, away from the city. Old Isaac led Madame Juliette's carriage towards Tyburn Street which, Chris explained, would years later become the famous Oxford Street. No-one could have foreseen the sudden end to the peaceful time they had experienced during the last weeks.

The crowd was taking over Tyburn. There were people coming from everywhere, making it impossible for the carriages to get through.

"What's happening?" Chris wanted to know.

"It seems we've chosen the wrong day to go out." Old Isaac said, frowning and looking at Madame Juliette. He tried to steer the horses round, but the guards prevented him, forcing him to stop. They aimed their bayonets and one of them reached out his open hand towards the old man, without saying a word and with an extremely unfriendly expression. Old Isaac seemed to be used to it, because he immediately reached into his pocket and handed the guard a piece of paper with the royal stamp on it. It was the official document that identified him as a free man. Sarah, scared to death, grabbed Chris's arm and bent her head down in front of the guards as a sign of submission. The men looked at her for a moment but when they saw Madame Juliette laying her hand on Sarah's head, they moved away. They ordered the old man to move the carriage and keep going. Elizabeth got hold of little Jonathan, squeezing up to Joseph who put his arms around them.

From one side another group surged forward:

"Give way! Give way to the condemned!" The guards yelled and pushed anyone who dared to cross them. Old Isaac kept the carriage to one side and asked everybody to be quiet. Behind them they saw the slowly moving carriage carrying the prisoners condemned to be hanged. The dreadful view made Chris feel queasy. The street sellers were swamped by a white crowd shouting, hysterically, "Death! Death! Death to the thieves and the blacks!"

From that moment on, everything happened too fast. Little Jonathan started to cry, afraid of the shouting and Old Isaac fought to keep control of the snorting and agitated horses. A woman holding a child in her arms suddenly appeared and ran towards the prisoners. Once there, she tried desperately to climb on to the cart but had to defend herself from the guard who pushed her away. As the woman renewed her attempts, the guard hit her with the butt of his musket on her chest. She fell to the ground, still holding the baby. Immediately Sarah had jumped off the carriage and rushed to the woman and was already bending over her.

"Sarah!" Chris shouted. The guard, interpreting Sarah's movements as an act of disobedience, raised his weapon to hit her too. Chris tried to jump off the carriage but Madame Juliette's strong arms held her back. It was Joseph who managed to fly at the guard. Everything turned to chaos. Chris was trying to release herself from Madame Juliette's arms and Elizabeth was calling out for her husband. The open carriage with the prisoners kept moving slowly, while other guards joined their companions and started venting their fury on Joseph, beating him to the ground next to Sarah. Then the guards forced him and Sarah to get up and dragged them away into the crowd. The woman with her baby lay on the ground without moving.

"Where are they? Sarah! Joseph!" Chris was desperately trying to catch sight of them, Madame Juliette still holding her arm. In the meantime Old Isaac had controlled the horses and was manoeuvring to leave the place.

"No, no! We can't go!" Chris was furious. "We can't just leave them!" When she saw that Old Isaac had no intention of stopping, she freed herself from Madame Juliette's strong grip and jumped off. She was not going to leave Sarah or Joseph there. She was not going to do that. Once on the street the crowd dragged her with it. She tried to look over her shoulder and walk against the flow but her efforts were useless. She was forced to move along with them. Suddenly the crowd stopped and started shouting again, "Death! Death to the black thieves!"

In a future century she would have looked up and admired the Marble Arch, but there was none to see. She was in the centre of Tyburn, the former village where executions were public spectacles. Tyburn, where people had erected large spectator stands so that as many as possible, for a fee, could see the hangings. She felt sick. The convicts were placed in a horse drawn cart, blindfolded, a noose place around their necks and given the chance to speak to the crowd to confess their sins. The drums started to sound and the crowd fell silent. The convicts refused to confess to crimes they had not committed and the cart was pulled away. Horrified, Chris saw their bodies falling and twisting and people approaching them quickly to pull their legs to help them out of their misery and avoid long and painful death. She had read about those events but she never thought she would find herself witnessing them.

Chris was petrified, staring at the scene. She could neither move nor breathe. She just stood there, her eyes wide open, until the crowd around her began to drift away and she heard the cry that brought her back to reality.

"Chris! Chris!" Sarah's desperate voice made her heart pound.

"Sarah?" she answered, but got no response and she started walking in circles, scanning the place until she saw her. Not far from where she stood, Sarah and Joseph were pushed into a closed carriage with small windows and iron bars. Joseph could hardly stand on his feet. Her first thought was to run over to them but she knew that would be a huge mistake. The guards would not let her get close. The sensible thing was to follow them and find out where they were being taken. Chris covered her head with her cloak and mingled with the rest of the poor people. While she walked, trying not to lose sight of them, unsettling thoughts crossed her mind. What would happen to them? How was she going to help them, now that Old Isaac, Elizabeth and Madame Juliette were not with her? Where were they? What if the guards hurt Sarah and Joseph? What if she got lost and could not go back to the lodging? Where were the guards going? Suddenly she realized that the street where she was looked familiar. They had walked along this road to get to Madame Juliette's house. Not all was lost. 'This means the Tower of London must be ahead,' she thought and she was right. The carriage went on down the street, turned, went on again and then stopped in front of the main entrance to the Tower. She hid behind the trees by the riverside. Two of the guards opened the door and pulled the chains fastened around Sarah's and Joseph's wrists. Both of them tripped and lost their balance, falling down. She made a move as if to set off running towards her friends but a command came from just behind her:

"You stay there, girl! Don't even think about it. You must not do anything stupid again!"

"Madame Juliette! You scared the hell out of me!"

"Well deserved, Chris. What the hell you think you're doing? What would have happened if they'd got you too? You're not thinking, girl!"

"How did you get here?" she asked, ignoring the reprimand.

"Old Isaac guessed they'd bring them here, but we couldn't be sure."

"Well, then I'm happy I did what I did. It wasn't a bad idea after all, was it? Now we only need to get them out."

"As I said before, you're not thinking. Come on, let's go back."

"Go back? We can't leave them there; we have to get them out!"

"If we get them out, it won't be now, Chris. Now do what I tell you, will you? We've got enough trouble."

"If we get them out! I prefer it when you're optimistic."

"And I prefer you when you use your brain. I'm just being down to earth, girl. Have you got any idea how many guards this prison has?"

"I don't care if they have a whole troop there." Chris was determined, "I don't know how, but we have to help them. I won't leave Sarah on her own there, nor Joseph."

"My God you're stubborn! You need to calm down first. At least we know where they are. Let's go back and plan."

"Wait, what's happening there? Are they not going in?"

"If it's what I imagine..."

Another guard came out of the Tower, gave some orders and Sarah and Joseph were forced back into the carriage. It started moving again.

Chris and Madame Juliette followed it closely along a few streets until they reached a group of grim looking old buildings.

"The old warehouses," Madame Juliette whispered with a big smile and a sigh of relief.

"Is there anything funny about this place?" Chris asked harshly.

"No, there's nothing funny about it." Madame Juliette frowned at her, annoyed. "It's a prison," she almost yelled but she smiled again.

"And that makes you happy? What possible reason could you have to feel happy?"

"What makes me happy, impetuous girl is that God is on our side! Come on, let's go home."

CHAPTER 16

"In the old warehouses?" Old Isaac asked Madame Juliette, once back in the lodging. "Thank you Lord, that is good news after all."

"Could somebody please explain to us why this is so good?" Chris demanded, looking at Elizabeth.

"The thing is, dear," Old Isaac said, "There are so many guards posted in the Tower that you can't imagine. We would have had no chance at all of rescuing Sarah and Joseph from the Tower."

"And?" Chris was still out of her mind.

"If they took them to the warehouses, the chance of escape is better if we can work out how to take advantage of it because they just use that place to lock up vagabonds or drunkards and there's never too many guards, maybe two or three."

All of a sudden Chris realized how irrational and impatient her reaction had been. "Madame Juliette, I'm so sorry I lost control. I just couldn't take it, I..."

"Don't worry, my dear, I was once young and sometimes impetuous as well. What we need now is a good plan. We can't be too confident, but we need to move fast."

Chris didn't see Old Isaac for the rest of the afternoon. Madame Juliette was busy in the house and Elizabeth spent the hours dedicated to Jonathan. Chris was distracted and no matter how hard she tried to pretend, she was worried and sad.

'She's a good woman,' Chris thought about Elizabeth, 'and a good mother.' Her mind went back to her own family and she tried hard to find one nice memory of her mother being affectionate to her, but she couldn't find any. The only memories of her childhood went back to her parents' preaching about her duties towards her younger sister. Michelle had been born prematurely six years after Chris and she had never forgotten that day. She could clearly see her father frantically walking up and down in the hospital, waiting for the doctors to tell him about the birth.

Her sister was born with a severe osseous malformation in her hips, and a heart problem. That day Chris's life changed. It seemed to her that she didn't exist for her parents anymore. Only Michelle counted; Michelle and her health problems. The following years passed between doctors and hospitals, check-ups, operations and medicines, special treatments and the constant reminder about how important it was to look after her little sister. When Michelle turned five, she underwent the last surgery on her hips that helped her to stand by herself. By then Chris had become used to not expecting much from her parents. They knew nothing about her. Only her grandparents had been there for her: interested in listening to her; answering her questions and concerns; playing with her; giving her motivation and incentives; spoiling her and correcting her when she did something wrong.

Looking after her sister had been no guarantee of getting along well with her. They were strangers to each other. Their only link was having being born to the same mother. Michelle grew up into a spoiled teenager who would rise to a selfish, capricious and manipulative woman. Whatever goals she had, she would achieve, captivating everybody but Chris and her grandparents. A sense of responsibility was never one of Michelle's characteristics; therefore, she always got the worst marks at school. She was still the most popular girl of her class, maybe because she spent more time in the director's office than in the classroom, paying attention to the teachers.

To compensate her for all her physical problems, life had given her an extremely sharp memory. After a quick revision she knew the correct answers allowing her to pass the necessary examinations. Her biggest weakness was that she lacked the capacity to love just for the sake of love.

When Chris finished school and applied for university, her parents seemed interested in her future, but of course they disapproved of her choice to study photography considering it, as Chris knew they would, one more of her wrong choices and mistakes.

"Kiss...Dad and Sadah?" Jonathan brought her back to reality. She sat him on her lap and hugged him.

"Soon, sweetheart, they'll be back with us very soon, I promise." Chris thought of her sudden promise. She had also promised Sarah to look after her, and now she was imprisoned. How was she doing? Was she cold and hungry? Who else apart from Joseph was there with her, in that horrible place? She missed her. She missed her a lot.

"We've got to plan something, Elizabeth," she told her later while having a cup of tea.

"I can't think of how we could fool the guards, Chris."

"I only hope that Old Isaac wasn't wrong about the guards and that this will all be over soon. In less than a week the ship will go, with or without us." Both women were silent after that. There was no need to express their thoughts. Both of them knew too well what the other was thinking. If the guards caught them trying to help the prisoners, they would probably lock them up too and the idea of being carried to Tyburn made them tremble. Chris looked at Elizabeth, admiring her strength. She was grateful because it was sort of contagious. What she didn't know was that Elizabeth was thinking exactly the same of her.

For the time being, the best and only thing to do was to wait and rest. Maybe tomorrow they would devise a plan.

So it was. During breakfast, while Jonathan played with the two wooden figures Sarah had carved for him, Chris stared fixedly at Elizabeth.

"What's wrong?" Elizabeth asked.

"I think I've got it," she smiled and Elizabeth looked surprised. She didn't tell her though, that her plan was based on a dream she had had last night. She didn't have to tell her that her grandfather was helping her to think, as long as the plan was good enough to rescue Sarah and Jonathan.

"It might be crazy, but with Madame Juliette's and Old Isaac's help, I can't see why it wouldn't work."

"What do you have in mind?"

Chris told her and shortly afterwards they went searching for Madame Juliette. They found her talking to Old Isaac, who had just arrived.

"Chris, Isaac might have a plan. He met some friends yesterday and they could help us." Madame smiled.

"Great, we can talk about your plan or we could think of bringing the prisoners the word of God during their last hours." Madame Juliette and the old man looked at each other wondering what Chris was talking about.

They spent the following hours discussing the rescue plan.

Dusk was falling. The Tower of London area and the old warehouses were very different from the rest of the city. While in some places fancy carriages were already transporting wealthy members of high society to various private and glamorous parties, in other parts of London the less fortunate started to fill up the inns where they could forget their worries.

The two figures approached the gates of the old warehouses.

"This is no place for you, sisters," said one of the guards in a deep, strong voice. "It would be better for you to go away."

"Any place is good to fulfil God's will, brother," one of the sisters answered with trembling voice.

"What are you looking for?"

"We only want to bring the word of God to prisoners possessed by evil, brother, and bring them some food and drink to ease their suffering for their sins."

"I can't let you in, sisters."

"What's happening here?" somebody shouted from behind them.

"Two sisters bringing food to the prisoners, Captain."

"We bring food and the word of God, brother. God will bless you for your good will. It's only food and drink."

The official checked the basket Madame Juliette was carrying and took one of the bottles.

"Let them in, Sergeant! If these prisoners make it to the gallows, it won't do them any harm to get there well fed, but we'll keep this!" the captain said smiling and hiding the bottle under his cape before he walked away.

"God bless you, brother," Chris said but she kept her thought to herself, 'If they are hurt, I'll kill you, *brother*, I promise.'

The women were led through a narrow, stinking corridor, dimly illuminated by a couple of torches. Inside they found a third guard who was caught by surprise at the sight of the visitors. He immediately grabbed his musket. "Put your musket down," the sergeant told him, "the captain gave them permission to see the prisoners. I will take them there myself." A few metres ahead he pointed to one of the cells from which they could hear pitiful pleadings. "These won't need anything, sisters. They will be executed in the morning." Then he led them to another cell and said, "You can see these ones, maybe they'll be luckier than the others."

"Aren't there any more sinners, my son?"

"No, sister, there's only this poor unfortunate and his two black bastard friends."

The two women approached the dungeon making the sign of the cross in front of the guard's face and whispering "God bless you, brother."

The guard opened the heavy wooden gate with wrought iron and said, "You can go in now. I will be back in a few minutes to help you out." He stepped back and moved away. They heard him whispering to his companion.

The stench of the little space made them nauseous. Once inside, and after adjusting their eyes to the darkness, they saw three figures, two of them clinging together. The other one was lying on the ground. They prayed it was them.

"We are here to tell you about God, brothers."

"Madame Juliette?" one of the sitting figures moved and stood up slowly.

"Shh... everything's fine, brother. God knows you regret your sins. Eat and drink and pray with us."

"Sarah, are you alright?" Chris said kneeling down over her friend. She took her hand and stroked her face affectionately.

"Chris..." she could hardly speak. They had beaten her and she seemed extremely weak.

"Tomorrow night, we'll come and get you out, darling. Please resist, you must be strong."

"Chris, I don't want to die, not here, not like this..."

"Don't speak like that, you won't die, none of you will die!" Chris hugged her and wiped away her tears. "Here, drink this and eat, you'll need all your strength tomorrow."

"You're risking too much, Juliette," Joseph said while eating and drinking eagerly.

"We won't leave you here, Joseph. Out there are two people who need you. Besides, it would have been impossible to stop Chris from doing something."

"Jonathan and Elizabeth, are they well?"

"They are just fine, fine and waiting for you."

"Can we give him some food?" Joseph pointed to the body lying on the ground.

"Who's he?" Chris wanted to know.

"He was caught stealing food. He only wanted to feed his family and they'll hang him for that and for being black."

Chris approached the body, held his face and gave him something to drink. The young man opened his eyes and said, "T-thank you, sister."

"Do you want to get out of here?"

"Of c-course, b-but how?" His mouth was full of bread and cheese.

"It's time to go, sisters!" the guard yelled.

"What's your name?"

"J-jeremiah."

"Don't worry, Jeremiah, you'll come with us too." Then she went back to Sarah, hugged her and after kissing her forehead she said, "Take this, keep this food. We'll come back tomorrow to get you out, ok?"

"Please take care, Chris, don't risk your life for me."

"Shh... just trust me, ok?"

The guard entered the cell and saw the three silhouettes down on their knees in front of the sisters. "...and save us from evil, Amen."

After the guard locked the gate again, Chris took another bottle out from the basket and handed it over to him.

"God won't see it as a sin if you share this wine with your companion as long as your captain doesn't see you, brother. The wine is produced in our convent. Our Lord knows how hard is must be for you, brothers, to spend such long hours here, just looking after these unfortunate sinners. We can bring you more wine tomorrow if you want."

The sergeant accepted the bottle, looked at Chris and drank from it. He took a breath, drank again and handed it over to his companion, who drank too.

"Of course, sister," he said gratefully. "You can come tomorrow and pray with those bastards but make sure you don't forget some bottles."

"Your captain won't get angry, will he? God is only asking us to ease the pain of the prisoners."

"You don't need to worry about him. The Captain won't be here tomorrow, only my two companions and me until midnight. Then they will change the guard."

"God bless you, brother. We'll see you tomorrow," said Madame Juliette.

Both women walked quickly and silently down the street until they lost sight of the warehouses.

As soon as they got home, Jonathan ran happily to throw himself in Chris's arms. Old Isaac and Elizabeth were anxiously waiting for them to hear all the details of the visit.

"We'll have to fool three armed men, Isaac," Chris said nervously after finishing the story.

"I don't see any problem there, child. I have the feeling everything's going to work out just fine. Besides, we can count on Jeremiah. You'll see, we'll sort this out and in a couple of days you'll be safe on board."

CHAPTER 17

The following afternoon, the women checked the details of the plan with Isaac. The old man would wait for them with little Jonathan and Elizabeth on the carriage a block away from the warehouses. They would have loaded enough food and water for two or three days. He and Madame Juliette would go along to make sure they were safe but for most of the journey they would be on their own. They had to reach the sea and continue along the coast until reaching the village of Eastbourne, where they would find the ship.

"We'll never be able to thank you enough for your help, Old Isaac."

"Don't think about that, Chris. Even if he knew he would get punished for it, Sarah's grandfather never hesitated in saving my life many years ago and this is how I can thank him, by helping his granddaughter and her friends."

"You know you can come with us, don't you? And you too, Madame Juliette," she added, looking at the big woman." If they find out that you helped us, you'll be in trouble," Chris said.

"We'll be just fine, dear, don't you worry. Besides, we're too old to start all over again somewhere else, aren't we, Isaac?" He nodded silently. Chris did not insist. She knew they were right. Madame Juliette would never abandon either her boys or her house, and Old Isaac's health wouldn't help him in a crossing like the one ahead of them.

The old man got up and left the room. He came back after a moment with two daggers. "It will be better if you take them." Handing them over to Chris, he continued, "They might be useful if you should have a problem." Chris took one of the daggers and observed it thoroughly. It was bigger than the one she had taken from the man in the house. Her mind flashed back to the cabin and, even though the memory was not a nice one, she knew she wouldn't hesitate to use the knife.

"Are you alright?" Elizabeth was holding her by the shoulders.

"Yes, I was just thinking how life can change so much and so quickly. Some months ago I never thought I'd kill someone."

"Don't think about that now, Chris. It's better to get ready; it will get dark soon."

Only an hour later, they realized it was getting dark faster than normal. The sky had been clear every day for the last week; now though the clouds started to cover the city.

"Heaven's helping us," Old Isaac smiled. "It will be easier to escape."

Dressed up in their religious habits, the women started walking towards the warehouses while Isaac and Elizabeth got on the carriage with Jonathan. They would follow them at a distance. By the time they got there, it was completely dark and pouring down. As agreed, Old Isaac stopped the carriage one block away from the warehouses. Waiting was agony.

The guards smiled at the view of the approaching nuns and said, extremely pleased, "Good Lord, sisters! You're very brave, coming down here in this rain!"

"Good evening, brother. The rain doesn't stop the Lord." They handed him one of the bottles and went inside. Madame Juliette greeted the other two guards and took two more bottles from the basket. They didn't wait to start drinking. After all, two nuns represented no danger and the night shift would only come at midnight.

"I'll open the cell for you, sisters," the sergeant offered, while sipping from his bottle. "Get up and pray for your soul, bastards!" he yelled to the threesome and turned his back on them, laughing. Joseph, Sarah and Jeremiah got up quickly.

"Let's pray, brothers," they said loud enough so that the guard would hear.

"Here, Jeremiah," Chris took from between her clothes one of the daggers and handed it over to him. The young man looked at it amazed. "Hopefully you won't need to use it." They waited some minutes, listening to the relaxed laughter outside until they heard nothing but silence.

Chris carefully opened the gate that separated them from the guards and poked her head round to check what was happening out there. One of the guards lay on the small table, gripping the bottle. The other guard had fallen to the ground.

"We can go now."

"What happened to them?" Joseph asked when he saw the bodies.

"Old Isaac put something in the wine."

"The other guard must be still out there," exclaimed Madame Juliette.

"I'll check," Chris walked towards the main entrance and came back in a hurry. "He's still there, we need to bring him in somehow," she whispered. But they had no time to think about what to do next.

The guard was already there, behind them and aiming his musket at Chris.

"Why aren't you with the prisoners in the cell, sister?" His voice was calm, but once he saw his companions and the others, he reacted furiously. "Go back to the cell!" he ordered pushing Chris too hard with his weapon. The sharp edge of the bayonet went easily through the thin clothes and Chris felt a stabbing ache at the side of her back that made her trip and lose balance. The guard, incensed, lifted the musket to hit Chris with its butt, but Jeremiah was quicker. Without hesitation he sprang at the guard and stuck the dagger in his chest.

"Holy God," Madame Juliette cried out. Joseph took her by the shoulders pushing her to the door. "Quick, we've got no time to waste, let's get out of here!" Sarah and Jeremiah helped Chris to get up and they ran away from the place.

They closed the huge gates, chaining them together and after locking the big rusted padlock, they threw the key into a stinking pile of rubbish.

After a few minutes the carriage moved away quickly and silently through the streets, while the rain still fell heavily.

Nobody said anything until Isaac brought the horses to a stop and said, "From here you'll have to go on by yourselves. The guards will be unconscious for some hours, but when they wake up they will find the other one dead and by then you must be really far away."

Sarah was the first in hugging him. "Go and fulfil your and your grandfather's dream, child." He kissed her forehead and looked at the others. "Forty miles from here, more or less, the road will part. Take the narrow path to the right. It will take you far off the main route but it will also take you to a small village where you'll be safe and able to rest. There look for the captain of the ship. Don't forget to give him this." He handed them a folded paper.

They said goodbye to Old Isaac and to a deeply moved Madame Juliette. Afterwards they thanked Jeremiah for his help. While in prison Sarah and Joseph had suggested he join them on their venture, but the young man had to go back to his family. "My family must be sad, thinking that I'll be executed. Now they will be happy to see me, thanks to you, my friends."

The three of them stayed behind, waving, while the rest of the group set off on the final journey that would take them to their destiny.

"I think heaven's still helping us. It seems that the rain is stopping now," Elizabeth said holding a sleeping Jonathan in her arms.

"It is, dear, it is," Joseph agreed from the front seat, where Sarah sat next to him. "Further ahead we'll need to give the horses a break."

"I don't think it's good to stop before we reach the place Old Isaac mentioned, Joseph." Chris made a huge effort not to show the pain in her voice, but she couldn't fool Sarah.

"What is it, Chris?" She did not wait for the answer. Sarah leaned on Joseph's shoulder and jumped into the back, sitting down beside her. In doing so, she accidentally brushed against Chris's injury, and she could not help moaning in pain.

"You're hurt!" she cried out worried, "Joseph, we need to stop!"

"No! Don't stop, please. I'm fine, we need to go on."

"But Chris..."

"I'm fine, it's only a scratch. Please, Joseph, we can't stop now." Joseph knew she was right. It would be dangerous to stop on the main road. He hoped that the horses could withstand the effort required as he whipped them on continuously, until they reached the secondary road.

They looked for a safe place to light a fire and were very pleased to find no sign of rain. The ground around was completely dry. After leaving little Jonathan sleeping comfortably on the wagon, Elizabeth helped Joseph to gather firewood.

"I'm sorry I will have to return the compliment and burn your wound to avoid an infection, Chris."

"Why are you sorry, Joseph?" she tried to smile.

"Because I was unconscious and you are not. Will you be able to stand it?" he was very concerned, after seeing that the scratch was not as insignificant as she had said.

"Do I have any choice?" Her voice was shaky.

"I'm afraid you don't," and while he put the dagger to the flames, he looked at Elizabeth and Sarah. "You'll have to hold her very tightly so that she doesn't move." They agreed, nodding silently. From then on everything happened very quickly. As soon as the red hot blade touched her skin, her whole body twisted with pain and all around her got dark. Chris fainted even before she could cry out.

She woke up and the first thing she saw was stars; millions of them. It was a cold but beautiful night. It took her a few seconds to remember what had happened. Then she noticed Sarah holding her hand and sleeping next to her. When she tried to move, the sharp ache made her grumble and Sarah woke up.

"You stay still, Stranger. Don't try to be brave." Chris didn't answer. She felt too weak to speak. She gently lay down again and surrendered to the care and protection her friend was offering. By the time she opened her eyes again, Joseph was checking on her wound.

"You'll be fine, but you must do the rest of the journey lying down without moving, otherwise the wound will open again and that wouldn't be good."

"Don't worry; I'll be a good girl. How late is it, shouldn't we go soon?"

"We'll leave as soon as you're comfortable on the carriage. First you need to eat something. Elizabeth cooked a nice meal with all the food Madame Juliette and Old Isaac packed for us." Chris ate unwillingly, while Elizabeth spoke to Sarah.

"Isaac asked me to give this to you." She said and Sarah reached out her hand to receive the small leather bag.

"But these are some of the jewels I gave him and all the money he got for the ones he sold!" She exclaimed in surprise after opening it.

"He's a good man, Old Isaac." Joseph said, giving Sarah a warm smile, "I'd say he was really fond of your grandfather and very grateful, too. I'm sure we'll miss him and Madame Juliette, don't you think, Elizabeth?"

"I hope they will be alright." Sarah's voice was full of melancholy.

"They will, dear, especially with Isaac knowing that at last he was able to do something for your grandfather." Elizabeth added.

"Well, ladies," Joseph said kindly, "as soon as we help Chris on the wagon, we can go. A ship is waiting for us!"

Joseph's and Elizabeth's plan when leaving their burned home had been to establish themselves in the city, but as life turned out, they had to change their plan. London was not a safe place to stay anymore, not even for Chris, so they had all decided to stay together and start a new life on that land beyond the sea.

CHAPTER 18

They arrived in the village at dawn and, even though it was unlikely that anyone would already be looking for them there, they set up camp on the outskirts to try to stay as hidden as possible. Joseph set off with Sarah to start looking for the captain and Elizabeth took care of Chris and little Jonathan.

"Everything's settled," Joseph confirmed happily when they came back around midday. "It was just as Old Isaac told us. The captain is an extremely nice and kind man and he'll let us on the ship. He was adamant in his warning though, to be prepared for a long and tough journey."

"When will we set sail?" Chris wanted to know, feeling much better.

"The day after tomorrow. That means we can stay here today to give you time to recover completely. I'll go back to town later to get us clothes, food and maybe some medicines or whatever could be useful for the journey." Chris was not listening anymore, she was lost in her thoughts and emotions.

"Are you all right?" Sarah asked when they were alone.

"Yes," she lied and forced a smile. "Just a bit worried about the journey ahead."

There was a lot to think about. She was thinking of their adventure coming to an end. She was afraid of whatever would come next. She reminded herself how useless it was to think too much. Was there, after all, anything that she could do to change the events? A long time had already passed and she was still here. Maybe there was no return to her century after all. Did she really want to return to the future? What did she have there, waiting for her? Of course her friends were there and also the new life she had planned. But here, she had friends now. These people had become such an important part of her life and she felt good with them and she knew they felt good about her too. She had a family now, she had fought for this family; risked her life, and she did not regret it for one second.

The day went by slowly but peacefully. Chris's wound was healing very well and early next morning she felt much stronger and in good spirits. They left the village as they took the road along the

93

sea that would lead them to the small port where the ship lay anchored, waiting to set sail. Some hours later they reached the top of the cliff which had a stunning view overlooking the village of Eastbourne. The rough waves slapped the coast furiously tossing the imposing ship, a three mast schooner whose sails were stowed ready to unfurl in a couple of hours towards a new adventure. From the distance they could see busy sailors loading barrels and bulky cargo, including some sort of wooden cages carrying what appeared to be poultry.

"There it goes, our food," teased Chris, reminded of similar ships in a movie about the French Revolution. 'And I thought my first cruise would be on a five star liner in the Caribbean,' she said to herself.

"If the captain was right, which I don't doubt at all," said Joseph, "one of those houses over there should be the lodging where we can rest until tomorrow."

The old cottage, where they would spend the night, was small but comfortable. After dinner, Chris insisted stubbornly in getting up and having a walk, even though the wound did hurt a little from time to time. She went out, walked slowly up to the viewpoint and sat down on a rock to contemplate the horizon, where the clouds had started changing colours.

"Hey Stranger," Sarah's whisper startled her.

"In two hundred years from today, somewhere out there will be a tunnel below the ocean which will bring both French and English coasts together."

"Below the ocean? I would be so scared to cross it! Did you?"

"No, I didn't actually. When I had the chance, I changed my mind at the last minute and I stayed in a beautiful French village in the countryside."

"Is there something disturbing you, Chris? You've been very quiet."

"Not at all, I was just wondering what's waiting for us there," she lifted her chin, her eyes fixed on the horizon.

"Do you regret it?" Sarah's voice was sad.

"Do I regret what?" she looked at her.

"I don't know, maybe having come so far?"

"You, Elizabeth, Joseph and little Jonathan are the only ones that I have now. After we agreed that they should leave too, maybe at first I wasn't sure, but now? No, I don't regret it."

"Everything will be fine, Stranger, you'll see."

"I know." But did she really believe that?

Sarah spoke again, "I want to thank you again for saving my life for the second time." Chris took her hand.

"Did you think for one moment that I'd wait to see you both being punished or even executed? We couldn't allow that, Sarah. Besides, you've helped me too."

"I love you, Chris."

"I love you too, my friend," Sarah's long kiss on her cheek made her feel her stomach contort. "I think we... we should go back. Tomorrow will be a very special day and we need to rest now."

Chapter 19

*H*ours before the sunrise, Chris was suddenly woken by Sarah's restlessness. She was mumbling incoherent words as if having a nightmare. After struggling to light the candle on the table next to the only bed in the room, she shook Sarah gently, trying to wake her up. Sarah opened her eyes, scared, and, despite the poor light, Chris could see her eyes full of tears. Sarah snuggled up to her side.

"You're here," she said snivelling.

"Of course I am and everything's fine. We still have a few hours. Go back to sleep," she said, holding her tightly and stroking her hair. Sarah stopped sobbing and fell asleep again. Chris instead, stayed awake, thinking of the ship and trying hard to imagine where they would end up. Any place would be so different to what she knew. What kind of adventures and surprises were waiting for them there? She was desperate to get some more sleep but her attempts failed. Unaware of the time sliding away, she began to feel very strange. The harder she tried to remember anything, the more blurred her memories became. Without realizing how it happened, she suddenly knew it. She knew she would not go.

"I will never board that ship," she whispered, "I won't do it; it won't be allowed." Her heart felt heavy and it was difficult to breath. She would miss Elizabeth and Joseph and that sweet little boy so much! And the mere idea of letting Sarah go was unbearable. She was so fond of her, she had got to know her, they had protected each other, she liked her presence, it was fun laughing with her, she enjoyed their chats and her companionship. She felt happy with Sarah. Her company had helped Chris forget her past and appreciate life for what it was. Sarah's voice brought her back.

"No grandfather, no, why?"

"Shh...Sleep, Sarah, sleep. It's only a dream."

But it was no dream. Sarah burst into tears and this time her tears seemed to spring up endlessly from the depths of her soul. Chris had to make a huge effort to stay strong and not fall apart. Sarah clung to her as if her life depended on their embrace. She knew as well that Chris would not board the ship.

"I don't want to go without you," she cried like a child and Chris didn't know what to do or what to say when their faces touched and

Sarah's lips brushed hers. She could feel Sarah's body shivering, looking for her. Or was it hers, shivering and looking for Sarah?

"I don't... I don't think this is right, I..." but Sarah's gentle and tender touch destroyed in a fraction of a second the strength of conviction Chris had had up to now. Her hesitation succumbed to a kiss that defeated any feeling of rejection from kissing a woman. It only lasted for a few seconds, though. Their intimacy was suddenly interrupted by the bright reflection of a light on the ceiling and then some sort of mist spreading all over the room. Shocked, they saw how the shape of a face was forming over them. It was only one feature, but each of them could recognize her own grandfather.

Embarrassed at being caught in what she believed a forbidden act, she called his name, "Grandfather."

"The sun will rise soon," the deep voice was coming from every corner of the room.

"Grandfather, I don't want to separate from her!"

"Everything is happening as it is meant to be," the voice continued.

"I'm not going," were Chris's only words.

"You'll meet again; you must wait until the time comes."

"You'll take care of her, will you?" Chris begged.

"You will both be looked after; you will both see me again. You won't recognize me, but you will see me again." On saying that, the figure began to fade and then there was silence again. The only noise they could hear was their heartbeats and both knew the time had come for them to say goodbye. This time Chris could not hold back her tears. There was nothing either of them could do. There were no questions, no answers and no possible explanations right now. Their only reality now was to lose themselves in each other's embrace.

The minutes or maybe hours, passed inexorably while they lay there holding each other, trying to keep back time. The noises next door soon marked the end, allowing only one last glance into each other's eyes, one last kiss and one last hug.

Joseph knocked at their door, hurrying them up. The captain wanted to set sail before sunrise. They were waiting for them at the old pier. Everybody was already on board ready to start their journey. Little Jonathan suddenly burst into tears when he saw Chris. As if knowing he had to say goodbye, he ran towards her arms.

"Hurry up," said Joseph gently, gesturing with his arm and starting to walk up the catwalk, but Elizabeth stopped him and pointed with eyes full of tears towards the women a few metres behind them.

"What?" he looked back and he understood immediately. They

embraced all together in silence trying to hold each other as long as possible, sharing their sadness. The fog, relentlessly and ruthlessly, started to come down, slowly swirling over Chris's head.

"Please," Chris begged to Elizabeth and Joseph while holding Sarah's hand. "Take care of her, take care of you and be happy in the new land."

Elizabeth held her tight, kissing her cheeks a few times, then gently took Sarah by her shoulders, forcing her to walk, but she clung one more time to Chris's neck and whispered in her ear, "Search for me in time, Stranger, somewhere I'll be waiting for you."

"I will, Sarah, I will."

Everything happened too fast after that. Whilst their friends started moving away slowly, Chris and Sarah were staring into each other's eyes, trying to find the last words they would share. Chris heard Sarah's whisper, "Until we meet again, my heart stays with you."

'And my heart goes with you,' she would have loved to say, but the words did not come.

Their images started to fade until they disappeared in the fog that now surrounded Chris completely. She felt her legs wobble and sank down to her knees on the cold, wet ground. There they were, the shivers running down her spine and the sensation of losing consciousness and, with it, the notion of space and time. Little by little her feelings ceased until she felt nothing. She wasn't cold, she wasn't hot. There was no sensation at all. An almost absolute silence fell about her, leaving only the echoing sound of her heartbeats, coming and going, crossing the infinite space, looking for home. She let herself go into the void. Her eyelids fell heavy and she let them close. She felt her body dissolving, becoming almost ethereal. She had to let go of it; to cross the boundaries of time and later take back its shape, wherever it was she had to go now. She lost track of time with the overwhelming tranquillity of a deep sleep, but she felt awake.

She was suspended on dancing and glaring clouds, breathing in fulfilment and serenity. There was no need to describe where she was and how she felt, there was no need for anything, because she was at one with unity. Multicoloured lights were swooping around her, loving her; she wished this sensation would never end, but it did come to an end. Just as when it started, everything began to fade again. She never knew what hit her, she only felt herself thrown a couple of feet. The only difference now was the scream, "Chris! Look out!"

"Sarah..."

CHAPTER 20

*I*t was dark when Chris regained consciousness. She opened her eyes and saw Anne, standing next to the bed staring at her. Next to her friend was a man, dressed in white. The room did not look familiar.

"W-where am I?" she asked completely disorientated and almost sobbing, trying to get up. Anne pushed her back, gently. Chris fell asleep again and by the time she woke up, Anne was sleeping on a couch, in front of her bed. The soft creak of Chris's bed woke her up.

"Hey, you're awake, finally! You've been sleeping all day. I was even able to go home and pick some clothes for you. How are you?" she asked cheerily, but clearly worried about her friend. She got no answer at all. Anne held her hand and asked again, "Chris, are you all right?"

"No."

"Can you speak? If you can't it's okay, you will, later."

No, she could not speak. She did not want to speak. She did not want to be there, back. She did not want anything.

"You got a hell of a blow, Chris. The doctor could not believe you had no broken bones."

"Blow? What blow? What doctor? Anne, where am I?" Chris glanced around her, but she did not recognize anything.

"Don't you remember, Chris?" Anne continued, "The doctor said it would be like this."

"What do I have to remember?"

"Well, I guess you didn't see the driver who ran over you. Some witnesses said that he lost control of his bike; others said he seemed as if he wanted to hit you. From where I was, I just saw how he hit you and how the bastard drove away without stopping! Thank God you're ok, sweetie."

"No, Anne. I don't remember anything. I only know that Sarah's gone."

"Sarah? Who's Sarah?"

"What day is today, Anne?" Chris was staring at the ceiling.

"What day? It's Thursday, but..."

"Thursday, what date?"

"What do you mean, what date?"

"Please, just tell me what the bloody date is!" she almost cried.

"Okay, okay, it's October 15th, but why?"

"It can't be, it's impossible..." Anne was taken aback by her friend's reaction.

"*What* can't be?"

Chris lost her self control. She looked around, refusing to accept what Anne was telling her.

"I'll call the doctor..."

"No! Please, don't do that." She pleaded with her eyes full of tears. Anne did not know what to do. She sat down on the edge of the bed and laid her hand on Chris's chest. Chris sat up on the bed and clung to her friend, bursting into tears.

"You've had a nightmare Chris, but everything's fine now."

A nightmare? No, it was not a nightmare. And it was not October 15th either. Anne was wrong. It was December and Sarah, Sarah had left on the ship, together with Joseph and his family. They were going on the ship when the fog covered her. Suddenly she calmed down. She let go of Anne, who kept looking at her, with concern as she dried her tears. Chris did remember. She could remember every single detail, every second experienced with Sarah in the past.

"The doctor said you received such a blow that you would be in shock when you woke up, and..."

"I'm not in shock! I'm... I'm..."

"What is it, Chris, what is it?"

"You won't believe it, if I tell you."

"But *what* is it, that I won't believe? That a drunken bloke hit you so hard that he threw you along the road? I saw it, Chris!" But Chris did not seem to be listening to her friend.

"I want to get out of here."

"We need to wait for the doctor and get him to allow you to leave hospital."

Chris was clever and conscious enough to realize that the doctor would never release her if he did not see that she was absolutely fine, so, when he entered the room later, followed by a nurse, she gave him a gentle smile. He smiled back and looked at the chart at the end of her bed.

"I can see we're feeling much better."

"Yes doctor, I feel very well and I'd love to go home."

"Well, I'm not sure..."

"Please, doctor" Chris looked at his identity card "Doctor Morris, I really feel very well. I promise I won't do anything silly and besides, there's probably someone out there who needs this bed much more than I do. I'm sure my friend will look after me," Chris added giving Anne a smile.

"You need to stay here tonight for observation, Chris. You can go home tomorrow morning first thing, but still *nothing silly* as you say, which means you can't walk nor move unless it's strictly necessary. Not even a shower for two whole days. After that you can move around very gently until you get back to your normal routine. The blow you received to your head must have been very hard to keep you unconscious for so many hours. Apart from that, you've only got some scratches, one worse than the others. I wouldn't usually talk about miracles, but if I have to, then I'd say we've witnessed one. I want to insist though, that you come again in three days for a check-up".

Chris was disappointed. She wanted to leave immediately, but she knew without the doctor's consent that was impossible.

Anne gave her a compassionate look and said, "I will look after her, Doctor Morris."

"Well then, I shall see you in a few days," he said and left the room.

She had a long night's sleep and the next day Anne finally drove her home. Chris just sat there, staring out of the car window, her expression lost and her lips sealed. Had it really been a nightmare as Anne said? Why this painful ache in the chest that prevented her from breathing normally? How could a dream be so real? It was not going to be easy to accept that. Chris could not get Sarah out of her mind.

"We're here, Chris." Anne had already parked, turned off the engine and grabbed her bag and was staring at her friend, but Chris had not noticed.

"I'm sorry, I was distracted." She got out of the car very slowly, feeling pretty queasy. They went in and Chris lay herself down on the couch.

"Don't you need to go to work?"

"Work?" Anne was taken by surprise. She was really worried about her friend. "Don't you remember we're off work for the next few weeks?"

"Oh, I do apologize Anne, I forgot about it!"

"Would you like a cup of tea or a coffee?"

"A coffee would be lovely Sarah, thank you."

Anne, already on her way to the kitchen, stopped in her tracks, turned round and frowned, but did not say anything when she saw Chris had closed her eyes.

CHAPTER 21

"Who's Sarah?" Anne asked handing her the coffee, "Why did you call me that? You did back at the hospital, too."

"There's something I've got to tell you, Anne, but there's a problem."

"And what would the problem be?"

"You won't believe me."

"I heard that before, too. Why don't you try me? I'm all ears and I'm really intrigued to know what's going on in there!" she said pointing to Chris's head.

"What would you say if I told you it wasn't an accident?"

"Well, if I hadn't been there, I'd say tell me about it, but I *was* there and I *saw* what happened, Chris."

"Maybe you're right, maybe you saw what happened *there*, but what you saw is not everything, there's more, much more."

"What are you talking about? I'm *really* worried, Chris."

"I'm fine, you don't need to worry. At least I'm fine physically." Anne lay back on the couch, looking at her friend before Chris continued, "I don't know how to tell you this, and you're not going to believe it anyway..."

"For heaven's sake Chris, will you stop that? What is it that I won't believe? What happened to you while you were unconscious?"

"To start with, two months passed," Anne lifted her eyebrows and her mouth fell open. She stayed like that as Chris explained, "I mean for you, here, only one day passed, but for me *yesterday* was two months ago."

"Well, I guess that's what the doctor meant by *shock*!"

"There's no shock, Anne. What I'm trying to tell you is that something happened with time. Don't ask me why or how, but I left the present for almost two months."

"You *left*? And where did you go, Chris?"

"From the tone of your voice I know you think I'm going mad and I don't blame you because it's really madness, but you've got to believe me. Just tell me something, have I ever lied to you?"

"No, you haven't, but this is slightly...different. I'm sure it's a traumatic state after..."

"It's not a traumatic anything! What I'm trying to tell you is that I travelled in time!" If Chris could have read her mind she would find out that Anne desperately wished Patrick was there. She was trying hard to make Anne believe what she was hearing. "I know this is crazy, but it's true and..." she stopped all of a sudden.

"And?" Anne shrugged, her eyes wide open staring at her friend.

"I can prove it to you!" Chris scanned the room looking for something.

"Prove it? Chris, what's wrong with you?"

"There's nothing wrong with me, where's my stuff, my clothes?"

"Your...I don't know, I...everything happened so quickly that...I guess it's in the bag they gave me at the hospital, but..."

"Where is the bag?"

"It's still in the car; I forgot about it, do you want it *now*?"

"Anne, please? Can you bring it?" Chris said with begging eyes.

She left the room and came back a few minutes later, with a big white plastic bag, still looking extremely upset.

"Did you check it?" Chris asked, grabbing it.

"No..." Anne was following her friend's movements to get everything out of the bag.

"Thank God!" she cried out when she felt the cloak with her fingers. She pulled it out, together with the rest of the clothes they had bought when they finally got to London.

"That's not yours; they must have made a mistake at the hospital!" Chris smiled when she checked the pocket of the cloak and took a tiny leather bag out.

"Why are you smiling? What's that?"

Chris handed the tiny bag to Anne and sat down, sighing with relief. Anne stared at the bag and opened it.

"What is this...coins? They seem very old, how did you know...if these are not your clothes...but it *is* the bag the nurse gave me..." Anne was terribly confused and distressed.

"These are my clothes Anne, I mean, they *were* my clothes until I came back, and the money is part of the money we used in London. Look at them, look at them very thoroughly." Anne did as Chris told her; she picked some and looked at them frowning.

"Where did you get these, Chris?"

"I brought them," she was still smiling, satisfied.

"You *brought* them? What do you mean by that?"

"What I mean, my dear friend is, that I brought these coins from the past."

"You brought them from the past..."

"Yes, to be precise from 1780. Anne, what you've got in your hands are two hundred year old pennies and shillings." Chris grabbed her cloak again and searched the other pocket. She took another leather bag and stuck her hand in it. "If you still don't believe me, you'd better check these."

"Jewellery?" Anne emptied both bags on the sofa. When she looked up back to Chris, she saw her crying.

"These coins and the few pieces of jewellery prove that I'm not making it up, Anne. It wasn't a nightmare. Everything was real, Sarah, the others...everything! You have to admit it; you *have to* believe me now. For some reason that I can't explain. Fate, God, I don't know, I went back to 1780...and now I'm back."

Anne could not take her eyes off the jewels. "Are these for real?" she asked but did not wait for an answer, "If they are, you've got a lot of money here, Chris."

"That's probably true," Chris said, aware that her friend had always been more driven by money than she was, "but what I really see there, is the reason for you to believe me and stop thinking I'm in shock or that I'm making this up."

They were silent for a long while. Anne tried several times to speak, but she just could not say a word. What was there to be said about what was happening? It was not easy to accept just like that; that time travel was possible. There was no reason for Chris to make up a story like that and, besides, the jewels and the coins were there.

"So?" Chris looked at Anne expectantly.

"So what?"

"Do you believe me?"

"I do and I don't."

"Maybe if I told you what happened it would make more sense, would you like to hear the whole story, have you got the time?"

"If I hadn't, trust me, I'd make it. So, where does it start? You mentioned you were gone for two months?" From Anne's tone, Chris knew her friend was finding all this very difficult, but could she blame her for that?

"It's not only about the time; it's about everything that happened whilst I was there."

"Go on, I'm all ears. Just don't tell me I was there as well, *that* would be impossible to believe."

"No, don't worry, you weren't there." Chris smiled.

"Sorry, I'm not trying to make fun of it, it's just...well, it doesn't happen very often that you leave a friend on the corner and a few minutes later she's knocked down by a crazy driver and when she wakes up she starts talking about time travel and, moreover, she's carrying a tiny fortune in jewels and some very old coins."

The phone rang and Anne jumped to her feet to answer.

"Patrick says hi, he's at Heathrow. He should be home in a couple of hours."

If Chris had been listening and looking at her friend she would have seen the relieved expression in Anne's face, knowing that Patrick would be there soon. Chris' thoughts were with Sarah and their kiss. That kiss seemed to have become more important than her whole adventure. Could she tell Anne about it? How would she react? She tried to remember if they had ever talked about same sex couples. Would she mind? Would she reject it, as part of Chris did too? Chris was afraid of voicing that secret and being repelled by her friend, so she decided to keep it to herself. There were too many other things to tell her.

On the other hand though, whatever happened, she shivered at the memory of Sarah's lips kissing hers; that kiss was surely the result of an extremely emotional moment before saying goodbye, especially after the experiences they shared. Why not? It had been just a kiss, nothing but a kiss and it was not worth risking their friendship for. If Anne thought gay people were inferior, different, sick or should be punished, so what? Why had she assumed that Sarah was the special person her grandfather said she would meet?

"Are you alright?" Anne interrupted.

"Hum...yes, sorry, where were we?"

"You were about to start your story."

The words did not come easily. They did not come at all. That simple kiss possessed her whole mind and she was feeling extremely upset. She had to tell Anne about it.

"Before I start telling you, there's something I need to ask you," and without waiting she said, "What do you think of relationships... when things happen between people of... the same sex?" Anne was taken aback.

"Excuse me? Why do you ask my opinion about gay people *now*?"

"Could you just tell me?"

"Okay, okay. I guess weirder things are happening just now. I don't mind them, Chris. I don't judge them. I like men, other women like women, men like men and some like both, so what?

"It's not normal!"

"Normal? Says who?"

"Well, those who taught us."

"Taught us what exactly?" It seemed to Chris that Anne was fiercely defending gays. "What is it that we are taught? That good and evil exists? Love and hatred? Light and darkness? Humbleness and pride? Feminine and masculine? What happens when something is neither one nor the other; just is? When something isn't either black or white? When you don't hate but you don't love either?" Anne paused. "It took me a long time, Chris. A long time ago I thought gay people were different. But things happen in life. When I first met gays I felt very unsettled, I tried to ignore them but finally I took the time to listen to their stories and I learned a lot and what I learned made me understand. Imagine what it feels to be young and *different* and be rejected by your family or, imagine being so afraid of their rejection that the person hides his or her real feelings and goes with the flow, marries someone of the opposite sex, has children and then somehow starts living a double life. I've seen it too many times. I don't know, Chris, one day I just found out that life is more than what we are taught to believe. What's good for you is not necessarily good for me and vice versa. I learned that a child who grows up in a criminal environment will recognize crime as *normal* because crime is what that person learned. Whoever grows up among people with no education at all will consider rude manners *normal*." Chris was mute.

"I believe like straight people, gay people can be good or bad, racist or not racist, honest or dishonest, fair or unfair. I just appreciate the goodness in people, regardless of their sexual orientation. Who am I to judge? If I had to judge anybody, I'd choose those who try to convince others to change their lives because *they* believe that *their* truth is *the* truth, but I'd rather not judge because I don't want to be judged by someone who might be *wrong*. There are too many chances to be wrong."

Chris remembered the moment many years ago when she had told Anne about her decision to move in with Steve. She also remembered her own family's reaction. How they disapproved of living with an unknown foreigner and worse, without marrying! She remembered Anne's only comment, *'Chris, are you sure? Are you happy? If you are, go for it and enjoy your happiness. Take advice but don't let others take your happiness away from you.'*

"Will you tell me how this has anything to do with your story?"
"You will find out after listening to it."

CHAPTER 22

Chris made sure to include every single detail in her narrative of the events. Anne interrupted her constantly, eager to know more.

By the time Chris came to the final part, it was almost two o'clock.

"...and when the fog started to surround me, I saw Sarah's figure fading into it and from then on, you know the rest." Even Anne's breathing was almost imperceptible. After a long pause she said,

"It's incredible, fascinating, how do you think it..."

"Do you believe me?"

"My friend, are you lying to me? Are you making all this up?"

"I'm not, every single word is true."

"Well, at the beginning I was seriously doubtful. I thought the blow had affected you really badly. After looking at those coins and jewels though, knowing the clothes you were wearing are very strange and listening to your story, yes, I believe you. Nobody in the whole world can make up such a story in such a short time."

"Thanks, Anne, it's a huge relief," she smiled.

"There is something I don't understand, though." Chris frowned at Anne's question.

"What is it?"

"Your sudden curiosity about what I think of gay people?" When Chris blushed without saying a word, Anne somehow just knew. "It was because you and Sarah...?"

"No, it's definitely not what you think, nothing happened!"

"*Nothing* at all?" Anne was actually enjoying herself, but Chris was not.

"No, well... yes, but... oh my God, I..." Anne stopped giggling when she saw how upset Chris was. She got closer and hugged her warmly.

"I don't know why it happened or how, I never thought something like this would happen to me, it was only..."

"It was only...?"

"It was only a kiss."

"Sweetie, I'm sure you'll get over this, it..."

"It's not only the kiss, it's everything: the journey into the past, that I still don't understand; meeting someone like her. You've got no idea how I wish I could just wake up and realize it was a dream, like you said. Maybe I'd know what to do." Anne wiped a tear off her cheek and let her offload her heart.

"I don't know what to think about the world, about life, about the way we live. What is real and what is not? How is it possible for everything to change so dramatically and so suddenly? What are we really? Why did this happen to me?" She paused. "When I arrived here in October, I just wanted to forget and start all over again and now I feel completely lost, a part of me is here and the other God knows where. All I wanted was to get Steve's memory out of my mind, forget about the plans we had, the house we were going to buy, his lies, his double life. I wish I could forget about my family, my own family, people whose only words were 'we told you'. And what happens? I meet a woman. A woman, for God's sake, and to make it just a bit more complicated, a woman who doesn't even exist! If I hadn't the jewels and the symbol, I'd think..."

"What symbol are you talking about?" Chris looked for it in the bag and passed it to Anne, who studied it thoroughly. "Does it have any meaning?"

"Supposedly, if the symbols are separated, fate will find a way to bring the two bearers together again."

"The symbols you said, is there another one then?"

"Sarah has the counterpart."

"What do you feel for her?" she asked.

"I don't know. When it all started I couldn't understand anything of what was happening – not that I understand now, of course. I still have moments where confusion overwhelms me. At first, I thought it was a joke from you guys – a very bad joke, by the way. As time went by, she and I... well we talked a lot and one day I realized that Steve's memory was fading. The pain I felt wasn't there anymore and the day came when I didn't miss him at all. The only problem is that now..." she paused and took the symbol and stroked it gently.

"Now what?" asked Anne.

"Now it's Sarah who I miss and I wonder what is worse, to miss a son of a bitch or a woman who existed two hundred years ago and who probably never survived the journey across the sea."

Anne had no idea what to say. The only thing she could think of was to hold her friend's hands and suggest, "Let's take it easy, okay? I'm sure there must be an answer. In the meantime, would you like me to cook something nice while you just relax?" Chris accepted gratefully, leaning back on the couch while Anne disappeared to the kitchen. Once on her own, all the memories came back to her.

'Where are you Sarah? I wonder what happened to you; did you fulfil your dream? I wish I knew if you miss me like I miss you.'

Anne came back, saying, "I need to go out for a while. I haven't got some of the ingredients. Will you be alright?"

"I'll be fine, don't worry," Chris said, with a not very convincing voice and stretched on the sofa, while Anne ran up the stairs to pick up her bag.

Before leaving, she saw her friend had already fallen asleep. She covered her with a throw and went out.

When Patrick came home he called out for Anne but got no answer. Without going in the sitting room, he went straight upstairs to drop his bag.

"Hey sleeping beauty, supper's ready." Patrick woke her gently.

"Patrick! Hi, I didn't hear you coming in, sorry." Chris said in a sleepy voice.

"That's because you were soundly asleep and I didn't want to wake you up."

"Anne's gone to the shops to buy some food."

"She did indeed, and came back a couple of hours ago with loads of yummy stuff. I was helping her in the kitchen while she updated me with the last news. Gosh, Chris, I didn't know about your new hobby?"

"What hobby?"

"Time travelling! Are you planning to take us with you next time? Just imagine, we could go back there, buy some land for peanuts, come back and find out that we own half of the land in Islington. Never mind how much tax we'd have to pay. Wouldn't that be fantastic?"

Chris could not help it, she had to laugh. "You're mad, Patrick, but a sweetie as well."

"How do you feel, gorgeous?"

"I'm happy to have you as my friends." Patrick squeezed her in a warm hug.

"Come on, you two, this is getting cold!" Anne shouted from the kitchen.

After a long exquisite supper and countless questions from Patrick, he said,

"I think we need help."

"Help? I would need to tell the story again to people who don't know me, Patrick. I'm not nuts enough to let anybody lock me up." Chris said firmly.

"I meant help from someone who *would* believe us. Someone who'd give us the help we're looking for," added Patrick pensively.

"What do you mean?" Chris said.

"Maybe..." both women waited for him to finish the sentence, "I know someone who knows someone..."

"That's far too many people already, Patrick; I told you, I really don't want to go around telling people what happened to me."

"Wait, wait, what I'm trying to say is that this friend, he knows a woman who might be able to help and there won't be any need to explain." Chris looked interested now and let Patrick go on. "This woman has experience in things that might be a little... *weird*."

"*Weird*? Is she a time traveller by any chance?" Patrick ignored Chris's sarcastic remark.

"Maybe, how can we know? We should give it a try."

Chris thought about it. What options did she have if she wanted to do something about her experience? She needed help to get over it; she knew she could not do it by herself. What about the chance that this person might be a fraud? As if reading her mind, Patrick added,

"I know there are many fake gurus around making money out of naive people, but I promise she's not like that." He was already picking the phone up and dialling a number. A minute later he came back with the note in his hand. Anne took it from him and read.

"Brighton?" She stared at him. He nodded. Chris jumped off her seat and repeated after her friend,

"Brighton... and didn't your friend want to know more, like why you asked for her details?"

"No, *nada*. I just told him I was asked and that I thought of him."

Noticing the enthusiasm in Chris' eyes, Anne said feeling relieved, "Brighton, here we come!"

"Are you both sure you want to help me?"

"Look," Patrick said, "if you think for one second we'll let you go through this once-in-a-lifetime event on your own, you're wrong. And besides, should you disappear again, I want to be there; remember our *business*?"

"As I said, you're mad, Patrick." But she laughed again and explained the joke to Anne, who thought it was a great idea.

"You're *both* mad!" Chris smiled again.

"Are you afraid?" Anne wanted to know later, "Because if you are, it might be better if we don't do anything."

"No, I'm not afraid, it's only that everything's changed so much and so quickly that it's hard to assimilate. I've also had this feeling since I came back, I'm trying to ignore it, but I can't."

"What feeling?" Anne spoke.

"It's as if someone were trying to get in touch with me." She held her head with her hands and added, "I know it sounds crazy, but sometimes I hear a voice calling me and if we have to go back to Brighton..."

"Sarah?"

"No, I thought it might be her, I wish it were her, but it's not. Somehow I can feel her, but this is different, it's sort of a call from somebody else."

"Well, maybe someone's with you." Patrick sounded convinced. He hadn't had any doubt at all Chris's story was real. Even though he didn't know her as well as Anne did, it seemed that he knew she was telling the truth. What he never mentioned was why he believed her so easily. Chris looked straight into his eyes, but she was not really looking at him. It seemed she was seeing through him. Without moving her eyes she whispered in hushed words,

"Everything's happening as it should, you'll meet again, when the time comes..."

Anne and Patrick glanced at each other in silent amazement.

Chapter 23

On their way to Brighton the following morning, Chris sat in the rear seat of the car, looking out of the window. Although different, it was the same road she and her friends had walked along some weeks and two hundred years ago. She remembered the moment when Joseph cauterized her wound. She touched her skin under her shirt and said in a low voice,

"The scar!" Patrick looked at her in the back mirror and Anne over her shoulder.

"What scar?" she asked frowning.

"I completely forgot about the scar, because it didn't hurt anymore. There you have another proof that I haven't made anything up." After saying that they fell silent. Anne was sorting soft music out and Patrick, who had been driving quietly, looked at Chris again and after some time he asked,

"What's on your mind, Chris?"

"I was going through that horrible day at Tyburn: the woman with the baby trying to get closer to her husband; the guards beating her; those hanging bodies and Sarah and Joseph forced into the wagon." Chris felt suddenly very cold.

"Why were they executed?" Anne wanted to know.

"Sometimes just because they had stolen food or a few shillings, we heard from Old Isaac."

"My God, it's so easy to forget we're talking only two hundred years ago!"

"How did Sarah manage while you were there?" Patrick spoke.

"Was she hiding all the time?" Anne added.

"That was not a problem, since we always walked around together. Old Isaac was a freeman and Joseph and Elizabeth made everybody believe, except for Madame Juliette of course, that Sarah was their servant. If anybody came close she stood back and silently, in this damn subdued gesture that the arrogant white despots forced them to take..." Chris voice changed to anger when she remembered all the humiliation Sarah and the other slaves had gone through. She paused.

Patrick broke the silence again, "Did you realize how dangerous it was for you to help them? I don't want to imagine what they'd have done to you if they'd caught you – even more if they'd found out about the jewels she'd stolen from an English lord!"

"If you'd only been there, Patrick. If you'd seen the horrible spectacle at Tyburn, you wouldn't have given a damn about the danger you were in," she sighed deeply. "You'd have reacted with the same scorn and done exactly what I did, I'm sure. You'd have helped her, without thinking of yourself but only of the unfair treatment she and thousands more black people were given. And about the jewels, it was me who convinced her to think of them as a poor reward for all they did to her. All these jewels, the ones that she gave to me and the ones she took, were far from being enough to make up for all her suffering, the years when she and her grandfather worked for Wesley without getting anything back. The abuse she had to take and her grandfather's death because he couldn't resist the torture. I can only hope that they made it across the ocean and that the jewels gave her and Joseph and his family the chance of a good life wherever they landed."

Anne turned her head and put her hand on Chris's, trying to calm her down. There was a new silence, mainly because Chris was unable to go on talking. The mix of anger and impotence that grew inside her were holding her words back. Besides, what was there to be said, given the circumstances? How could she know if they had finally made it to their destination? The passion in Chris's words made them feel the story much more vividly and intensely than in the beginning.

It was Anne who said, after a while, "You did what you could to help her and the others, Chris. I know you think it wasn't enough, but you helped them. You were there with Sarah until they left and that should make you feel better."

Chris grasped Anne's hand tightly and whispered with a voice full of melancholy, "It's a poor consolation, my friend, a poor consolation."

Patrick remained silent.

By the time they reached Brighton, it was still early but the pouring rain darkened the town. Some traffic lights were down, which made their driving through the traffic jam even more painful, but finally they made it to the hotel.

"Anybody thought about bringing an umbrella? The weather forecast didn't say anything about rain," he said, while parking the car on the road across from the hotel. The women gazed at each other and shrugged. With the recent events there was no wonder everybody had forgotten the rule of always carrying an umbrella, never mind the season.

"I'll make sure we always carry one in the boot in future, darling."

The receptionist could not hide his amusement at the sight of the drenched threesome standing in front of the desk. "Welcome to the hotel, ladies and gentleman. I'm sorry I haven't got good news about the weather. I just heard the forecast and it doesn't seem very good for the next few hours. On the contrary, we are expecting the storm to get worse during the night."

"Oh, never mind," Anne smiled ironically, "we love the rain."

After taking her wet clothes off and enjoying a long shower, Chris went downstairs, sat at the bar and asked the barman for the wine list. As she looked up to thank him, the picture over the bar caught her eye. It could have been a coincidence, but it still made her shiver. The painting showed the exact scene at the pier two hundred years ago, when she had kissed Sarah and her friends goodbye. With dark, almost ghostly colours, the artist had managed to reflect on the canvas the scarcely visible masts of the schooner, its sails totally unfurled, the dim daybreak shaded with dark grey clouds. The fog was also there.

"It looks pretty real, doesn't it?" The voice next to her made her jump off the stool.

"Sorry, I didn't mean to scare you!"

"Patrick, don't worry." Her eyes went back to painting. "It's just as if the artist had watched the scene through my eyes."

The barman came back with the wine list, and she said, "Would you like to choose the wine, Patrick? As long as it's red I don't mind."

"Hum, don't ever tell my family but, could we have a bottle of the Chilean Shiraz and three glasses, please?" He ordered and then to Chris, "Are you alright?" Chris waited until Patrick had tasted and approved the wine and the barman had gone.

"I'm fine. It's weird though, to know that only a couple of days ago I was around here, well, further east, towards Eastbourne, but two hundred years ago."

After a moment she spoke again, "Patrick, do you believe in other lives?"

"I do."

"Just like that, *I do*? Don't you have any sort of doubts about it?"

"Nope, no doubts at all," he sounded convinced.

"If you do believe in other lives, how do you imagine them? Do you think they are related? Is your current life the continuation of a previous one or something like that?"

"I couldn't tell you, Chris. I'd love to; the truth is I don't know." His voice was wistful, as if he, also, were looking for answers. "Maybe it's our lives that continue or maybe it's only what we learn that continues."

"Forever? As in for all eternity? We are born, over and over again?" Chris was not very convinced about that. Although everything had changed since her grandfather's death, she had always been much more matter-of-fact. It suited her more to believe that life started with birth, ended with death and that was it, but she could not deny that things had changed. She had changed. Crossing the time barrier had forced her to face a completely different world, different lives, different people and different emotions, which were turning out to be impossible to ignore. It disturbed her. As did the memory of Sarah and not knowing what had happened to her.

"I don't know, or I want to believe, I guess, that it's until we reach some sort of a state or place. I haven't got a clue what to call it. To be honest, when I think about it, I try not to go too deeply into it, it can be really wearisome not finding the answers."

"You tell me!" Chris' smile was sad. "There are so many things I'd like to know now."

"I'd rather think that the answers will slowly crop up, Chris. But I do understand how difficult it can be to stop the anxiety of not getting them immediately."

"You know what, I try so hard to convince myself that all this was just a nightmare, but I can't fool myself. I know I didn't dream it, Patrick. It wasn't a dream from which you just wake up and that's it. That would be easy, but it's not the way it was. I didn't die either, nor was I reborn into another body. I *was* there, you know what I'm saying? I was there!" She pointed at the painting and stared at him. "Do you believe me? Do you believe all that Anne told you?"

"Yes, I do."

"How can you do that?"

"What do you mean, how can I do what?"

"How can you be so sure about trusting me?"

"Well, the thing is, Chris, I have no explanations about how or why this happened to you, everything's very different to..." he paused.

"Different to what?" Chris noticed Patrick's hesitation and gave him time to speak.

"There is something I need to tell you, Chris," he finally said with trembling voice.

"You can tell me anything, but are you ok?"

"Yes, yes, I'm fine. Listen, remember I told you my friend knew somebody who could help?"

"Yes, he gave you the name and the address."

"No, he didn't give me the name. He just reminded me how to get there."

"Are you telling me that you know the person we'll meet?"

"Yes, I do. I came to see her once, but my reasons were completely different from yours. I think that in the end though, it all might be connected."

CHAPTER 24

"Since I can remember," he began after moving to sit in front of the fireplace, "I've had this recurrent nightmare, until one day I told my mother about it. As a little boy though, she could easily convince me that it was due to the stories that I had heard, the movies I watched or the books I read. As time went by, I found out that she was really terrified just thinking about this and I knew she wouldn't ever help me to find out why I kept having the same dream. One day I just stopped dreaming. The nightmare was gone and it didn't come back for a long time. I had almost forgotten about it, until some years it came back; the same old nightmare, night after night." Chris was listening attentively.

"I didn't tell my mother. She was living with me at that time but she was ill and very frail so I decided it wouldn't do her any good to know. On the contrary, it would have just made her feel worse. I didn't have any very close friends so I couldn't really talk to anybody, so I kept it to myself. I tried to ignore it, but the nightmare was there every night. After Mum died I couldn't stand it anymore."

"What was it about?"

"I used to see myself chasing someone...I mean, I saw a man on a horse chasing someone, but I knew it was me, although he didn't look like me. Then, I... this guy on the horse captured the man with a rope and dragged him along and laughed."

Patrick stopped so after a minute or two Chris asked him if there was anything else he could remember.

"There is more. I could see the face and the body of the poor guy, bumping along the ground, the wounds that opened up, and I just laughed! I would usually wake up soaking in my own perspiration, with the face of that man following me everywhere I went."

"Could you recognize him?"

"No, but I do remember that he was... I knew he was..." he looked at Chris and paused, as if afraid of telling her.

"He was what? Why do you stop?" Suddenly she knew. She opened her eyes wide and stared at Patrick.

"Are you saying that you were...?"

"Yes. In that nightmare I was one of the damn slave hunters."

His confession made him look sad. Chris was shocked, staring at the flames. She recalled the moment she had killed the man with the pitchfork.

"How can you be sure of that?" She did not want to believe what Patrick was saying.

"I came here."

"I don't understand."

"I told you, when my mother died, I couldn't stand it anymore. I did a lot of research on dreams and then I decided to find out more through a regression."

"A regression?"

Patrick nodded. "A friend helped me to find the person who could do it and we ended up here. The woman we'll meet is the same woman I met a couple of years ago and when I heard what you said about the ship setting sail from here, that immediately brought back to my mind what she first said." He paused.

"What was that?"

"That my nightmare was like a link between this and a previous life." Chris was astounded by Patrick's words. "I had never seen her before but I felt she could see through me and she was adamant about my not having the regression; she said I wasn't *ready* to do it. She also made it very clear that nobody could really help us by answering why or how but by teaching us to see that the true answers are the ones we find out by ourselves, searching in our hearts." Patrick had a sip of his wine and continued, "After that, time and reflexion helped me to find out why I hated black people."

"Did you? Why?" Patrick being racist was a shocking revelation for Chris.

"Out of pure racism, I thought, but it wasn't that. It was part of a past which at some point would take its toll."

"That's what you meant by learning? In a previous life you were a slave hunter, you chased them, you killed them and you were reborn into a life where you hated them? If you hated them before and hate them now, I'm sorry Patrick, I really can't see much learning there. What happens to you when you come across a black person, especially in a place like London, where black and white are so obviously normal and accepted?" Chris was filled with disappointment. She thought she knew her friend's partner but she didn't. She was talking to someone who probably considered himself superior to black people.

"Chris, I know what you must be feeling and thinking, and after going through your experience you have the right to hit out at me, but trust me, you'll be pleased to hear the rest of the story."

"Will I?"

"Oh yes, you will. I did learn something and I paid an excruciating price for the things I did in one of my previous lives. You get the punishment from life itself, believe me." Chris didn't interrupt him again, waiting for him to continue. "What I mean by that is that when I became *aware* of my previous acts, when I *saw* the damage I had caused, even if I wasn't conscious of it in this life, things changed and somehow my racism started to lessen. It wasn't such a strong feeling anymore, although I still couldn't get very close or really mingle with black people, no matter how hard I tried." Patrick sighed, "One day, the friend who helped me to find the woman we'll meet tomorrow, introduced me to another of his friends and it happened that I fell madly in love for the first time in my life." He looked straight into Chris' eyes when he said, "*He* became my first boyfriend."

Chris' jaw dropped. "*He*? Are you telling me that you're *gay*? What the hell are you doing with Anne, then?" That was too much for Chris, she was so unsettled that she made a move to get up and leave, but Patrick grabbed her arm saying,

"Please Chris, please let me finish and then I promise you can do whatever you feel like."

"I don't understand!" Chris shouted.

"You will. When I first met Paul nothing happened, we just talked and met a few times for a drink. Albeit not completely, he helped me to get over my prejudice towards black people; every time we met I got to know him a bit better. We found out we had so many interests in common and one day it just happened. We started a relationship that wasn't easy at first. I loved him, but somehow a part of me hated him as well."

"You hated him because he was a man?"

"No, I hated him because he was black." Chris's composure and understanding was hit by Patrick's words like a formidable blow.

"That part of me always tried to run away from him but never succeeded, because I was so attracted to him. He was remarkably kind, the way he thought about life, his self confidence, his tenderness, his joy of living. I had never met anybody like him before. As time passed, the remaining traces of my racism vanished and everything felt so right, so good."

She felt as though she was sinking in the couch with the heaviness of Patrick's story. This man was her best friend's partner and he was talking about his love for another man. She did not care at all about Paul being black, what bothered her was what was Anne doing with him? She let him continue, without realizing that his eyes were full of tears.

"We had so many plans, good friends, we had it all. Until the day we had the accident. It was pouring down, the motorway was slippery... the lorry moved unexpectedly into our lane... I lost control and we crashed. When I woke up in the hospital, after I don't remember how many hours, they told me he had died instantly."

"Patrick... I don't know what to say." Chris was astounded.

"Don't say anything, Chris. We're friends and I wanted you to know why I believe in other lives. I wanted to share with you my belief that life always pays us back. Maybe it takes more than a lifetime, but everything comes back, sooner or later. I hated black people and life taught me I was wrong. Real justice lies beyond human understanding. Of course there are many who don't believe in anything. For them any strange event is either sickness or a trick of the mind. The thing is I don't care about these people now. Everyone has the right to believe whatever suits them best. I don't expect anything in this sense; I don't expect anybody to believe what I believe." He paused and looked at her.

"The woman you'll meet tomorrow, she knew everything, my whole life was an open book for her. She taught me about our free will to make decisions in life. She said other things too, which I didn't understand then, but, as time passed and events occurred, began to make sense. If I've told you about this, it's just because it happened. Everything has its right time and I guess it was the time for you to know this story." All that was fine and Chris could probably understand, but what bothered her was still there.

"I think you need to tell me about Anne, Patrick."

"That must really baffle you, doesn't it? It did confuse me too, trust me." He smiled warmly and continued, "Anne is the most amazing woman I've ever known and I'm planning to spend the rest of my life with her. Let's say that she was and still is my free will."

"But you are gay!"

"And you're wondering how a gay man can love a woman?"

"Actually I do and I would like to know why you're with her."

"After Paul died," his fingers were circling the edge of his glass, "I thought I'd never recover. I lost everything: the interest in meeting people; of going out; of getting on my feet again. To be honest I just wanted to die, but my beliefs were there and I couldn't ignore them. They were so strong that they didn't let me do anything crazy. If I was going to be born again, I didn't like the idea of dragging into the new life, the heavy burden of killing myself. I believe if someone can't get over some painful life event, this event will, like it or not, recur until you deal with it, until you accept it and learn from it."

"So, what did you do?" Chris thought what she might possibly have had to learn from meeting Sarah.

"I worked like mad, nonstop, which is how I managed to improve the editorial firm my father founded in London.

Everything was going so well with it that we decided to expand and open a branch in Italy. Of course I had to learn Italian and I got myself registered in the Italian Language Institute where..."

"... Ann was working," she finished for him.

"Exactly," he laughed, "It's so funny to remember how we met. One day I was running late and..." Chris stopped listening. She thought how handsome he was, how beautiful his smile was and all of a sudden the memory of Sarah came to her.

"Chris, are you alright?" Patrick's touch on her arm brought her back.

"Yeah, sorry, I was gone for a moment."

"Sure you're ok?"

"Yes, I was just remembering how Sarah and I met but, hey, you were telling me how you and Anne met!" She changed the subject and he continued,

"I was running late and I entered the usual classroom. They had changed the teacher, but that wasn't unusual. I sat down in a desk close to the door and next to Anne, whom I thought was a new student. Only when I heard the teacher speaking a language that I couldn't understand, I also noticed that my classmates were not the same. They had changed the room as well! I grabbed my things again, embarrassed. Anne looked at me and by my expression she knew what had happened. I hadn't blushed in a long time, believe me. Later that day, she approached me in the cafeteria. We laughed about the incident and from the very first there was a special bond between us. I guess I felt safe because she was a woman. One day I just opened up to her, told her everything and we became very good friends. It seemed so natural to spend our free time together, that I never noticed how my feelings were changing. When I did I panicked, but not for long, only until I realized I had fallen in love with her and she with me and Chris, I really want to spend the rest of my life with her."

"How can you explain all this, Patrick?"

"I don't try to do that anymore."

"But I need to, I'm scared." Chris said.

"Scared? Why are you *scared*?" Anne asked approaching from behind. She kissed Patrick and sat down next to him. He poured her a glass and told her about their conversation.

"And why is it that you're scared?" she was adamant to know.

"Maybe it's my pay back that scares me, or maybe I'm afraid of not doing the right thing from now on."

"You shouldn't think about that now. Tomorrow's an important day and I want you to know that no matter what happens, we'll be with you."

CHAPTER 25

Chris could not sleep that night. The torrential rain, gale and cracking thunder kept her awake and so did all her memories that came flooding back. She tried so hard to understand but, at the same time, she wished that she had imagined everything. Then she wished she could blame everything on the bike rider; to believe that the blow had caused her some sort of post traumatic hallucination. Unfortunately, she knew that was not an option. The jewels and the symbol were enough proof and so was the round-the-clock memory of Sarah. She thought of Patrick's story and of Sarah's last words, "Search for me in time, Stranger, somewhere I'll be waiting for you."

"How, Sarah?" she said out loud, "Tell me how can I find you; how could anybody find you after two hundred years?" She closed her eyes, trying to fall sleep again, trying to accept what Patrick had told her, that somehow she would find the answers within herself.

At dawn the storm finally eased and complete silence returned. Just when she was about to cross the boundary between consciousness and unconsciousness, she heard the calming and familiar voice: "Everything's happening as it should, child. You will meet again, when the time comes."

The following morning, with the storm over, the sky was amazingly blue and clear and Chris felt surprisingly calm. Last night's fear had miraculously vanished, but she did not associate that with the voice she had heard.

"How do you feel?" Anne asked her when they met for breakfast.

"Now that you ask, I think I feel great, despite everything. Probably because you're here with me, I feel safe and relaxed."

As soon as they reached Eastbourne, Patrick opened the map and showed Anne the road which would lead them to their destination.

"Where this road ends we'll have to leave the car and walk," he added. "You'll enjoy it, it's a beautiful path."

Once there, they started walking silently, enjoying the stunning view. Far on the horizon, the now quiet waters of the English Channel met the black clouds which carried the storm to the French coast. Chris's tranquillity disappeared as soon as they reached the viewpoint. "My God!" she exclaimed.

"What's wrong?" Anne asked, taken aback.

"This is the place; this is where we first saw the schooner!" She looked around and stretched her arm towards the few houses. "The lodge where we stayed was somewhere there."

"That's where we're going." Patrick added.

The place appeared deserted, except for the old woman sitting at the front door.

"Just the same as the first time." He looked at the old lady, "she was waiting for me too."

"How could she know?"

Patrick shrugged and added, "Don't ask me, she just knows."

The old woman indeed seemed to be waiting for them. She was wearing a long dark skirt down to her feet. One could only see her shoes, which seemed to have walked thousands of miles. An old, worn cloak on her shoulders fell down to her waist, whilst her hands lay crossed resting in her lap. Her almost white hair was neatly combed back, showing a wrinkled face that hid too many years. The visitors approached the woman, greeting her shyly.

"The storm's gone," she said and stretched out her arm towards the coast. "But there is always another one coming." They looked at each other silently and puzzled. Chris felt awkward when she saw the woman getting up and walking towards her, but as soon as she laid her hand on Chris' hand, a sudden peace overcame her.

"Come with me my dear," the woman whispered and the two of them paced slowly to the edge of the cliff. Once there, she spoke again, looking at the horizon.

"The fog protected them while they sailed away from the coast, but the crossing was long and difficult and many of them didn't make it. They drowned in the depths, along with their dreams of a new life. But there were others whose strength helped them to reach their destination, even if it was not the one they expected to reach. The ocean hit them once again, the furious clouds darkened the sky and the rage of the wind and the rain lashed the ship against the rocks. Only those who clung to their hopes survived. They jumped overboard into the sea, fighting desperately to reach the shore."

Every bit of colour had drained from Chris' face and she could hardly breathe. Who was this woman? How could she possibly know what had happened two hundred years ago? Was she there? Had she made the same journey that Chris had? Were Sarah and her friends amongst the survivors?

"Too many questions at the same time, don't you think?" This time the woman was chuckling. Chris' heart was pounding. "Don't worry, child. Very soon you'll find the answers to all your questions. Your heart will tell you if they made it."

"Wait a minute, who are you? Can you read my mind?"

"That is only one more skill that we learn along the path," the old woman said.

"What path?" Chris' voice was trembling now. "What is this all about?" She wanted to run away, but she felt frozen and sank down, sitting beside the woman now.

"You need to believe in yourself, have confidence and learn how to listen to your heart."

"Have confidence in what? That something impossible is happening to me?"

"Only those things which we don't believe in are impossible, child. Anything we don't *know* seems inexplicable until we find the bridge between the reality of what we know and the truth of the unknown."

"Can you tell me who you are?"

"We've received many names through time: sometimes we're called guides; mystics; sometimes we're just insane; sometimes we're called angels..."

"Oh yeah, sure," Chris smiled sarcastically, "And I've been so good that I've been honoured by meeting an angel. You'll have to excuse me, lady, but it's sort of hard to accept all this."

"Do you doubt about the kindness and love that you carry in your heart?"

"What kindness? What love? Are you laughing at me? If I'm so kind and loving as you say, shouldn't I get some of the same in return instead of going through things that bring only pain, disappointment and despair?" Chris cried defiantly.

"My dear, these things you mention are our debts, debts that we've left unsolved and which must be paid sometimes, as you say, with pain and disillusion, but once they are resolved, you have free will."

"What free will?"

"We can choose to move on or stay at the point where our soul stagnates."

"Sure, and I'm right at that point, am I?" Chris felt overwhelmed by her own rebelliousness and unease.

"Yes, you are. I'm telling you again, child, you can choose to trust and listen to your heart or stay in the stage of distrust and stop moving on, because you're afraid of the unknown. Only you can decide the path you'll take."

"As easy as that, hum? Is it the one or the other? Just tell me, how can I trust, how can I accept a destiny, how can I accept something that I don't understand? How did all this start? Is it maybe true that all our life is written from the very beginning? If that's right, all that we've learned, what's the point of that?"

"The teachings are omnipresent; they exist to show us the paths when we're ready."

"But what's the point of learning all that I have, if I suddenly find myself travelling in time and meeting people who I won't see again, people for whom I had... have feelings that I can't accept?"

"When you told the young woman you'll look for her in time, why did you do that?"

Chris blushed.

"How... how do you know that?"

"Why did you say what you said?"

"Well, I suppose it was an impulse I felt at that moment," she said, as if apologising.

"Was it an impulse or were you listening to your heart?" The old lady smiled warmly. "Is that what worries you most, your feelings for that woman? Are your feelings for Sarah what you are fighting inside and you struggle because part of you accepts it and the other part rebels, only because that person was a woman like you?"

"Before I came here, to this country, there was someone in my life."

"And you were disappointed with what you found out." Chris looked at her, frowning.

"You know about that too? How can you know about everything?"

"I too chose a path when it was my time to do so."

"You *chose* what you are?" The woman nodded.

Chris continued, "There have been moments since I came back, when I've felt strong enough to move on, accepting the unknown, but there are also moments when I feel desolate and lost as if losing my mind. It's then that I wish this hadn't happened, when I wish I could forget and go on with my life."

"It's all right to feel lost and struggle amid doubts, but there's something you can rely on and that is, you're not alone, you've never been alone." The woman got up and began to walk back slowly.

"Don't go..." Chris pleaded. The woman turned around and looked at her, waiting for her question.

"Why me?"

"You asked for it."

"I asked for it? I asked for this?"

The woman nodded one more time silently and then she said, "It is very important not to forget what you've learned during your journey." As the old woman concluded she moved away.

"Why are you going? Won't you tell me more? Will I see you again?" She yelled to the woman in despair. She didn't hear the answers; she felt them in her mind. 'The time will come when you will listen to your heart again.'

The old woman disappeared into one of the houses and Chris was overwhelmed by a feeling of loneliness. There was only the breeze; the rest was emptiness.

For the next few minutes she considered her options. She could try to understand how all this happened, how it was possible to travel in time, or she could just try to accept it and forget, as Patrick had. He accepted his beliefs and his life before and he did the same now, with Anne. Could she do the same? Would she feel so lost and so confused if she had only travelled in time? She realized it was not really the time travelling which upset her the most; it was her feelings for Sarah that were driving her mad. When the woman said that she had asked for it, did she mean that in a previous life she had *asked* for this to happen? She thought of Sarah again and the events of the past hit her mind, as if trying desperately not to be forgotten.

'You need to believe in yourself, have confidence and learn how to listen to your heart,' the woman had said, 'until we find the bridge between the reality of what we know and the truth of the unknown.' Guides, mystics, angels, choosing between moving on, let our soul stagnate... it was all too much.

"Chris, are you all right?" Lost in her thoughts, she had not heard her friends coming back from their walk.

"Chris?" Patrick asked again and she looked at them.

"Are you ok?" Anne wanted to know.

"Yes. We can go now," she said and got up, abruptly. Anne and Patrick glanced at each other but said nothing. Then the threesome went back down the same path, walked past the old woman's house, headed towards the car and drove back to Brighton in complete silence.

Later on, whilst having dinner in the restaurant at the hotel, Anne could not help asking, "Are you going to tell us what happened there?"

Chris hesitated at first but then said, "I think it's better to forget about all this."

"Forget about it, just like that, as simple as that?" Patrick could not believe his ears.

"Yes, forget about it. What really happened was that I had a strange nightmare, a sort of disorder resulting from the blow the biker gave me. I will go on with my life."

"But Chris, aren't you making the decision too quickly? You know it wasn't a nightmare and even less a disorder of your mind. What are you talking about?"

"You're right, Patrick. Maybe it wasn't a nightmare, but I can't be sure of that and I can't find a logical explanation of what happened either. So, the right thing to do now is not to run into more problems. I don't want to ask more questions that have no answers."

"You call all this experience a *problem*? Do you think that by fooling yourself you'll easily forget and keep away from *problems*?"

"I'm sorry you disagree, Patrick, but at the end of the day I'm the one who decides here, right?"

Anne, who had been quiet so far, reacted immediately to Chris's sharpness, "Patrick's only trying to help, Chris."

"Well then, don't help me anymore. If you excuse me now, I just lost my appetite." Chris left the table and disappeared through the door and up the stairs.

Once in her room, she threw herself on the bed and burst into tears, wishing she were dead.

Chapter 26

During the days that followed the Brighton episode, Chris was another person. To Anne's and Patrick's astonishment, and as if by magic, she seemed to have erased what happened from her life. Not knowing what to do, they went back to work and Chris seemed happy with it. She got up early every day to run or walk, came back one or two hours later and, after she had showered, she went out again.

Patrick didn't mention the subject again and any attempt Anne made was frustrated by Chris with a simple and brief, "Forget it, I already did."

"It's hard to believe it was so easy for her to forget," Anne told Patrick one day whilst working in the garden.

"I don't think she has forgotten, baby. Rather I believe she's having a hell of a time, struggling inside and she won't last much longer. I'm afraid sooner or later she'll collapse."

"Maybe you're right, but if you ask me, I'm not quite sure what the best option is: the attitude she's adopted or facing something which is so..." she couldn't find the right word.

"Unnatural?" Patrick helped her.

"Yes."

"Well, although I can't compare what I experienced with Chris's time travel," he paused, stopped digging and approached her, "I found you and I'm far from regretting it."

"Have I told you lately how much I love you?"

"Hum... I'm not sure how much that is..." Patrick whispered in her ear while cuddling her.

"What about... as much as to spend the rest of my life with you?"

"Only one life?" he giggled and was about to kiss her when they noticed Chris's presence.

"Sorry, I didn't want to disturb you," she said starting to turn around.

"Don't be silly, there's nothing we can't make up for later," Anne said looking at Patrick mischievously and then again to Chris, "How are you sweetie?"

"I'm ok," she said with a voice full of melancholy having seen her friends so in love. Sarah's image came back to her with all its power. The more she denied her memory and the intense feelings for her, the more she missed her.

"Are you sure you're ok?" Patrick frowned.

"Yes. Listen, I was thinking, I'd like to treat you both to dinner tonight, and you choose the venue." After spending the evenings on her own, at the theatre, the movies, reading or watching television, this was her first clear attempt in many days to come closer to them again.

"We've got a date, darling. Shall we say the Southbank?"

"That would be lovely." Anne was happy to see her friend was up to socializing again.

After dinner she gave them the news.

"I've decided to do some travelling; first to Jordan and then Africa." Anne and Patrick looked at each other.

"What are you going to do there? You've already been!"

"I need to go away, Anne. Go away from these streets, from the memories, from everything, I just can't..." she burst into tears.

"Chris..." Anne began, but Patrick stopped her by putting his hand over hers. Chris went on, without noticing Patrick's movement.

"I can't deal with this anymore. Every day is worse than the one before. It doesn't matter what I do, where I go, how I distract myself. If I stay here, I'll go mad." She paused and so did her friends, respecting her need to let everything out.

"I keep on seeing things, feeling things."

"Seeing things?" Anne could not help asking, "What do you mean by *seeing* things?"

"Well, I didn't tell you because I was so determined to forget, but the fact is that I've had fleeting visions."

"Fleeting visions?"

"One day when I was having a coffee, I heard a strange noise and I looked out of the window." Chris was playing with her glass. "Everybody was there, all mixed up, people from the past and people from the present. Then, one night, I opened my eyes, when I couldn't sleep, and I saw people talking in front of me! Last night..." her voice sounded scared; "last night..." she could not go on. Anne took her hand, reassuringly and gave her strength to continue. "Last night I saw them again and one of them looked at me as if trying to tell me something. I turned the light on; trying to convince myself it was just an hallucination or a reflection from the window. I rubbed my eyes over and over again, but they were still there, talking to each other and looking at me as if waiting for me to do something."

"Chris," Patrick said firmly, "I don't think it's a good idea at all for you to go anywhere right now."

"But I can't..."

"You listen to me now," he said firmly. "Everything that happened was real. You know it wasn't a dream. You've got to stop running away."

"Dammit, Patrick! What can I do?" Chris was very close to a nervous breakdown.

"First thing, stop denying what happened."

"Ok!" She yelled back, "I don't deny it anymore. It happened to me. I also accept that now I've got these people from the past calling me. What now? Do you think by voicing it everything's going to be just fine?"

"It depends on *how* you say it, *how* you accept it and it depends on what you want, Chris."

"What do you mean by *how* to accept it? I said it, I accept it!"

"Yes, you did say it, we heard it." He looked at Anne, "But do you feel you're accepting it or is it just words; because just words are definitely not an acceptance. When you accept something you don't need words, it's a feeling that you get inside. Can you feel it?"

"What do I do after accepting?"

"Well, it might be good if you ask yourself what you *really* want. Never mind how crazy your wish might sound."

"What do I wish? As if choosing a course? As easy as that?"

"Yes, as easy as that." Patrick said confidently.

Chris thought about the question. What did she really want? Forget? Give away the jewels to a museum? Bury or throw the symbol into the Thames, to see if the memories drowned along with it? Did she want to go on with her previous life? Go back to her job and find another Steve somewhere and fall in love again? Have children, a house and a dog and live happily ever after? What was it, what did she want?"

The answer did not take long to find and to her astonishment, she did feel it was the truth. She felt it as if it were written somewhere deep in her heart.

"I want something impossible, Patrick. I want to find Sarah."

PART III
THE SEARCH

CHAPTER 27

*T*he sun was slowly setting on the horizon in front of Bahia
Esperanza, the little village in northern Brazil, whose name only
appeared occasionally on an old map of the area. Although located
less than a hundred kilometres from Itapicoca and just a couple of
hundred kilometres from Fortaleza, it was a real nightmare to get
there. One could well say that its inhabitants were right to believe
that Bahia Esperanza was protected by the gods. The only and
almost impassable access road frightened the tourists off. By sea, the
reefs acted as heavenly guardians, preventing the cruise-ships or
even the smallest boats from approaching and invading the
paradise-like beaches of white sand, crystalline water and palm
trees waving happily in the breeze. Whoever dared to reach the
place by air faced the risk of being subsumed by a tangle of tropical
vegetation. Bahia Esperanza was indeed a paradise protected from
the world, and the people of the village were grateful for it.

For Joana, another working day at school was just coming to its
end. She taught the children to read and write and gave them basic
life skills. She told them about the many opportunities they would
have if they were ever to decide, as grown-ups, to leave the village
and go for the life in a big city.

There was no telephone nor electricity in the village. Television
had not reached them either, keeping their lives unaffected by the
influence of its news on the state of the world, wars or political
greed.

Since their ancestors had settled two hundred years ago, the
people of the village since had known very well about the world out
there in the 21st century. This isolation had never prevented them
from being aware of how life in big cities had developed. Somehow,
though, there was a special bond between the place and its people.

Joana herself had wondered many times what it was that kept
her there. The answer was always the same. She could go away for
a short period of time, but she would always come back. Every
single patch of ground of that paradise was etched in her mind, in
her heart and in her skin. Everybody who knew her, knew well that
Joana's bond to Bahia Esperanza would be difficult to break.

That day she was not deeply concerned about the reasons why

she did not want to leave Bahia Esperanza. Her mind was somewhere else. She did not remember either, as she used to do, the stories she had been told of how her ancestors had arrived on this continent, escaping from white persecution. That day was special.

Just one more test to correct and she could go home and pack what she would need for the next few days. She locked the door of the school and headed home. It was still too early to go down to the beach to enjoy, as she had many times before, the moment when the clouds began to change colour as the sun set far away. That evening she would not be there, she was going with Roberto to the city. The only existing shop in the village needed provisions and he was the one in charge of doing it. Once a month he loaded his old truck with handicrafts and handmade blankets and took them to the market in Itapicoca. With the money he would get for them, he would load the truck with provisions and different store supplies, including materials for the school. This time he was going to Fortaleza and Joana thought it would be a great opportunity to visit her friends Lucia and Mama Elsa. They had always lived in Bahia Esperanza, until the day Lucia had decided she wanted to live in the big city. Two years ago she had moved there, taking Mama Elsa with her.

As soon as everything was packed, she sat down on her bed and thought about her decision to go with Roberto. Things were happening to her, things that she did not understand. Many times she had dreams and she had read about them just to have a better understanding of their meaning. Most of the recent events though, were not only dreams. The first time it happened was a week ago; then yesterday. She was reading on the beach and, from time to time, she felt the urge to look at the sea, waiting for it to happen again. She stayed there for another hour, until the sky began to lose its brightness and at the same time the clouds danced for her, changing shape and colour up to the moment when they too faded, leaving the stage to the stars and the moon which, later on, would illuminate the tropical night. She decided not to wait anymore and got up, with a last glance, just to check. There it was. She gently rubbed her eyes to make sure it was not an illusion. She looked again and it was there, just the same as the previous days. It was a ship; the same ship as before. The first time it happened so quickly that she thought it might be some sort of replica of an old schooner, offering the tourists the option of dinner and dancing whilst sailing along the coast. When she saw it the second time, she thought it was very strange that it was not decorated, as it should have been, with garlands, lights and little multicoloured flags. Now, during its third apparition, there was something else that drew her attention. This time the ship was closer to the shore and completely silent, no music at all, just silence. She stayed very still, trying to distinguish something. It was not music that came to her ears. First it was only voices, but then the voices turned into screams and there were many people on deck. That was definitely not a ship for tourists. She could not see their faces, but she did see that everybody was moving rapidly around, with raised arms, as if waving. Suddenly the calm sea turned into a fury and the waves, formed out of the void, started to hit the ship mercilessly. Only a few seconds later the sky was covered with black stormy clouds, firing lightning to destroy the ship. Joana was paralysed. A horror movie was playing just in front of her. The ship was washed towards the reef and it seemed that the captain, if there was one, could not do anything to prevent the disaster. The crash was imminent.

Joana was terrified. She wished her grandmother had been there to explain what was happening; why these hallucinations occurred.

The ship's bow crashed against the rocks and the schooner broke into pieces and, between waves and darkness, Joana could see the bodies, some of them falling into the sea and others jumping overboard in desperation, trying to save themselves. In a few minutes the furious sea had swallowed the ship and the storm left, satisfied. On the now peaceful sea, the remains of masts, barrels and sails floated, serving as life rafts to the survivors who fought to reach the shore. As quickly as everything appeared for Joana, so it disappeared from her sight and the bay was again the beautiful and peaceful bay it had been just before.

"Joana?" the call and insistent knocking at her door brought her back. "Are you ok? I was worried as you didn't answer." Roberto was standing at her front door.

"Yes, I'm sorry, we can go now." She picked up her stuff and left the house, absentmindedly.

"Great, we've got a long drive ahead." Roberto smiled.

CHAPTER 28

"Joana, you're here!" Her friend flung her arms round Joana's neck, happy to see her. "I heard the roar of a truck and, I don't know why, but I knew it must be you!"

"Lucia!" They kissed and hugged each other and after exchanging a few words and agreeing he would pick her up next Sunday to go back to Bahia Esperanza, Roberto left the two women.

"I've missed you so much; you can't imagine how I've been longing for our chats since we moved here," Lucia said happily.

"Well, that's the price you have to pay for abandoning us in Bahia Esperanza!" Joana smiled back, clinging to her friend again and kissing her on both cheeks. "Where's Mama Elsa?"

"She's asleep; I guess she'll be delighted to see you, although I think she knew."

"She knew what? What do you mean?"

"You know her, she's always had this ability of foreseeing things, and earlier today when she woke up she said, '*I can sense we'll see Joana very soon.*' Joana wondered if it was mere coincidence: her hallucinations; her need to talk to Mama Elsa; the old woman's presentiment.

"Jo, are you ok?"

"Yes, I'm fine, it's only that..."

"That what?"

"Well, things have been happening, Lucia and maybe Mama Elsa can help me to understand."

"What do you mean by *things*?"

"It might sound crazy, but if it had happened only once I wouldn't really mind, but they occur so frequently." The soft, gentle call for Lucia from the other room interrupted their conversation. She responded immediately and a moment later she came back, pushing the wheelchair in which Mama Elsa sat.

"Mama Elsa!" Joana ran to her and hugged the smiling lady.

"Bless you, my dear child, you're here."

"Yes Mama Elsa, I'm here. How are you?" Joana asked getting down on her knees and holding and kissing the woman's wrinkled hands.

"Old and tired child, old and tired."

"Tired maybe, Mama Elsa, but old? You know you'll never be old!" The threesome laughed out loud.

"I'm sorry I came so late," Joana apologised. "You were sleeping."

"Don't worry, child, I have plenty of time to sleep and to sit in this chair! I wanted so much to see you!" Mama Elsa stroked Joana's face.

They chatted and laughed for a long time and the young women forgot about their previous conversation. Lucia told her friend about the job she had got three months ago in some important travel agency and, from her expression, Joana knew the city had conquered her friend's heart. She would probably never go back to Bahia Esperanza, which made Joana sad. But soon Lucia's happiness overwhelmed her and she felt happy for this woman who was not just a friend, more a beloved sister. Suddenly, she thought maybe she, too, would give up her job in Bahia Esperanza and end up here. The question was, for how long could she be away from home? Joana told them later about how much effort her students were putting into their work and how much they knew now. She also told them about their friends in the village and how much everybody missed them.

"What about Roberto?" Lucia asked mischievously.

"What about him?"

"Don't you have anything to tell us?"

"I don't know what you're talking about!" although she knew too well.

"Come on, Joana, you know he's mad about you!"

"I know, Lucia, I know and I love him dearly. Maybe one day. The truth is that I don't really know." Joana was aware of Roberto's feelings and so many times she had thought about accepting him, but had still not made up her mind. There was something stopping her, as if she was waiting for something special to happen.

"Too much waiting..." Lucia warned her.

"It is so good having you here, child." Mama Elsa's words were a lifesaver. Joana was happy to change the subject.

"I'm happy to be here too, Mama Elsa," she paused and added, "You knew I'd come, didn't you?"

"Tomorrow, child, tomorrow we'll speak."

That night, in her room, Joana thought about Lucia's words. Was she ready to accept Roberto and commit to a long term relationship? Was it love she felt for him? What would happen if she accepted him and later on found out she really loved him as a friend? Would she stay alone? What about this feeling of waiting for someone special to come? No matter how much thought she put into it, loneliness was definitely not a good reason to be with someone forever.

Although she had never been in love, she dreamt of a love that would go beyond just having a companion. Tiredness overcame her. She closed her eyes and soon she was deeply asleep.

Some hours later she woke up, startled. She was sweating and her whole body was trembling. She turned the light on, wanting to feel she was safe. 'My God, it was only a nightmare,' she thought, relieved, but not convinced. How could a dream be so real? Her first impulse was to get up and wake up Lucia but she did not do it. That would give the dream more significance than it really deserved. She turned off the light again and tried to go back to sleep. The dream fought to come back, but Joana finally managed to fall asleep again.

The following morning, Mama Elsa was already awake and waiting patiently for her. Lucia had gone out.

Joana started to speak first. "Mama Elsa, strange things are happening."

"I know, child."

"You know? How can you know?"

"The time has come for the past to meet the present; the time that will show you your path in this life, a path that was interrupted."

"What are you talking about, Mama Elsa? I don't understand a word."

"You will, as soon as I tell you what I've been asked to pass on to you. Maybe many of your questions will remain unanswered for now and you'll need much patience and faith to listen to your heart. I know I'll be gone soon."

"Don't say that, Mama Elsa, you won't go anywhere."

"Don't be afraid or sad, baby. You'll understand when you hear what I have to tell you." Joana sat down on the floor next to the woman's chair and rested her head on her lap as the old woman started to speak.

"You know the story of our ancestors, how they arrived here. You know that many of them were escaping." Joana nodded silently and respectfully.

"They risked their lives and crossed the seas, not knowing where they would get to, but for the black slaves any place was a better place than England in the 18th century. During the journey, many of them died, some starved, some became ill and others were not strong enough. Many storms took their dreams to the depths of the ocean. Only the strongest survived the last storm which forced them to swim to shore. They survived in this land which took them and gave them the chance to be free."

"The beach..." Joana whispered, "The scenes on the beach! Mama Elsa, I saw something..."

"Tell me about it, child."

"It was a ship. At first I thought it was my imagination, but then there was a storm, the ship was wrecked against the reef and the people fell into the ocean, screaming and they swam desperately to the coast. Then everything disappeared, like a movie that had been shown on a huge screen set up on the sea before me. Mama Elsa, why did I see that? How did you know I would come?" Joana's easy life teaching children suddenly became complicated with things she could hardly comprehend.

"I know it's difficult to understand or accept, Joana. It was for me too. I can't explain to you how it happens, I can't say why. Answers don't come when we want them, they come when we're ready to accept them. There is something I can tell you though and that is, life is much more than what we see through our eyes. There's something else beyond the physical things we can perceive by touching them; there's something else beyond the sound we can hear. We know very little about time and space and we learn slowly."

"Are you saying I won't get an answer to what's happening?"

"I'm saying you will when the time comes. First you need to develop faith and patience."

"What about what you know, Mama Elsa? How did you get your knowledge? Is there something else you can tell me?"

"Yes, child, there is. Two nights ago your grandmother appeared to me in my dream as a sign that the time had come for me to tell you, as I have, about the past meeting the present. When I saw her, I knew you'd come."

"You mean, you saw grandma like I saw the ship? Why? What for?"

"Among the people on that ship, Joana, there was a woman called Sarah." The woman held Joana's trembling hand, reassuringly. "This woman kept alive in her heart her wish to meet again the one who risked their life to save her and helped her to fulfil her dream of freedom."

"And this woman, Sarah..." Joana was afraid to ask, "In what way is she related to me?"

"You, Joana, are the last of her daughters through time."

"I can understand that, but..."

"What you've seen, what you've dreamed, all of it, is part of a previous life of yours."

"A previous life of mine?" Joana was shocked. She suddenly remembered things she had long ago forgotten, stories that her mother told her when she was a girl and the moment when she, herself, asked her not to tell her anymore.

"I thought my mother's stories were just that: stories," she paused, "and now you say that I've had a previous life? How can I be sure that happened? That what I've dreamt isn't just a result of my imagination?"

"Whether it was your imagination or it was real, only you will find out, Joana, if you keep Sarah's wish as your own."

"But I don't want..." she stopped, realizing she could be about to tell a lie if she finished the sentence.

How many times had she caught herself dreaming on the beach, that one day someone special would come into her life? And had she not thought about it only yesterday, although many years ago she had decided it was a silly, childish dream, something that only happened in movies and in books? She also remembered last night's nightmare.

"Mama Elsa, last night I had this strange nightmare. I was fleeing, I mean I saw myself fleeing from a hut, but I know the woman in my dream was me, and I felt a blow which made me fall, then more blows. Mama Elsa what was all that about?" Joana saw the woman's eyes full of tears.

"It means, child, that the woman of your dream was indeed you, that woman was Sarah, and she lives in you now."

"No, Mama Elsa, that can't be, this is madness. No one in their right mind would accept such a thing, nobody! What I had was only a dream, a nightmare. I'm not her, it's impossible, I can't be her!" In her panic, Joana stood up and moved away from the old woman, staring at her in disbelief and shaking her head. She backed into the door, opened it and ran away.

CHAPTER 29

She walked aimlessly, without noticing the time. She could not get Mama Elsa's words out of her mind and her head was about to explode. '*That woman is you, that woman was Sarah, she lives in you, she lives in you now...*' She looked around and realized she was in a park. There were people hanging around, walking, young people laughing, couples lying on the lawn, talking, kissing, children playing. Everything seemed unreal. Her vision clouded and the silhouettes got all mixed up, the voices and the laughter assaulted her senses and Sarah's name was everywhere. The next minute she noticed everybody staring at her and approaching her, chanting '*Sarah, Sarah...*' Her vision faded more and more, her legs trembled and her strength seemed to be leaving her body. She could hardly breathe and it was then that she heard the voice.

"Joana!" Roberto managed to catch her, just before she fainted.

When she woke up, her friend was staring at her, "How do you feel, sweetheart?" Roberto was really concerned.

"Where am I? Roberto, what..." Joana looked around and saw Lucia too, sitting right beside her and suddenly she remembered everything.

"Roberto, I want to go back to Bahia Esperanza," were her only words. Roberto and Lucia glanced at each other.

"Joana," Lucia protested, "Why? What happened? When I came back Mama Elsa was so quiet and looked so concerned, when Roberto brought you home unconscious!" She paused when she heard the old woman's voice calling her. Lucia left the room but came back almost immediately. Looking at Lucia's face, Roberto knew something was wrong.

"What is it?" he asked.

"Mama Elsa, she wants to see you, Joana. I've never seen her like this before." Joana got up, trembling.

As soon as the old woman saw her, she said, "Joana, things don't always happen as one would like them to." Every word was a struggle. "You must believe that you'll find the answer." She looked at Lucia and stretched her arm out, pointing to a small box on her night table. Lucia handed it to her. Mama Elsa opened it with effort and took out a strange symbol, which she then handed to Joana and said "Joana, your grandmother asked me to give it to you, you must keep it until the time comes." Mama Elsa's voice was fading away.

Joana took it without paying much attention, but pleading, "Mama Elsa, please don't speak, you must rest."

"I will rest, child. Don't be sad. I've been waiting for this moment for a long time." She could hardly breathe now. "I have enjoyed every day of my life, now I must go. Be happy, Joana."

"Mama Elsa!" Lucia was by her side, holding her hand and struggling to hold back the tears. The woman stared at her for a long moment, as if trying to find something in Lucia's eyes. Finally she smiled and put her other hand gently on Lucia's.

"To ránti iwo lode, obini. To gbò iwo okán anti bojutó lówo'oun nigbáti na koja ri mó pelu na ore... ni na agbará mbè 'lowo imò, lò-na, obini..."

Joana did not understand; why was Mama Elsa telling Lucia to remember her path and to listen to her heart? Why was she telling her to look after her when past and present meet? Why was she telling Lucia she had the power of knowledge? The truth was that she did not understand anything that was happening.

Whispering her departing words, Mama Elsa sighed deeply and peacefully and closed her eyes for the last time.

Two days after the funeral, Roberto asked Joana whether she wanted to leave or stay.

"I'm staying, Robertinho. I can't and I don't want to leave Lucia alone now." This was true, but she was also not sure whether she wanted to go back to Bahia Esperanza after all Mama Elsa had said to her. She was afraid of going back to the village, to the memories, to the beach.

"All right, but I'll come back soon, to see if you've changed your mind." He hugged her and kissed her goodbye. Then he pulled Lucia towards him, kissed her gently and gave her a long, deep look, as if trying to comfort her and give her strength.

Later that night, the two friends decided to try to take their mind off it all and went out to have a drink.

"I can't believe she's gone." Lucia was terribly affected by her loss. "Can you tell me what you two talked about? It seems that after she spoke to you, there was no reason for her to stay alive anymore and you, you have been so quiet these days. Remember when you arrived? You said strange things were happening." Joana knew too well Lucia was not going to give up until she found out. "Are those things related to what Mama Elsa told you? Or to the symbol she gave to you?"

"I can't tell you anything about the symbol, Lucia. I have no idea why she gave it to me; I can only guess she wanted me to keep it. What can I tell you? There's no point in hiding it from you." Joana told Lucia about her nightmare, about her hallucinations on the beach and about her ancestors. Lucia was astounded.

"So, after all this time you're not Joana, but...what's her name?"

"Sarah," Joana whispered and then she asked, "Do you think this relates to what she said to you before she died?" Lucia answered with a shrug; she was determined not to think about it.

After a moment's silence, Joana spoke again, "I wonder who Sarah was waiting for. You know, this is really hard to believe, but on the other hand Mama Elsa wouldn't make it up, would she?"

"I don't think so. What are you going to do?"

"I've got no idea. I only know I once had a quiet and peaceful life in Bahia Esperanza and now my head's all messed up with unreal situations, mad things about the present mingling with the past and, if it wasn't enough, someone tells me I'm not who I think I am but someone else. Does it mean that I've lived a life that's not mine? I don't know my friend, I don't know." She paused and continued, after having a sip from her cocktail. "Everything's very weird, one part of me denies every little bit of this story and says forget it, forget it, while the other half," she paused again, pensive, "while the other half tells me everything could be true."

"What will happen if everything turns out to be real after all?" Lucia was speaking now. "If in the end everything's true. Where is that person Sarah was longing for all this time, going to come from? How? What if some strange guy shows up, dressed in a funny old way, knocks at your door and says," Lucia lowered her voice, '*Hey Sarah, I'm here, as I promised!*"

Both women giggled, more hysterical than amused.

"Maybe the sensible thing to do is forget about everything and live here in Fortaleza, look for a job or, maybe I could finally accept Robertinho and have a family with him."

"Without loving him? Joana, I know I always make fun of you two," Lucia was serious now, "but committing to him, wouldn't it be like leading him on, giving him false hope?"

"What if I could grow to love him? He's always been so nice to me and he is very handsome."

"You're not serious, are you? Why don't you just stay here as you said? At least for a while, until this is all over? Of course you'd live with me. Maybe you could even work with me at the agency!"

"The agency? Lucia, for God's sake, what would I do there? I don't know, I'm not sure about anything right now."

"Come on, you've always been optimistic, don't stop now. You didn't collapse after your mother died, nor after your grandmother's death and now you'll give up because of something that we don't even know is real?" Lucia was thinking of Mama

Elsa's last words to her. She knew too well that the old woman had had no choice as fate had set the rules in her case, but Lucia was not ready to accept a destiny which she did not want. She had to convince Joana to forget about this and stay in Fortaleza. Of course she was overjoyed when her friend said,

"Maybe you're right, maybe the best thing is to forget it and start my life all over again, here in Fortaleza."

CHAPTER 30

W hen Chris got home from her early run, Anne and Patrick were about to have breakfast in the garden. The autumn morning was beautifully warm and Chris joined them after her shower.

"That was very brave of you, to get up so early after such a late night," Anne said as she poured her friend a cup of coffee.

"Thank you both for coming with me last night. I really appreciate your words. I must say that I do feel better after admitting that I'd love to find Sarah again. Of course I feel terribly sad because I can't see how this could happen... but anyway, somehow it helps."

"Will you tell her now?" Anne whispered to Patrick.

"Tell me what?"

"Well, it's only that last night, before I went to sleep, I had this idea..." he loved being mysterious.

"Come on, darling, tell her!"

"Alright, alright! Chris, we decided to go on with our lives, didn't we?"

"Yes...and?" Chris was eager to know what they were planning.

"What would you say if you and I work together?"

"Right. Doing what? I know nothing about publishing."

"You don't need to."

"Please explain?"

"I will. You know the business is doing very well, the staff is managing perfectly and I could have lots of spare time. I have been thinking of diversifying into another industry."

"And that would be...?"

"Tourism."

"Right, and what would I do in a tourism agency? I'm not a salesperson, Patrick, and tourism is all about sales. Besides, what do *you* know about tourism?"

"Nothing, but when I'm interested I learn extremely quickly and you, you've got a lot to offer!" He stopped to have some coffee.

"Did you know about this, Anne?"

"Oh, yes, he told me all about it today. Was it at five in the morning, sweetheart?" Anne looked at him ticking him off for waking her up so early. He kissed her on the cheek.

"And what do you think?" Chris asked.

"I think it's a great idea, I'm looking forward to it."

"I'm still waiting to hear about the skills I bring."

"Your responsibility would be publicity and designing leaflets and magazines; lots of photography involved."

"I don't know what to say!"

"That's easy, say yes. This might be a good chance to start a new life." Anne said smiling.

Chris did not need too much time to become as enthusiastic as her friends were. The offer was too tempting and she had nothing to lose. She also knew she could not continue to be idle for much longer.

That breakfast turned into their first very long business meeting and by the end of it they had already made their first three ambitious decisions: the first one being the opening date; the second the destinations to offer to their, as yet, nonexistent customers; and the third decision was to put all their efforts into achieving both simultaneously.

The winter was definitely coming and the exotic scenery of the paradise-like beaches of Brazil was the perfect destination to offer people who, by December or January, had had enough of a long winter.

The following weeks became a hive of activity which distracted Chris from her restlessness. Choosing the appropriate location for the office, the amount of bureaucratic paperwork to get a business legally up and running, the recruitment of the right staff and, of course, the contacts to be made with the different airlines, stopped her from dwelling on Sarah and a deep-seated longing to find her. If she let her thoughts run free it would mean losing control of her life once again and she just could not allow this to happen. It was madness wishing to find her after two hundred years and, for the time being, her only reality was to go on waking up every day in the 21st century. There was nothing else; there could not be anything else. Strangely enough, after confessing to her friends her deep wish to find Sarah again, she no longer saw weird people from the past walking around, she did not wake up with nightmares at night, she did not hear voices either. It seemed she had done the right thing and life was being good to her.

She dedicated what little spare time she had left, to do some research and reading about those topics that, until now, had never been of any interest to her; topics like reincarnation, life after life, events or stories about unknown dimensions or travelling in time. And when her friends questioned her about her reading, they had long chats about it, without mentioning anything that could bring back sad memories.

At the beginning of December, everything was organized and, although not officially open yet, the agency had already organized all-inclusive holidays for its first customers.

"As the business is doing very well, I was thinking," Chris said to them during dinner one evening, "since we haven't had real holidays, we could have a working holiday." Anne and Patrick looked at each other surprised and Anne reacted first, wondering if it was the right time to do that.

"Why not? We can afford it and we need to get a real feel for the places we're planning to send our customers to. Am I right? We could spend some time travelling around, ensuring that we had first hand information. By the beginning of February we'd be back, ready to settle everything for the opening. By then the staff will have finished their probationary period. Besides, the Office Manager is doing an excellent job."

Anne and Patrick needed no more than a moment or two and a few glances to get enthusiastic about the idea.

Two days later, the threesome got on board Brazilian Airlines Flight 937 to their first destination; the city of Belem.

The first weeks in Brazil passed between cruise ships along the Amazon River and the Brazilian coast. They had their first break in Fortaleza, which was unanimously chosen as the perfect venue for Christmas and New Year.

It was in this city where everything began to get confused again for Chris. It did not matter how hard she tried, she just could not get away from Sarah's memory. She came to her mind with increasing intensity. She could laugh, she could enjoy herself, meet people and socialize and converse with her friends, but all of a sudden she would find herself thinking of Sarah and how she could find her. She thought so much of her that her heart ached. Over and over again too, her grandfather's words came to mind, '*You'll meet again, when the time comes...*'

More cruise ships and flight connections took them down to Rio de Janeiro and by the end of January, they were back in Fortaleza, from where they would soon catch a plane and return to London.

They visited more than a dozen hotels, many of which would appear as highly recommended by their agency, but at the end they registered at the Caesar Park, on Rua Beira Mar, between Iracema Beach and the Yacht Club.

Alone in her room and enjoying the beautiful sight over the beach and the Atlantic Ocean, Chris wondered what it was that attracted her so much to this city. She now had the same feeling as on her arrival in Fortaleza.

"You're very quiet today, dear," Anne said, sipping from her cocktail on the hotel's terrace.

"It's this city, there's something about this place..."

"I'm sure it's just our running around, visiting all these places during two months. Maybe you need a holiday without touching your camera!"

"Maybe, but I doubt it, Patrick. I need more than two months running around as you say, to feel eager about holidays. It's something else, it's..."

"Could you be a little more specific?" Anne was curious. She and Patrick had already noticed and talked about her sudden mood changes.

"I've got this sort of a premonition, a strong and crazy premonition that I still can't define." Anne and Patrick glanced at each other again.

"And this premonition has to do with Sarah?" Patrick's comment made Chris tremendously tense. Suddenly she did not want to speak anymore, regretting what she had just said.

"Is it possible that she's here?" Anne's remark was audacious and she knew it might upset her friend, but she just smiled nervously. What could she say to that other than make a joke of it?

"Yeah, sure, and can you also tell me how it could happen, after two hundred years? Gosh, she'd be *very* old."

"I thought this sort of questioning was over." Anne paused to speak after a few seconds again. "Do you think you've been fooling everyone all this time? If you think that, maybe you fooled yourself, but not us. Your eyes don't lie, Chris."

"What about you, Patrick? Do you think the same?" she defended herself.

"I only know," he was playing with his glass, "that I've got a strange feeling."

"You know what?" Anne said firmly. "I don't need to have any premonitions to know that maybe the three of us have been trying to fool ourselves, just keeping busy with the business twenty-four-seven and thinking that everything was normal again, but that's not true! And since we're in the land of *Macumba*, why don't we try to find somebody who can help us?"

"You mean somebody like the woman in Brighton?" Patrick asked immediately.

"That's exactly what I mean, why not?"

"Two hundred years ago, many of the natives and slaves who were living here, fought against the prohibition of popular cults. Some of them worshipped Shangó and they said he had a woman, Yansan, who was his sister, goddess of the winds and the storms. Others said she was his counterpart, that both of them were bisexual gods, and at the same time they were one..." Chris gazed into the distance. Anne and Patrick looked puzzled.

In the little restaurant at the other end of the city, only a few streets away from Parque Do Cocó, Joana and Lucia were having a drink after work. Joana was reading the last part of an article found in an old magazine: '...goddess of the winds and the storms. Others said she was his counterpart, that both of them were bisexual gods, and at the same time they were one...'

"Where did you get that?" Patrick asked intrigued.

"Where did I get what?" Chris appeared to be recovering from a trance.

"What you just said!"

"I wasn't saying anything, Patrick. I was just thinking about something I read somewhere." All of a sudden she went still and turned pale. Anne held Patrick's hand firmly and said,

"I don't like this. Chris, are you feeling alright?"

"Do you want me to answer your question, Anne?"

"Which one?"

"The one about if it's possible that Sarah's here."

"Can you?" Anne was frowning.

"Yes I can, she *is* here."

"How can you know?"

CHAPTER 31

"What else does it say?" Lucia asked but she had no answer. Joana was looking over her shoulder, as if searching for someone.

"What's wrong?"

"Nothing, I just thought I heard someone talking to me."

"I was asking what else is in there," Lucia insisted.

"Oh, that's it. It's just an old magazine I found somewhere. Lucia, would you mind if we go? I'd like to have a walk."

"Not at all, I need to go back to work anyway to sort out some things for Nereu. I want to tell you about it, it's important."

"What is it? Can't it wait until tomorrow?"

"Nereu's selling the agency."

After Mama Elsa's death, Joana's worries about going back to Bahia Esperanza and facing again the apparitions on the beach, did not go away, so she decided the best decision was to stay in Fortaleza. The old woman's story about this woman Sarah made her also afraid and, somehow, the presence of her friend gave her strength.

Two days later she received Nereu's offer to work with them and, as the weeks passed, she got more and more used and attached to the attractions of living in the city, to Lucia's friends and of course to the amazing opportunities to learn. Considering the resources available in Bahia Esperanza, being in this city was like being in the University of Life. Of course she missed her friends and the children at school, but escaping from her fears and her inability to deal with the unknown were enough reasons to stay away from home.

Everything had worked fine for Joana until a month ago, when she started having the nightmares that became recurrent during Christmas and New Year. She also started having those moments when no matter what time of the day, she felt as she had a while ago, as if somebody were calling her.

"Why does he want to sell if the business is doing so well?"

"He knows that and he's not extremely happy about the idea, but you know his family lives in Portugal, don't you?" Joana nodded. "Well, his mother called him a couple of weeks ago with bad news. His father had a stroke and although he's recovering, he won't be able to go back to work. Nereu's youngest brother is not ready to take over, so there wasn't much of an option for him. He wouldn't just leave his mother in full charge of the hotel they run in Lisbon, it's too much for one person. He's going back to take over himself."

"But why sell the agency? Why not just keep it?"

"That's what I said, but he's made up his mind and as you said, the business is doing so well that he's already had some offers."

"That is a real shame," Joana said, discouraged. "I was really enjoying the job."

"I know, dear. It seems we'll need to look for another job, unless of course the new owner decides to keep the staff." She wanted to be optimistic.

"Do you think that could happen?"

"We'll see, maybe tomorrow there'll be good news."

"Why tomorrow?"

"That's why I need to go back now. Nereu's having a meeting with one of the potential buyers and he asked me to go with him. I need to put some information together. I must go now, are you coming?"

"I don't think so. If you don't mind I'll have a walk and I'll see you later at home."

"Are you ok?" Lucia could see the deep melancholy in Joana's eyes.

"Yes, I'm fine, I just need some fresh air," she lied. The truth was she needed some space to think about the upsetting feelings she was having and this was definitely not a good moment to bother her friend with them.

The following day, at the Caesar Park Hotel, while waiting for Anne and Chris to have breakfast, Patrick was chatting animatedly with the manager. He could not wait to tell Anne and Chris about it.

"I have some very interesting information for you, ladies," he said when they showed up.

"Did you find somebody who can help us?" was Anne's guess. She was still thinking of last night's conversation.

"No, sorry, it's not that, yet. Maybe there are other steps to be made first."

"What do you mean?" Chris was puzzled.

"Maybe we could find a good reason to stay around a bit longer and sort out things."

"Could you be a little more specific?"

"The thing is, that while I was waiting for you just now, I was telling the manager about our business and he told me..."

"Come on, baby, speak! Why do you need to be so mysterious?" Anne urged him.

"Okay, okay, this man told me that a very good friend of his is planning to sell his business because he's moving to Portugal."

"What business? You're not thinking what I think you're thinking, are you?" Anne knew Patrick too well.

"Why not?"

"Wait a minute, what are you talking about?" Chris was lost.

"It's just an idea that came to me during our chat," he paused. "Maybe we should think about having an agency down here. What do you think?" He paused again, staring at them, waiting for their reaction.

"Isn't it a little adventurous? We don't know anybody here, we don't know how things work and, besides, we haven't had the opening in London yet." Chris remarked.

"We don't need to discuss it now, but maybe you could do it," he gestured to Chris and seemed extremely confident.

"Me? Who told you that I want to live here?" Chris tried to look surprised but her friends knew her too well. After all, during their first week in Fortaleza she had driven them crazy, talking about how beautiful and fun this city was and how she could perfectly imagine herself living in a city like this. She'd always dreamt of living by the sea, she found the weather great and the people were charming, welcoming and happy.

"Aren't we going a little too fast, love?" Anne was worried about Patrick's impulsiveness.

"As I said, it's just an idea, sweetheart. I think though, that when opportunities arise, one should take them. Why don't we just try to establish some contacts?"

The women looked at each other again and after a while Chris said,

"There's nothing to lose if we just speak to this man, right?" Patrick got up immediately, with a satisfied smile like a boy who had just got what he wanted.

"Don't you think this is crazy, Chris?" Anne said.

"Crazier than the rest of last few months' events, my friend?" she said, relaxed while finishing her coffee.

"Everything's sorted." Patrick was still smiling when he came back. "It seems that this man, Nereu da Silva, is having a meeting here today. The manager promised he'd make an appointment for us to have dinner with him. In the meantime ladies, what do you think about a little sightseeing?"

CHAPTER 32

That morning, Joana woke up with a start, dripping with sweat. She looked around frantically, but on recognizing her room, she calmed down. She was safe at home and Lucia was still asleep. It was the same nightmare she had had in Bahia Esperanza, only this time there was something different in it, something else. She had heard caring words telling her, *'You'll be fine, you'll see. I'll take care of you and we'll make your dream come true.'* She wondered why she had dreamt the same thing again. Who was with her, looking after her? And this person had called her Sarah. Joana was scared.

It was still very early but she got up and made a coffee. She did not want to think or remember Mama Elsa, but she could not help it. *'You're her, my child, you're Sarah.'*

Lucia found Joana in the living room holding the coffee mug tightly between her hands, her tearful eyes lost somewhere in the room.

"Joana, what's wrong?" As she did not get an answer, she insisted, "Sweetheart, what's happened?"

"It's back, Lucia," she whispered.

"What is back?"

"The nightmare, the same nightmare, something's happening Lucia and I don't know what." Lucia sat down next to her, thoughtful.

"I've been hearing someone calling me, someone who's very close. What am I going to do, Lucia?"

"Let's take it easy, okay? I don't know yet, but we'll sort this out, you'll see." She wondered if she believed her own words. "Now, why don't we get ready to go together to the Caesar Park?"

"I'd rather stay here and then go to work."

"I don't want you to be by yourself, not now, please? We can go back to work later and decide what to do." Joana hesitated but finally she agreed.

"Alright, I'll come with you."

Later that morning, Lucia was parking her car not far away from the main entrance to the hotel. At the same time, Anne and Patrick were waiting for Chris, who was about to get into the rented car. But before doing so, she lifted her head to look around, her hand holding the car door. Her heartbeat raced and she felt her stomach contracting. Patrick, who had already started the engine looked at Anne and shrugged, wondering what was holding up Chris.

"Come on, partner, what are you waiting for?" Chris turned around and scanned the place. Apart from the few tourists and the two hotel porters, there was only that other car parking just then, nobody else was there. 'This is impossible, I can't be so wrong. Sarah, are you here?'

In the meantime, Joana put her hand on Lucia's arm, as she was taking the car key. Lucia looked at her in surprise. "It's happening, Lucia," she felt a lump in her throat and her heart was beating fast.

"What is happening?"

"Somebody's calling me, Lucia, right now!" She got out of the car quickly and looked around. There was nothing there, just the two hotel porters, a couple of tourists and that car with three passengers driving away. Her heartbeat calmed down and the lump in her throat disappeared.

In the meantime Anne, looking over her shoulder, asked Chris, "You feel alright, Chris?"

"Yes, it's gone now," she paused and added, "I'm sure, Anne."

"Sure of what?"

"That she's here." Anne grabbed her hand and looked at Patrick, who was very silent. He seemed to get very distressed when Chris experienced these things.

They drove along Av. Beira Mar to Rua Baraô de Studart, crossing Av. Da Aboliçao to reach, as the people of the Rent-a-Car had suggested, Parque Do Cocó. With more than four hundred hectares, it was the biggest urban park in South America and therefore one of the main attractions of the city, especially because of the thousands of native flora species grown there.

They parked the car next to the amphitheatre located in the park and set off on their walk. After almost two hours of wandering around, they found a cafeteria in a pergola and sat down to rest. They asked for some cold drinks and it was then that Chris saw the old woman sitting on a bench, not far from where they were. The woman, dressed in a very simple way, was feeding the pigeons, systematically throwing crumbs that she took out of her bag. It was not her feeding the many birds that caught Chris's attention, though. There was something familiar about that lady and she could not resist the impulse to approach her. Anne and Patrick watched her silently.

She sat down next to the woman, watching the pigeons vying desperately for the scattered crumbs.

"Do I... know you?" Chris asked shyly.

"I come here every day to feed them," the woman whispered, ignoring the question.

"There are lots to feed," Chris said.

"Yes, there are. They get very impatient, all of them, but they also know that at the end they will get their food, at the right moment..." she paused, "Like these pigeons, people get their answers at the right time, my child, not earlier." Chris fell into a sort of trance.

"How do we know when the right time comes?"

"You just know, you feel it, you're feeling it..." Chris closed her eyes.

"Grandfather..."

"Chris?" Anne and Patrick were standing right in front of her. "Why did you come to sit here on your own?" Anne asked her, intrigued.

"I'm not alone, she..." but when she turned her head there was nobody there.

"Where's she gone?"

"Who?" Anne looked worried.

"The old lady." Patrick whispered.

"What old lady? What's going on here?" Chris and Patrick did not hear her. They were staring at each other.

"Did you see her?"

"Yes, Chris. I saw her."

Later on that night, back in the hotel, Anne said, "Why do you both feel and see things and I don't?"

"I might have an idea, sweetheart," Patrick said gently.

"I'd love to hear it, love."

"I think Chris and I met in a previous life." For some reason, Chris did not look shocked by his remark. At this point anything was possible. Anne, though, was not relaxed.

"I'm not sure I like this anymore. I really don't know what to do."

"There's nothing you can do, love. Just be, be here with us. There's nothing we can do either. I guess we'll just need to wait."

"Wait until the right time comes..." Chris added, strangely relaxed.

The manager approached them to tell Patrick that his friend was waiting for them.

"Shall we go, ladies?"

"That's the whole story. Now you know why I've decided to sell my business." Nereu had told them about his family hotel back in Portugal, about the agency he had in this city and about the selling conditions." Then he added, "If you want, you can come and visit it tomorrow."

155

"We'd love to," Patrick said looking at them smiling, satisfied. "Is it okay with you if we come at noon?"

Once Patrick and Anne returned to their room after dinner and as Patrick pulled off his shirt, he said, "You were very quiet during the meal, darling."

"I'm scared, Patrick."

"Scared of what?"

"Of everything, of these weird things that both of you feel, of what happened to Chris in the park. What if something terrible happens? We don't know how to fight this kind of..." she hesitated, looking for the right word, "situation. It's pretty paranormal, Patrick." He held her tightly against him, stroking her hair.

"I guess we need to believe that nothing bad is going to happen, sweetheart. If you think about it, somehow everything has been happening by itself, as if following a natural course."

"I'm also worried about Chris."

"Why?"

"I don't know how it could happen, but what if she does find Sarah? What will happen then?"

"Well, there are a couple of options, I'd say," he said mischievously while he lifted Anne's chin, kissing her lips.

"Like what?" She put her fingers on his lips, gently rejecting his kiss.

"First," he speculated, "she could find an amazingly wise woman who could teach her many things, or she could make a very good friend or maybe she could..." he stopped.

"She could what?"

"We can't deny she could find her soul mate."

"Her... oh no, I don't believe that. One thing is to have had this brief and insignificant experience with Sarah, but you know, she's not... she's not like..." Anne frowned as if not believing her own words and added, "No, come on. She definitely..."

"*Brief and insignificant experience*? Do you really believe it was just a *brief and insignificant experience*?" He repeated emphasising every word.

"Do you think there's something she didn't tell us?"

"No, but if you look into her eyes when she speaks about Sarah..."

"You're not telling me you think she fell in love with her?"

"That, my love, is exactly what I think."

"You're wrong! You're out of your mind! Chris would never fall in love with a woman!"

"Why not?"

"Well, because she... she likes men, she loved Steve, I know her, she... she..."

"She *what* baby?" Patrick's clumsy fingers where trying to unfasten her blouse, but she ignored his silent message.

"She..." He did not let her speak. He was kissing her again, still struggling to undo the buttons of the blouse which prevented him from feeling her naked skin.

"Patrick..." she gasped.

"Hum?"

"Tell me something," she managed to ask, just as his lips kissed her neck and moved down to her shoulders, "Please..." He growled and looked at her tenderly.

"You never..."

"Never what, my love?"

"All this time we've been together, you've never missed..." It was true that she knew and accepted all about his life, but it was also true they had never again spoken about it. Not because she did not want to, but because she had been afraid of his answer. Patrick stepped back a bit, still holding her.

"Paul? My previous life?" Anne nodded, looking down.

"No, no. Look at me, darling. Look straight into my eyes and listen to my words," he said holding her face. "I missed him very much for a long time, you know that. It was hard to lose him and to realize I'd never be with him again. I caused him great pain when I first rejected him but after that, as I told you, we were very happy and I will never forget what we had. Wherever he might be now, I'm sure he feels the same."

"Do you think he was your twin soul?"

"I don't know for sure, but I think that's unlikely. If that were true, why would life have torn us apart? Of course I might be wrong."

"And don't you miss...?" She blushed.

"Being with a man?" she nodded shyly again, "No, I don't." He answered emphatically, kissed her and added, "Anne, the same as Chris has no answers to what happened to her, neither can I explain the change in my life. What I do know is that far beyond my being a man and your being a woman, I feel you're so deep in my heart that the thought of not being with you drives me mad. My life without you would be meaningless. I'm extremely happy with you, you're my friend, my companion, my lover and your body's the only one I want. I miss you when we're not together. You're my everything and I want to share my life with you."

"I love you so much, Patrick." Their clothes fell in a pile on the floor and they gasped for each other and kissed hungrily at first, then gently, while their fingers explored each other's body. They made love over and over again until they lay, exhausted, in each other's arms and fell asleep.

Patrick did not sleep as he normally would after making love to Anne. He kept on waking up during the night, soaked in sweat. The nightmare that had left him so many years ago was back. This time he knew it would stay and torture him. He could see himself clearly, wrapped in a dark cloak, a thick beard hiding almost all his face and his long hair, under a wide brimmed hat, falling untidily down to his shoulders. Although, in his dream, the man was far from being gentle and as well built and attractive as Patrick was, he knew it was him. The man looked happy and satisfied after catching his prey. He had her in the house, after beating her because she would not stay still. Patrick moved restlessly in bed. The woman was trying to escape now and he could not allow it. He took a lump of wood and threw it towards her, knocking her down. He pulled her inside again, kicking her and pushing her in to the corner. As he did so, he felt a presence and looked over his shoulder. Somebody was touching him.

"Baby, are you ok?" Sleepily, Anne clung to him, "What's wrong?" She woke up completely when she felt his sweaty chest. For a while he did not say a word. He held her tightly to him, seeking her protection.

"It's back, sweetheart, the nightmare is back."

CHAPTER 33

"I can see you didn't sleep very well either," said Anne when she met Chris having a coffee. Chris's eyes were gazing into the distance, admiring the beautiful sunrise.

"Why, did you have nightmares too?"

"Me? Oh no, I slept like a baby until Patrick woke me up. I have never seen him so distressed before."

"What do you mean?"

"He was scared like a child."

"Scared? Why?"

"I don't know, he wouldn't say why, but he said the nightmare was back. Then I fell asleep again and, when I finally woke up, he was sleeping so soundly that I didn't want to disturb him. After all, it's very early."

Chris wondered if it was the same nightmare he had told her about in Brighton. If it was, why was it coming back now? Was it really possible that they had shared a life in the past? Then she thought about her own dream and the memories of her last moments in the past all came back together; Sarah, her kiss, her eyes. Anne's voice brought her back.

"Do you really think you'll see Sarah again?"

"I don't think, I know," she sounded scared of her own certainty.

"How can you know something like that? It happened more than two hundred years ago," she hesitated. "This is all so weird!" Chris was quiet. Was there anything she could say?

"If it becomes true and you meet her again, here, now, have you thought about what you'll do?"

"What do you mean by what I'll do?"

"I mean exactly what I said. What would you do if you had her in front of you now?" As Chris remained thoughtfully silent, Anne persisted, "If you're so sure that it will happen, will you perhaps call her by her name and say, 'Hello, it's good to see you again, what have you been up to all this time?' How will you know it's really her? Do you think she's going to be exactly the same, a perfect reincarnation? Will she recognize you?"

"Haven't you got any questions left?"

"Sorry, it's only that..."

"Don't worry, the truth is, I know exactly how you feel, the problem is that I haven't got any answers to your questions apart from I don't know. What else can I tell you?"

"Why don't you start by telling me what you think when you remember her? What do you feel?"

"I feel melancholy, I feel touched and eager to know that she's all right, wherever she might be. I'd like to listen to her again, to watch her laugh and I'd love to..." She held back the words, knowing that she had already said too much.

"Patrick is right!"

"Right about what?"

"He says..."

"Oh come on, Anne, what?"

"You're in love with her!"

"Don't be silly, how can you say something like that? Do you think that too?" Chris was extremely upset.

"I'd prefer not to think, if you ask me, but I can't help noticing that expression in your eyes when you speak about her. Just now, a few seconds ago, you said you'd like to... what, Chris? What would you like to do if you met her?" Anne was merciless.

"Hug her, okay? Hug her!" Chris blushed and her voice rose and turned defensively, "What's wrong with that? Don't I sometimes hug you, or you me, with no reason?"

"Well, yes, we do, but..." she smiled mischievously, "you don't look at me like that."

"Like what?"

"Well, with eyes overflowing with love."

"You're mad. Both of you. Missing someone doesn't mean you're in love, does it? I knew I should have kept my mouth shut."

"Why do you get so upset about this? After all, you're the one who's sure you'll find her again. Besides, that is and was what you wanted, isn't it? It doesn't matter how hard you try to deny it, you're convinced that somehow your times are coming together again and as soon as you meet her again, you won't have any choice, sweetheart."

"Any choice about what?"

"To face your feelings for her."

"Do you really think I could ever accept falling in love with a woman? Why should I?"

"Why shouldn't you? What do you achieve by hiding your feelings? I don't know what it is, maybe you're afraid?"

"Afraid of what?"

"Afraid of people gossiping."

"That *is* absurd, Anne. I don't give a damn about what people say." Chris had never been so rebellious and confrontational with her friend.

"Or maybe you think this only happens to other people and not to you?"

Chris did not say anything for a minute, then she got up and said, "I think I'll go for a walk now."

"Ok, you do that my friend. As we've been saying, time will give us the answers, won't it? I'll go upstairs to check on Patrick."

Chris left the hotel and hurried down to the beach. It was a beautiful day to walk and maybe to take some nice pictures, although her mind was not really into photography. Anne's words were driving her crazy. Her friends were nuts and, if they were not, they had a good imagination. That was it, their imagination. She could not be in love with a woman, of course she could not. What future was there for two women? Patrick's case was different. He had left his past behind to find a normal life.

'I'm not really in love with you, Sarah, no way. I miss you, yes. I miss laughing with you, talking to you, feeling you're there, telling you about this world. That's it, Sarah, my 18th century friend, I just miss you a lot and I'd love to see you again.' As she kept walking down the beach she saw two people coming towards her, two women. As they came closer she heard them laughing. They looked happy, like two friends sharing their free time, chatting about this or that. Chris wondered whether they had a secret. Now she was getting mad. She could not possibly go around wondering if there was a secret between them whenever she saw two women. They passed by and gave her a friendly smile, as if they knew her. She greeted back, looked over her shoulder and saw they were looking at her as well. They were giggling and holding hands.

Chris looked away, towards the horizon, fixing her eyes on the ship approaching the coast. Her mind jumped back to the old woman in Brighton. What was it that she said, about having faith and listening to one's heart and not forgetting what had been? Her eyes rested again on the ship.

"It can't be," she whispered to herself. She rapidly took her camera, adjusted the zoom and shot several times. The ship came closer and she shot again. She put the camera down and in that fraction of time, the ship was gone. When she got back to the hotel, Anne and Patrick were asking at the front desk for her.

"Here you are!" he said with a smile when he saw her coming. "Let's go, it's time."

"Time to what? Oh yes, the agency."

CHAPTER 34

*A*t the time Anne had been interrogating Chris about her feelings for Sarah, on the other side of the city Lucia was walking sleepily into the kitchen to prepare their breakfast. The aroma of freshly made coffee greeted her. She saw Joana snuggled up with eyes closed on the couch, a mug between her hands.

"Are you alright?" Joana looked at her silently.

"What's wrong, why are you crying?"

"I'm not crying."

"No? And what are these?" She swept a tear off her cheek. "Did you have another nightmare?" Joana nodded and the tears rolled down freely.

"Was it that bad?" She sat down next to her, holding her hands, but Joana said nothing. After a few minutes, when she stopped crying, she said,

"I don't understand what I dreamt of."

"Was it not the same dream?"

"No, this time it was something completely different."

"Come on, tell me, it will make you feel better."

"There was a man, Lucia. I was very afraid and tried to escape from where he was holding me prisoner. He hit me. I mean, he hit her, but she was me."

"She? Who's she?"

"Sarah, I was Sarah and then, then the man was gone and I woke up and there was somebody next to me."

"Somebody else? Was it the same person you dreamt of before?"

"Yes."

"Who was it?"

"She was..."

"Who, Joana, who was she?"

"A woman."

"And what happened? Did she speak to you?"

"No."

"No?"

"She and I... we..."

"You what? Tell me, Joana."

"We were kissing."

"Kissing?"

"Yes, kissing."

"And?"

"We were alone, I don't know where, and in my dream I was dreaming as well, but I don't remember what. I just remember that I woke up and cried and she was holding me and then I was telling her I didn't want to *leave* without her, and then, then we kissed." Lucia was silent. She was not shocked at Joana's dreaming about kissing a woman. It was not Joana's words full of melancholy that upset her, nor the pain she felt in her friend's heart. There was something else, far beyond Joana's words. Lucia knew she could not go on denying the past. What was happening to Joana was a sign. Mama Elsa had told her, she had to help her.

"Lucia, I've never been with a woman, I don't know why I dreamt what I dreamt." But Lucia was not listening, she was thinking.

"Tell me more about the dream, tell me what happened afterwards."

"I don't remember anything else, just my words pleading to this stranger, the kiss and then... the fog! It was cold and her silhouette was vanishing, I was going... I do remember my last words to her... Lucia... I asked her to look for me in time... I was telling her that somewhere I'd be waiting for her... Chris! Her name was Chris... and it was so real..."

After a long while and a couple of coffees, Joana finally calmed down and they went off to work.

Patrick parked the car outside Nereu's agency and said, "You've been very quiet, Chris, is everything all right?"

Anne hadn't told Patrick about their earlier conversation. Chris was scanning the shops around and stopped all of a sudden.

"Listen," she said, "I've got to do something, I'll see you later, ok?" and she sped off, leaving them standing there, puzzled. She crossed the street towards the shop with the 'print your own pictures' sign.

Once in the shop, she pulled the memory card from her camera and inserted it in one of the computers available for self printing. Her fingers were trembling.

In the meantime, at the agency, Nereu was welcoming Patrick and Anne and introducing Lucia.

"Chris apologizes, Nereu, she couldn't reschedule another meeting," Patrick lied.

Lucia reacted immediately, raising her eyebrows. Was it not the name Joana had given her earlier? Could it be just a coincidence? The problem was she did not believe in coincidences. She tried to get more information.

"Chris?" she asked.

"Yes, she's our partner," explained Patrick.

Then Nereu spoke again,

"Joana, who also works for the agency, will join us as soon as she finishes dealing with some customers."

The meeting went on without Joana or Chris being there. They shook hands with Nereu to seal a pre agreement on the deal and left his office. Lucia led them to the foyer, where they met Joana.

"Here you are!" Lucia smiled. "Joana, this is..." but she could not go on. Joana's eyes were fixed on Patrick's. She was pale, as if she had seen a ghost. Before anybody had the chance to say a word, Patrick took Anne by the arm and almost dragged her out of there.

"Patrick, for God's sake! What's wrong with you?" Anne yelled at him, shocked. "I hope you have a damn good explanation for your weird behaviour in there! We just made a scene!" Patrick was not listening to her. He was walking so fast that it was difficult for her to keep up. "Patrick!"

Back in the agency and realizing what had just happened, Lucia held Joana's trembling hands. "Are you all right?"

"It's him!" Joana whispered, still in shock.

"What do you mean by *him*?"

"It's him, Lucia. The man in my nightmare!" Lucia's thoughts were all of a sudden confirmed. She put her arm around Joana's shoulder, reassuringly.

"His eyes..." Joana added, stammering, "His eyes were full of hatred, Lucia. He's come back, he's come for me!"

Chris left the shop and walked towards the park with the pictures in her pocket. She sat down on a bench, afraid of looking at them again. Had it been her imagination? She silently hoped so, but she knew she was fooling herself. Those pictures were the proof that everything that was happening was real.

"You've still got so many doubts, child, why?" Chris jumped off her seat, caught by surprise. Where did she come from? The old woman who she had met feeding the pigeons was right there, sitting next to her.

"I'm sorry, I didn't mean to scare you."

"It's fine, I was just distracted." She realized her apology was silly.

"Your doubts are the things upsetting you."

"Who are you?" she asked directly, hoping the answer would be as straightforward.

"Sometimes they call us guides; mystics; other times we're just insane, and sometimes we're called angels..."

"It can't be!"

"Child, it's time for you to remove the veil of doubts in your heart. You listen but you deny what you hear..."

"I want to understand why and how this is happening!" she exclaimed in despair.

The old woman looked straight into her eyes and it took Chris only one moment to become aware of who she was sitting next to.

"You? Here?" The woman gave her a warm smile. "How can you be here? It's impossible! Never..."

"Never doesn't exist, Chris, nothing is impossible."

Chris remembered their encounter in Brighton and felt how past and present were coming together.

"I've chosen it?" she asked and the woman nodded.

"Yes, child. You did."

"And Sarah?"

"She knows you're here."

"Please tell me, just tell me why she..why a woman? Did I choose that too?"

"Energy transforms itself, child. It must take all existing shapes to reach knowledge before becoming light again."

Another flashback was occurring in Chris' mind; that magazine she found back at the airport and the psychiatrist's remark about having many lives. It was true, then.

"She knows?"

"She's finding out. Everything's happening as it should." Chris thought there was sadness in the old woman's eyes, "Also for those who have challenged fate."

"What do you mean by that?" She knew though, and she did not want to believe it. "No, you don't mean Patrick...do you? Anne told me his nightmare was back!"

"Only what one doesn't let go comes back child, only what you don't accept comes back to you, over and over again."

"Does it mean that Patrick and that slave hunter of whom he dreams," she hesitated. "Could he hurt Sarah, even if it's not Patrick who wants to do that?"

The old woman nodded sadly and Chris could see clearly now.

"Sarah will need your help one more time."

"Will you be with me?"

"You know I will, as long as you want me to be with you."

"I mean like this," the old woman smiled and said,

"Your faith, Chris, set it free! Now you must go, child."

Chris threw her arms round her neck, kissed both the woman's cheeks and sped off. She wanted so much to hang onto the strength she was feeling right now.

CHAPTER 35

*B*ack in the hotel, she went straight upstairs to her friend's room. Anne was alone.

"Where's Patrick? What's wrong?" Anne did not look very well.

"I don't know. After the meeting he became so upset, he dropped me here and said he needed some time on his own, to walk and think."

"Why did he get upset?

"How the hell do I know?! Everything was fine until he saw that woman."

"What woman?" Chris jumped and her eyes stared.

When Anne finished telling her the details of what had happened, Chris paced to the window, thoughtful. Then she looked at the envelope she was still holding and said,

"There's something in here that you should look at, Anne."

"Now? You want me to look at pictures now?" Anne asked in disbelief.

"Yes, please, now. It's important." Anne did as she asked. She looked at them over and over again, trying to convince herself.

"When did you take these? Did you see it?"

"Of course I did, today." And, after a while, "You said Patrick got upset after meeting a woman?" Anne nodded. "What did she look like?"

"I can't remember, everything happened too quickly."

"Please, Anne, try to remember her."

"Well, as tall as me, thin, her hair long to her shoulder and her eyes, I've got to say she had beautiful eyes and her look... but why are you asking?"

"Was she white?" Chris closed her eyes, hoping to get the answer she wanted.

"No, she was a mulata." Chris' heart jumped, making it hard for her to breathe. Her voice trembled when she said, "Anne, I think the woman you saw was Sarah, and I'm afraid Patrick got upset because, somehow, a part of him knew who she was." Anne's jaw dropped.

"What are you saying!?"

"Didn't Patrick mention to you the recurring nightmare where he saw himself chasing someone?"

"Yes, a long time ago, but what is the connection with this?"

"Last night the nightmare came back."

"Yes, but..."

"Everything fits, Anne. Patrick's nightmare, the dream I had last night of Sarah, this encounter with... Joana, you said?" Anne nodded. "His reaction, my encounter with the old woman, everything fits."

"What old woman?"

"I'm saying that everything's true, Anne. Times are coming together, don't ask me why or how, but the present is mingling with the past, that's what I'm talking about. I'm saying that two hundred years ago Sarah escaped the slave hunters and I'm saying that now Patrick has found Sarah."

"Wait, stop it there, please! I thought you were the one supposed to find Sarah."

"Yes."

"Well, then? How come you're saying that it's Patrick who found Joana... or Sarah, or whatever?"

"I'm assuming, Anne, that Patrick and the slave hunter in his nightmare are one, the same as Sarah and Joana. It seems as well that they're finding out who they are, if they haven't already."

"Come on, Chris. You really expect me to believe this? That I've been living and sleeping with a slave hunter from the 18th century?"

"Yes. Well, no, not really, I don't know, but it's happening, Anne."

"But *what*, my God, is really happening?" Anne was losing control of herself. "Oh, no, wait. What you're saying is that the slave hunter, who couldn't get Sarah two hundred years ago because you helped her, is possessing Patrick in order to capture Joana, who's being possessed by Sarah?"

"Partly." Chris looked calm, but she was far from being calm.

"You're driving me mad."

"It's not about spirits taking possession of human beings, Anne. At least I don't believe that. I'd rather say it's the same spirit, reincarnated."

"Do you believe that Patrick was that slave hunter and his hatred towards black people is so big that he's still chased by his..what do they call it?"

"His karma." Chris thought for a while and went on thoughtfully, "The reaction he had when he saw the woman Joana, who I say is Sarah, means that a part of him recognized her and because his other part didn't know what to do, he just took you out of there in despair. Maybe he's adopting two personalities that are fighting within him and one of these personalities can hurt Sarah."

"Patrick, hurt someone? That would never happen, you know that. You'll see, as soon as he comes back you'll see he'll be the same person we know."

"I hope so, I really hope so."

"I need a drink. Do you want to join me?"

"Yes, I do."

They sat at the bar, silent for a long while. She had not mentioned it, but Chris thought there was something wrong in all this.

"I'm afraid to ask what you're thinking now."

"There's something I don't get."

"Don't tell me," Anne's voice was full of a worried sarcasm, but Chris ignored it, deep in her thoughts.

"In the cabin, I killed that man. If Patrick could recognize Sarah, how come he hasn't recognized me all this time?"

"This is too much; could we please drop the subject?"

'Grandfather, who's Patrick?' she asked in her mind.

That same afternoon, Lucia and Joana decided to go back home early. Each lost in her own thoughts; they could hardly concentrate on working. Lucia walked silently, whilst Joana's pace was nervous and she constantly looked around, as if sensing someone following her.

"Joana, why did you say this man was looking for you?"

"Because I escaped."

"You escaped?"

"Yes, I escaped Lord Wesley."

Lucia remembered Mama Elsa's words and she knew she could not ignore events anymore. Once home, Joana went to her room. She took the symbol Mama Elsa had given her, looked at it carefully and clasped it between her hands. "Chris, where are you?" She sank down on the bed and after a while she was soundly asleep.

Chris, on the other side of the city, could not sleep in spite of feeling exhausted. Sarah was so near, only a couple of kilometres and she did not have the courage to go and see her.

"I don't understand you, Chris," Anne had told her. "No matter how hard you tried to hide it, you've spent months remembering her, wishing you could see her again and now that she's so close, if she is Sarah of course, you don't dare!"

It was true. She did not dare and she knew perfectly why. She felt embarrassed by the memory of their kiss. And she was afraid of how Sarah would react when they met. Would she recognize her? What had the old woman said? She said that Sarah was finding out and that she would need her help one more time. How much did she already know? How was she going to help her? The truth was, she did not have the courage to go and see her and she did not know if she would ever have it. She took the symbol out of her bag and pressed it to her chest.

The knocking at her door woke her with a start. It was still dark. Anne stood in the doorway, pale. "What is it?" she asked sleepily.

"Patrick hasn't come back, where is he?" Chris looked at her watch. It was just before six.

"And you've waited until now to come and tell me?"

"I was waiting for him but I fell asleep on the bed and I just woke up. What are we going to do?"

"We'll go looking for him."

They went downstairs to the front desk, but there was no message from Patrick.

"There's only one place where we can start looking, you know that, Chris, don't you?"

By the time they left the hotel, the city was already awake. The agency would probably be open when they got there. As the car was gone, they took a taxi after leaving a message in case Patrick came back in the meantime.

Once in front of the agency, they saw somebody was already in. Chris felt her heart was in her throat, but she calmed down when she saw the woman in there was not Sarah. They went in. Lucia immediately recognized Anne and approached them, smiling.

"You must be Chris." She looked around as if looking for someone else, "is your friend not with you?" Chris and Anne glanced at each other. Lucia seemed to be annoyed by his absence. She went to the telephone and dialled a number, but she did not get any answer.

"I thought Joana came to work early today, but I was wrong and she's still not at home," she looked at the telephone, "*and* my car is missing."

"Lucia," Chris said, "if you're Joana's friend, there's a story you should hear."

"Is there even more than what I've heard already?"

"Well, maybe. It's important we share what we know," Chris added.

A couple of hours later Lucia was aware of every single detail of the last months, from the very first moment that Chris arrived in England. She, on her side, told them everything she'd heard from Joana. Finally, she looked at the pictures of the old schooner that Chris had taken the previous day.

"You didn't meet me yesterday because of these pictures and now she's not here either. It seems fate is planning an uneasy encounter." She paused and then asked, "Have you got any idea where Sa...sorry, Joana, might have gone?"

"No, I don't, and I don't like not knowing after seeing the state she was in yesterday."

"What did she last say to you?"

"She referred to your friend as the 'man who's looking for me'. She also mentioned a man called Lord something."

"Wesley." Chris sank down on the visitor's sofa.

"Yes, that's the name."

"Did she say anything else?"

"No, she went to sleep very early. When I checked on her later, I didn't want to wake her up. She'd fallen asleep on the bed, with the symbol Mama Elsa gave to her before she died." Chris took hers from the bag and showed it to Lucia.

"It's identical to this one." The threesome went silent for a long while. Anne started walking up and down the room, until she stopped and stared, through the window full of holiday ads, at the figure across the road.

"Chris," she mumbled, stretching her hand out, but when Chris looked in the direction Anne was pointing, she did not see anything.

"What was it?"

"She was there, I'm sure!"

"The old woman?"

"Yes!" Anne shouted and Chris ran out. The street was empty.

"I think it's a sign."

"A sign? A sign of what?"

"Lucia, did you say your car was missing?" The woman nodded.

"Where is this place, Bahia Esperanza?"

"Do you think she..." Lucia paused, thought for a second and then said, "If Joana went there..."

"Where else could she have gone? Bahia Esperanza is where Sarah arrived two hundred years ago and I think it's where we should go too."

Lucia made a couple of telephone calls and then she said, "Okay, let's go then."

"But what about Patrick? We can't just leave him here!"

"Anne, I'm sure that if we find Sarah, we'll find Patrick." She looked at Lucia and said, "We need a car."

"It's sorted; one of those calls was to a friend who'll stay here, because Nereu's leaving today. We'll take my friend's car."

Chris could not care less about who would stay at the agency and look after the business. Her only interest right now was to find Sarah and Patrick.

CHAPTER 36

One hour later, the car was on the highway to Bahia Esperanza. "How do you manage to stay so calm, Chris?" Anne wanted to know.

"By trying to believe that everything's going to be just fine, I guess. After all, things are happening without us being able to do anything about them, aren't they?"

What she did not say though, was that she could feel the presence of the old woman with them. And *that* was giving her the strength. She also felt peace when she thought of Sarah. Imagining her asleep with the symbol in her hands comforted her. She did not mention either the other mixed feelings that flooded her mind. They were so strong that they seemed to have the power to freeze her. She was anxious because starting to accept her feelings for a woman was taking its toll. She was going to belong to a part of society which was too often attacked, judged, mocked and condemned by so many people who, in their ignorance, considered themselves *better* and *normal* human beings. Chris had too much to think about, she could not allow herself to look anxious. She tried to put her thoughts to rest by asking,

"You've been very quiet too, Lucia, what's on your mind?"

"I was thinking of Mama Elsa, wishing she was here. And of other things, too."

"Was she your mother?"

"I loved her dearly, but she wasn't my real mother," her smile was sad. "I was one of many babies abandoned to their fate in the doorway of some unknown home. In my case I was really blessed, because I was dropped at Mama Elsa's front door, in Bahia Esperanza. Her home was humble, as many in the village, but I never lacked anything. She taught me, with love, all she knew, even the truth about my origins. And she always said that I shouldn't hate my biological mother but forgive her. And to do that I made up a story which I repeated constantly to myself for a long time, until I believed it was my real story. It was about a black man, my father, and a white woman, my mother. They were desperately in love and she got pregnant. But her family would never accept their daughter having a baby with a black man. They tore them apart. The truth is probably very different, but as the years passed I didn't care anymore. I had Mama Elsa and her presence and love meant everything to me. Of course fate played a part, too, as it is doing now."

"What about the 'other things' you were thinking of?" Chris knew she was pushing Lucia, but she was curious.

At first Lucia hesitated, but finally she gave up and said, "All these events: your encounter in the past with Jo... with Sarah; now her and Patrick's disappearance; the nightmares that made them believe they were somebody else; these old women that show up for you just at the right time; everything relates to something that Mama Elsa said to me just before she died and also to what she taught me many years ago."

"Do you want to tell us about it? Can you do it?"

"Yes, there's no point at all in keeping it a secret or denying it anymore. Not now."

"Why should anybody keep teachings a secret?"

"I don't know, I guess I was afraid. I always dreamt about leaving Bahia Esperanza and getting a good job in the city, I dreamt about having lots of friends, fun, but now I know I can't escape my fate, which is always to be there for my people."

"I don't understand what sort of teachings can scare you? What is it that you fear?"

"The unknown."

"Would you mind explaining?"

"What do you know about *Macumba*?"

"*Macumba*?" Chris was startled. Anne was very silent in the back seat. "Not very much, to be honest. It's about rituals, isn't it? White magic, where believers worship their saints to get something?" Lucia nodded in silence. "But I thought *Macumba* was practised in the area of Rio, am I wrong?"

"No, you're right. I mentioned *Macumba* because so many people, when speaking of Brazil, speak about Rio, so there is a chance you'd heard of this cult." She paused and continued, "There are many names for religious cults, depending on the region of the country. There is *Xangó, Babassue, Umbanda, Batuque, Catimbó*, for us in the north, it's the *Candomblé*."

"I hope you're not saying we'll have to resort to these rituals to find Patrick?" Anne said, concerned.

"I wish I could say there won't be any need," she looked at Anne through the back mirror, "but I'm afraid we'll have to."

"How does *Candomblé* relate to you and Mama Elsa?" Chris asked.

"Mama Elsa was a *mae do Santo*."

"A *what*?" Anne asked again.

"It's the name given to those women who have the knowledge and preparation to initiate people into the cult and to lead the rituals and the people."

"And how or why did she become a *mae do Santo*?"

"Her mother was *Yoruba*."

"Do we have time to hear the whole story?" Chris was eager to know. Lucia looked at the car clock.

"We'll get to Bahia Esperanza in about one hour, more or less. So if you want to know, we do have enough time."

"Do we really want to know, Chris?" Anne did not sound happy about what she was about to learn.

"Oh yes, we do, Anne." Chris made herself comfortable and paid attention to Lucia. Lucia began:

"The *Yoruba* was a tribe divided into different kingdoms which existed for more than a thousand years in Africa, until the early 19th century. They started to fight each other and too many died because of the wars that lasted many years. Later, many of the survivors were captured and sold as slaves to work in plantations. Some of them were taken to Cuba, some were brought here. Among them was Mama Elsa. Please," she paused giving Chris a quick glance, "if you're thinking of calculating her age, don't. You wouldn't believe it." She sighed and then continued, "She was a King's daughter, but the slave traders never took any notice of that."

For a few seconds, Chris's mind jumped to the past, to the moment when Sarah told her about her own family.

Lucia went on, "At that time, the Catholic Church was fighting to convert the blacks and although many apparently accepted the conversion, it was only to obtain benefits that made their slavery more bearable. They kept their own beliefs hidden, giving each of their *orishas*, their African deities, the name of a catholic saint. That's how the *Santería* started, with all its different cults. The *Candomblé* is one of them. The followers of *Candomblé* believe in different lives, everyone having their fate written at their birth in the house of God in Heaven. When this fate is not met," Lucia sighed again, deeply, "the person is punished by his *orisha*, and he or she will reincarnate over and over again, until the debt is paid."

"In other words, the karma," Chris interrupted. Were Sarah and Patrick now experiencing their punishment?

"My God," Anne whispered, "but doesn't it count how good someone is during his life? What happens to all the kindness and love that someone can have or give? Doesn't it count at all?"

"Of course it counts," Lucia explained, "but how much it counts, is decided by their own *orisha*."

173

"I'm sorry to say this, Chris, but sometimes like now, I really wish you'd gone somewhere else to start a new life, not to London." Chris was hurt by her friend's reaction, but she understood how anxious Anne felt, thinking that Patrick might be in danger. She tried to ignore her by keeping silent, but Lucia did speak clearly,

"Anne, there is no coincidence at all in what has happened to all of you."

"What do you mean?" both asked at the same time.

"If Joana's and Patrick's lives are linked from previous times, your life, Chris, is linked to Joana's too, as well as to Patrick's."

"Why, for something that I did before? The old woman in Brighton told me that I had chosen."

"That is right."

"Does it mean, according to the *Candomblé,* that I, too, have an *orisha*? And that I have to face my karma?"

Lucia's answer was categorical, "Yes."

"But how can I know..."

"What your's is?"

"Yes."

"Haven't you thought that maybe you're already experiencing it? Every time that we have to accept situations that seem so unfair, or difficult, or strange," and she emphasized, "when we reject something or someone..." Chris knew exactly what Lucia meant. "I've told you all this, because I believe Patrick and Joana will need..."

"A ritual." Chris finished for her. Anne shrank into the back seat. She did not want to listen anymore. Chris took a deep breath and said,

"Is that what Mama Elsa taught you?"

"As a Yoruba Priestess and following the tradition, she received the teachings that passed down from one generation to another."

"What about you? You were not her real daughter. Why did she teach you?"

"The tradition says, if a *mae do Santo* doesn't give birth to a daughter, the gods will send her someone to be taught and I was abandoned at her door. First I had to be initiated and only if both *orishas*, Mama Elsa's and mine agreed, then I'd be allowed to take the place of a real daughter for her."

"And were you initiated?"

"Yes, when I was very young. At that time I didn't reject receiving the knowledge, but as time passed I didn't show a real interest and Mama Elsa didn't force me to. I guess she knew that one way or another, sooner or later, I'd meet my fate. I'd say my destiny started to come true when she took me in, then when Joana and I became close friends, and even now, after so many years, fate shows up again. Otherwise I'd have never met you or Patrick. Nereu and the agency, too, are links in this chain of events in our lives."

"What will we do now?" Chris wanted to know.

"First we need to find them, and perhaps..." she glanced at Chris, "we'll have to initiate you." She waited to see Chris' reaction.

"Initiate me? Oh no, thank you very much, but I don't think so. It really doesn't seem a good idea to me."

"I don't know, we shall see."

Chapter 37

The rest of the journey passed in silence, each of them dealing with their own thoughts. Lucia was finally accepting that she could not avoid her destiny anymore; Anne, was desperately wishing to be with Patrick at home, working in their garden; Chris, for her part, was visualizing herself in a previous life as someone with the power to judge and to punish; oblivious to the fact that life would ask for its toll, no matter how many lifetimes it took.

When they reached Bahia Esperanza shortly after midday, it was pouring with rain and the clouds had darkened the sky. Lucia drove straight to Joana's house near the school, where, only three months ago, her friend used to teach the children of the village. "This is strange," she said standing in front of the house.

"What could possibly be *strange* around here?" Anne said full of sarcasm.

"The door's open." She went in and looked around. Chris and Anne followed her and stopped behind her.

"It seems somebody was here before us," Anne commented at the sight of the mess. Lucia looked at Chris, who asked quietly,

"Do you think...?"

"Good God, could you please finish your sentences?" Anne spoke again, this time bad tempered.

"Yes," answered Lucia, "I think Joana was here, but so was somebody else and it seems that somebody was looking for something." They all ran out as they heard the roaring engine.

"Robertinho!"

"Lucia! You're here!" but immediately looked disappointed when he did not see Joana. He looked at both women and waited for Lucia to say something. After being introduced, he asked after Joana. Lucia replied,

"She couldn't come, Roberto, but promised to do so next time." The three women exchanged a glance.

"That's a real shame; I was hoping to see her. Are you staying long?"

"We don't know yet, maybe a few days."

"All right then. I just wanted to check whose car that was. We don't receive many visitors around here, as you must remember. I need to go now. Don't leave without coming to my place to catch up, okay?" He left and the women went back to the house.

"Aren't you going to tell him about Joana?" Chris asked.

"Not unless there's no option. I know him too well, Chris. He's a sweet and nice man and a very good friend, but he wouldn't believe a word of our stories. He has never believed in *Candomblé* either and, if he thought Joana was in danger, he would call the police straight away and let me tell you, we do not want the police here."

"What are we doing now, where shall we start looking? I don't like the idea of Joana lost somewhere out there and Patrick after her."

"Joana would never get lost in Bahia Esperanza, Chris. She knows this place like the back of her hand. If she chose to hide here it's because she knew she'd be safe."

"What if he followed her? If he did in Fortaleza, he must have come all the way down. None of us could have got here if it wasn't for you or for her."

"She'll know where to go, don't worry. We used to play hide and seek all over the place and Joana always won."

"There's a problem, Lucia, you're talking about Joana, what if it's Sarah who..."

"I know what you're thinking."

"Then explain it to me, please. If, as you said, Joana believes she is actually Sarah or if she believes she's two people at the same time, what will happen to Sarah? Will *she* understand what's happening?" In spite of her confidence in the old woman's words and although two hours ago she might have believed everything was going to be fine, Chris could not help worrying about what Sarah, not Joana, was feeling right now.

"It will indeed be much harder for her, you're right," Lucia said, knowing this was going to be hard to hear. "But Chris, at some point she'll have to decide who she wants to be. One of them will need to go, leave so the other can live." Lucia looked at Anne and said, "It's the same for Patrick."

"Are you saying that Patrick might die?"

"Well, sort of die. If he allows the hunter's mind to be stronger, his mind will give up and abandon him. He'll stop being who he is. That's the point when it matters who Patrick is now, how he has lived his life so far. It's like when someone dies, the spirit is judged for its actions during its lifetime. In Patrick's case both minds, both consciences will challenge each other and the stronger thoughts will beat the weaker. At that moment, this *orisha* will give him free will to decide."

"Is that the free will the old woman in Brighton was talking about?"

"You could say so."

"But what happens if both minds are equally powerful and both want to stay?"

"Let's hope that won't happen."

"But *if* it happens?" Chris wanted her question answered.

"It wouldn't be good for either of them."

"Why, what would happen?" Chris insisted and Anne knew she would not like the answer Lucia was about to give.

"Just imagine two powerful minds fighting inside one mind, call it the good against the evil, if you want. A constant fight..."

"The person loses his mind." Chris said and closed her eyes. She had to believe, she had to have faith.

"That's why the tributes the *orisha* receives during the *bembe* are so important, it's the only way we can help Joana and Patrick."

"What's that now, tributes and *bem*-something?" Anne asked, distressed.

"According to tradition, we have to offer the *orishas* a *bembe*. It's a sort of party which they are invited to share with us. If the *orisha* accepts the party and approves the gifts then it possesses the leader of the *bembe* or the one who's been initiated or both, and starts participating in the dances, sharing the rhythms and the chants."

"What sort of gifts are we talking about?" Anne spoke again.

"Food, alcohol, multicoloured dresses, music," she paused. "Sometimes though, it's necessary to sacrifice an animal." Anne was feeling sick.

"How will we know what to offer each one?" Chris did not sound very happy either.

"We know what every *orisha* likes. It's more or less the same as for any of us. All of them have their preferences, even whims that might make them happy."

The storm began to ease as they talked. Chris was distractedly looking out of the window when she heard the voice in her mind, *'The waves hit them one last time, the furious clouds darkened the horizon and the rain blew the schooner against the reef, and they jumped into the sea, in a last desperate attempt to reach the shore.'*

'The beach... I must go to the beach,' she said to herself.

"We should go to the village and get some supplies and maybe we could find out if somebody saw Joana or recognized the cars."

Chris did not answer Lucia's suggestion but Anne welcomed it.

"Great, I'll come with you, staying here is driving me mad." Looking at her distracted friend she repeated, "Chris, let's go?"

"Actually, would you mind if I stayed? I'd love to have a walk."

"Be careful, Chris, there's still unexplored jungle to the north where you could easily get lost if you went too far away from the coast," Lucia warned.

"Don't worry, I won't go far."

After giving her the directions to reach the beach, Lucia left, followed by Anne.

Chapter 38

*T*he clouds were gone and the burning sun's rays hit the soaking ground. The heavy tropical humidity invaded the place. She walked through the forest following the winding path until she jumped out of her skin when a little monkey – the smallest she'd ever seen – flew over her shoulders.

"Hey there, don't be afraid; it's not you I'm looking for!" The tiny animal stopped not far away and looked at her with a funny screech as if imitating a child pleased with a prank. Chris left the forest behind and the amazing beauty of the landscape opening in front of her took her breath away. She immediately remembered Lucia telling her about how much time Joana used to spend in this place, the same beach where she first had her hallucinations of the schooner.

"This is it, then, the place you finally reached two hundred years ago! Now I understand why you like it so much here!" she said as if Sarah were listening. "It's absolutely stunning, and so peaceful!"

The colour of the sea, the white sand and the palm trees covered with climbing ferns, everything fitted perfectly in this paradise. Then she saw the reef '...*and the rain blew the schooner against the reef...*'

Chris took her shoes off and walked into the warm water until it was up to her knees, paying no attention to her light trousers which were sticking to her legs. She could almost hear the screams of the survivors, fighting the waves in their desperation to reach the beach.

She felt a shiver running down her back. Someone was there, she could feel it. She turned round and scanned the place. Whoever it was had no intention of showing themselves. Fear and anxiety froze her for a while, but she managed to get hold of herself and started walking back along the path. Her sense of fear told her to go back to the house, but her impulsiveness was stronger and her steps led her exactly where Lucia had warned her not to go, into the forest.

Oblivious to the passing of time, she finally realized she was lost. Her panic grew as the minutes went by and there, there it was again, the feeling of being observed. She could blame herself for being so stupid in ignoring Lucia's warning, or she could try to be calm. The gentle crack of dry leaves behind her made her jump and she spun round.

"Patrick!" she yelled, not sure whether to run away or approach him. Noticing the look in his eyes she realized that the first option would have been useless and the second absurd, if not almost suicidal. She stepped back, but he was quicker. With an unnatural strength, fuelled by hatred, Patrick grabbed her arm and dragged her a few metres, only to throw her against the bushes.

"Patrick!" she shouted again in despair, but he did not seem to recognize her. She managed to get up, but another blow took her down again. She felt her whole body trembling, until she finally fainted.

When she recovered, she was still being dragged, but with difficulty. She tried to free herself from his grip, to get up and look around, but the nausea came back and she felt the stabbing pain in her head. She groaned and her captor stopped and bent over her, brushing the hair off her face. That is when she saw her.

"Sarah!" the dark curtain engulfed her again.

The next time she recovered, she was lying on the grass and someone was holding her. It was dark and she could only hear the sounds of the tropical night and the waves crashing smoothly on the beach. She did not dare to move or even to breathe; scared of giving away that she was conscious again. She felt a hand on her shoulder and her heart beat so fast that she could feel it in her throat. That hand was too gentle to be the one which had hit her before. It could not be Patrick and besides, she had seen Sarah! But of course it could have been her imagination. She went on looking for excuses to stay still. She knew too well who was holding her, but she was also finding it difficult to breathe and did not have the courage to move and confirm that the person was indeed Sarah. The easiest thing to do was nothing, just stay there, waiting for something to happen. Her heartbeat began to ease. In her head she heard Anne's words during their last conversation at the hotel, *'If you should meet her again...you'll have no options, you'll have to face your feelings...'*

After a while Sarah moved slightly and she could hear her soft whisper, "Chris, you'll be all right." But Chris was still frozen and did not say a word. Sarah laid her head gently on the ground and got up.

"Sarah..." Chris's voice was a murmur. Sarah lent over her again and their eyes met in silence. Sarah was the first to show a shy smile. "You know... who I am?" What a silly remark, she thought immediately after speaking, but Sarah smiled again and said,

"I did ask you to look for me in time, Stranger, remember?"

"Yes, you did." Chris finally managed a smile. She had worried so much about knowing what to say, only to realize now that there was no need to worry about it. It seemed that was something she had to learn as well. There was absolutely no need to force conversations; it was much easier to let words flow naturally.

"It's weird, you know? I've thought so many times what I'd say when...if I found you again and..." Sarah did not let her finish.

"Do I need to go again?" she said with tearful eyes and Chris felt the lump in her throat coming back.

"No, of course not, why do you say that?" She finally found the courage to straighten up and hug her friend. They clung to each other for a long while until Chris said, "We can't stay here, Sarah, Patrick might come back."

Sarah stared at her with surprise, "Who's Patrick?"

"You don't know who Patrick is?"

"No," she shook her head, frowning.

"And Joana, do you know who Joana is?" Sarah shook her head again.

"How did you get here, Sarah?" Chris was recovering her confidence now, as fast as Sarah seemed to start losing awareness of what was happening. She looked around, scared, trying to answer Chris's questions.

"I don't know... I was walking... I saw you on the ground, unconscious and then...I don't remember," she said despairingly, falling on her knees next to Chris, who took her in her arms again.

"It's okay, Sarah, it's okay."

"What's happening to me? Why can't I remember?"

"You're just confused, Sarah," she lied. "You'll see, as soon as we get back to the house, everything's going to be all right again." Sarah was not listening anymore; she went into a trance, her eyes completely lost in the void.

Chris had to find their way back, there was nothing else to do, just go back and take Sarah to Lucia. This time other words came back, '*Sarah will need your help one more time.*' Chris started to pray for help which came instantly, with the tiny monkey's scream that startled her. She smiled, took Sarah's hand and pulled her, saying, "Come on, I've got the feeling somebody will show us the way out of here." Sarah did not say a word, she followed Chris, subdued and quiet.

The tiny monkey flew from branch to branch, showing them the way. As they moved forward through the jungle, trying not to trip, the sound of the waves became louder and louder. They finally found the path to the house.

Once near the beach, Sarah stopped and looked at the sea.

"I recognize this place, the beach..." but Chris pushed her gently, towards the house. Her calmness was slowly being replaced by the feeling of being watched, which became so strong that she forced

Sarah to run. Only at the sight of the house and the lights in it, did she feel relieved. When she saw Lucia and Anne in the porch she knew they were safe.

"Good Lord, Chris, where have you been?" Lucia stopped when she saw Joana, still staring into the distance as if not really aware of her surroundings. Lucia looked at Chris, waiting for her to say something, but Chris just shrugged silently. They went back into the house.

Once in the bright room, Anne looked at Chris with the clear intention of telling her off, but she saw the awful bruise.

"What happened to you?" she asked pointing at Chris's forehead. Only when Chris put her hand up to her head did she feel the stabbing pain. She had to tell them, but Anne would definitely not like the story. She said nothing. Chris looked at Sarah, still standing there, frozen, and Lucia, staring at Joana as if recognizing somebody else. Lucia took Joana's arm and led her to the bedroom. Joana followed, as if hypnotized.

Chris and Anne watched them, noticing how Lucia pushed Joana, gently, forcing her to lie on the bed, lowering her head and whispering, "*Moruba arube, moforibale tie orisha wani busi tie ilé.*" Chris and Anne exchanged glances.

"What did you tell her?" They asked Lucia when she came back.

"I greeted her, calling her sister and prostrated myself in front of her god who's come to bless her home. Her *orisha* is with her, we need to get ready."

"Get ready for what?" Anne asked. Chris stayed silent. She was *ready* for whatever Lucia had in mind, at least she thought so. She knew that the last month's events were coming to an end. The only thing still missing was to know if fate was going to grant her wish or not. She had also noticed how Lucia had changed. Somehow, she looked more mature, confident, and she radiated calmness.

"Our *orishas* are calling us to enjoy and share with them."

"What does it mean?" Anne did not understand what was going on.

"It means we're having the bembe, is that right?" Chris said looking at Lucia, who nodded. Anne did not say anything else.

"Is Joana all right?" Chris asked again.

"She really doesn't realize what's going on. It's like being hypnotized. That's why we need to prepare the *bembe* as soon as possible, to welcome her *orisha*."

"Do you know her *orisha*?" Chris asked and Lucia nodded.

Anne disappeared into the kitchen and came back with a bottle of wine and three glasses.

"I need a drink, anybody want to join me?" she asked, already pouring a glass for herself. Lucia and Chris did not pay any attention to her invitation, both had heard Joana moaning.

"What's going on?" Anne said when she saw Chris going into Joana's bedroom.

She sat down on the bed, next to her friend who had her eyes closed. She looked unsettled and her expression, fearful. She mumbled things that Chris could not understand, so she bent over her and gently stroke her head.

"It's okay, Sarah, nobody's going to hurt you, we won't let them, I won't let them."

"That man..." Sarah stuttered with trembling voice and grabbed Chris's arm, "That man is looking for me; his eyes are full of hatred."

"You're having a nightmare, sweetheart." She held her hand, until finally Sarah relaxed and fell asleep. Chris left the room.

CHAPTER 39

"Can you still feel it?" Lucia asked and Chris nodded. "Feel what?" Anne instinctively jumped off the sofa and flew to the door, "Patrick? Are you talking about Patrick?" Both women reacted immediately, trying to prevent her from going out, but she was already half way there, yelling back at them, "If Patrick's out there I want to see him!" Lucia and Chris ran after her and a few metres away from the house, Anne stopped in her tracks, trying to find him in the dark.

"Patrick!" she called, "Patrick, darling, it's me." She took another step and stopped again when she saw him. He was staring at her, frozen. His hair dishevelled, the beard already covering his face and his muddy clothing gave him the appearance of a beggar. His look, fixed on Anne's, seemed to soften slightly. Anne took another step towards him but she was held back.

"That's not him, Anne. That man is not Patrick! He's the man who attacked me today!" Anne looked at Chris with horror.

"We can't help him Anne, not yet." Lucia said.

Chris looked at Patrick and saw how he looked at her and how the tender look he had for Anne, changed into a furious one, eager for revenge. Realizing what was happening, Lucia put her hand on Chris's shoulder.

"Woman!" They heard a voice that was not Patrick's. "You have crossed my life again, this time I shall come back for you and for her!" He stretched out his arm, pointing at the house.

Chris had no idea where she found the courage, but with trembling legs she moved one step forward and shouted back to him, "And I shall be waiting for you. I will get in your way as many times as necessary, until you leave her alone and go away!" The man groaned and stepped back, disappearing into the thicket.

The women went back in and locked the door. Anne, pouring another glass of wine, sank onto the sofa. Chris went to check on Sarah.

"She's sleeping soundly," she said when she came back and, moving towards the table, poured a drink for her and another for Lucia, who was looking extremely annoyed.

"What's wrong?" Chris asked her.

"What the hell were you thinking when you spoke to him out there?"

"I didn't think, I just said it, I just felt it, and I will keep my word, why?"

"You don't realize what you did, do you?"

"Yes, I do, I defended Sarah!"

"No, you didn't do that." Lucia lowered her look.

"What do you mean?"

"What you did is allow your *orisha*, through your uncontrollable emotions, to challenge his orisha." Chris lost her colour and Lucia went on, "Do you remember what I told you in the car, about initiating you?"

"Yes, but how does this relate to what just happened?" she retorted.

Anne, silently sipping from her glass, thought it did not matter what happened from now on. She would not interfere nor say a word. She had no intention of sharing a ritual if it meant her being involved as a guest too. One thing was to respect other people's beliefs, quite another to become part of them. Chris could decide for herself.

"At some point in time, your life and Joana's were linked, you know that. Now you've met again and your feelings for her will either make you stay together or part. It will be your choice again. A moment ago your *orisha* spoke for you, using your feelings. Your *orisha* showed you one path, which is staying with her, the other path, only you know it."

Chris thought a long time about Lucia's words, until she found the answer in her heart.

"The other path would be to leave." She stared at Lucia looking for a sign that she might be wrong, but she did not find it.

Leaving meant deserting Sarah, again. Two hundred years ago it was not Sarah who had left after all, boarding the ship. Chris knew now that it was her own deep wish to return to the life she knew better, which had decided for her. She had been so afraid to face her feelings for that woman that she chose to leave, without really knowing what she was doing. She also knew that now she was free to go again, if that was what she wanted. But leave Sarah again? This time to leave meant to leave Sarah but to abandon her friends as well. The toll fate was taking was higher this time. To stay meant to help them and face once and for all her new feelings. If she left, her karma would probably follow her. Was she prepared to live the rest of her life knowing that sooner or later fate was going to ask her to settle her debts? To leave meant not only to leave Sarah, but also to forget her feelings. Could she do that? Could she really get her old life back? Had she not tried already? On the other hand, would she be able to be happy with her new life?

'Energy transforms itself, it must take all existing shapes to reach knowledge before it becomes light.' She remembered these words and also the ones she had read in that magazine at the airport in Madrid, *'We have not one, but many lives,'* and even more words came to her mind, *'As you do, so it will be done to you; as you judge, so you will be judged.'*

Lucia, as if reading her mind and sensing her distress, came to her rescue.

"It's late," she said. "We should get some sleep, tomorrow's going to be a tough day." They looked at Anne, waiting for any reaction. She only stood up, looked at them and said,

"What? I haven't said a word! I know I want Patrick back and it doesn't matter anymore what must be done. I won't interfere with whatever you do, Lucia."

She and Lucia made themselves comfortable in the room while Chris went into Joana's room. She was sound asleep. Quietly, she picked up her bag with the few things they had collected from the hotel before leaving Fortaleza. She put on another T-shirt and lay down on the bed next to Sarah, watching her.

"It's amazing, Sarah. It's two hundred years in the future and you're exactly the same person: your eyes; your features; even your hair is the same. It's as if time hadn't passed after all. Is it perhaps possible that..." She gently pulled down Sarah's blouse and looked at her naked shoulder. Even the scars were there! She covered her again and thought, still watching her, 'I was so sure I didn't have prejudices about these feelings and you... you showed me how wrong I was.'

Just before falling asleep, she heard the words, *'You will meet again, when the right time comes.'*

"Grandfather," she whispered.

"Chris, you're here," Sarah said half asleep, stretching her arm over Chris and hiding her face in the curve of Chris's neck. Chris kissed her forehead and said,

"Yes, Sarah. I'm here."

CHAPTER 40

Chris woke with a start, frightened by the sudden movement at her side. Sarah was sitting on the bed, looking at her. She said, stammering, "W-what? H-how?"

"Sarah, what's wrong?" Chris rubbed her eyes and leaned on one elbow. Sarah was as white as paper.

"Sarah?" Chris realized what was wrong and she called for Lucia, who came in straight away, half asleep and trembling. At the sight of Joana's expression, she approached her, took her arm and said,

"Are you ok, Joana?"

"Lucia, what's happened? How come I'm here, in my own bedroom? And..." she was looking at Chris, now, who exchanged a glance with Lucia.

"Don't you remember anything?" Lucia asked, but Joana just shook her head, not taking her eyes off Chris, who had started to feel really uncomfortable under her scrutiny.

"Come with me, my friend," Lucia pulled her gently out of the room.

Chris lent back on the bed and covered her face with both hands. Try as she might, she could not remember ever having felt so embarrassed in her whole life. Lucia's scream made her jump.

"Joana!"

Anne was standing, leaning on the doorframe. She did not look very good either.

"*That* is a seriously confused woman, Chris. She ran out after hearing from Lucia what happened yesterday and Lucia ran after her."

"And what do you expect? How would you feel, if all of a sudden, among other things, first you're told by someone whom you trust beyond everything, that you're not who you believe you are, but someone who lived two hundred years ago, and then you are told that somebody from the past is back and wants to kill you?" Whilst speaking, annoyed by Anne's comment, Chris was getting dressed.

She went out of the house and saw Lucia speaking to Joana, and without thinking, she approached them. But Joana went back to the house, walking past her without looking. Understandingly, Lucia squeezed Chris's arm and ran after Joana again.

Chris did not want to go back to Joana's house, so she walked down to the beach. She needed desperately to be on her own. What did she see in Sarah's eyes; surprise? No, it was not surprise. Her eyes were eyes of uncertainty, distrust, fear, as if saying; go away and leave me alone. She stopped by the rocks, chose one of the biggest and sat on it.

"Isn't it ironic, granddad?" she started talking to him as if he was there with her. He was, after all, her confidant. "It took me so long to accept these feelings, accept the fact that for some reason I need to go through this experience and, as soon as I accept them," she smiled sadly, "she runs away, scared! It's not that I don't understand, her, you know? How couldn't I? It's just that...if she pushes me away, well...at least Lucia is here to help her." She paused in her thoughts and after a while she went on talking to the sea. "Is it that she's afraid of her free will too, granddad? If it's Joana who stays at the end, she doesn't know me; perhaps we won't even be friends, we won't have shared memories and maybe she won't have any sort of feelings, which means, I guess, she'll continue her normal life...I know, I know...," she continued her monologue, "one day I'll get the answers, when the time comes..."

She also thought about her comfort now, which was that Sarah had at last done it. Two hundred years ago she had made her dream come true; she reached far beyond the horizon and, two hundred years later, she could live in the world that Chris had put so much effort into describing.

Knowing that cheered Chris' heart. She felt good because she had helped her. More important than being friends now, in the present, she knew deep in her heart that what really mattered was to know that Sarah would be all right and happy. All of a sudden, Chris realized that the way she felt now was different. Her feelings, especially those she had for Sarah, did not include selfishness. It made her nostalgic, yes, but not sad. She was ready to face her destiny, whatever it was, because she believed now that this destiny would, maybe one day, offer her happiness as well. Chris smiled.

"Are you talking to the sea?" Chris shuddered and gave a little jump when she recognized the voice behind her.

"Sorry, I didn't mean to scare you!" Joana was standing there, her arms crossed.

"You didn't! Well, maybe just a little bit."

"Are you?"

"Am I what?" She felt shy and awkward, not able to take her eyes off Sarah's.

"Talking to the sea?" Chris smiled but said nothing. Who was she talking to, Sarah or Joana?

"I've done it too, many times... may I?" she gestured pointing to the rock.

"Of course," Chris moved and Sarah sat down next to her.

They were silent for a long while, looking at the waves crashing against the rocks in front of them. It was Sarah who spoke first.

"I wanted to apologize, I wasn't very nice to you before."

"You don't need to apologize, after all, this is not a very normal situation, is it?" She could hear her heartbeat.

"Lucia told me everything, Chris," she explained. "But I still can't work everything out in my mind and... and I want you to know," she hesitated, "that I feel very bad because I can't remember and if I do remember bits, then I don't know what's real and what's not." Chris lifted her hand to her chest and grabbed the symbol, showing it to Joana.

"Is this real for you?" Her words were shy but, at the same time, full of hope. Joana remained still, but she got hold of her symbol and smiled back, stretching out her hand with her symbol in it.

"I want to ask you so many things, Chris, but I don't know where to start. I've had so many dreams, since I was a little girl, here, in this place. When I told Mama Elsa what was happening to me, first I thought it was a nightmare, that fate was playing a joke on me, but afterwards I thought I was going mad and even now..."

"You're definitely not mad, Sa...sorry, Joana."

"What do you want to call me?" Joana looked at her deeply.

"I'm so used to Sarah," she answered with no hesitation.

"Well, then I'll be Sarah for you."

"Yes, you'll always be Sarah for me," she blushed, "but for you? Who will it be?" Sarah opened her mouth, but hesitated. Then, she said,

"I'm very scared, Chris. Lucia told me what we need to do to find the answer. She also told me about Mama Elsa's teachings."

"Weren't you sad that she didn't tell you before about them?"

"Not at all, I know she had her reasons for not telling me. I don't judge her for that."

There was another silence, which Chris broke this time. "I'm glad you're speaking to me," she dared to confess and added, "It means a lot to me."

"Why?" the question took Chris by surprise and she looked down to hide her blushing face. Sarah noticed and smiled.

'Because I've realized that I love you,' Chris would have loved to say, but she did not. Instead, she just said,

"Well, I'm glad because I wouldn't know how to help you, if you didn't speak to me!"

"Hum..." Sarah smiled.

"What does hum mean?"

"Can I ask you something?"

"Of course, you can ask anything."

"What are you going to do when all this is sorted out?" Sarah asked.

"What am I going to do? Well..." 'if you asked me to stay I would,' she thought but instead she answered, "I'm not sure yet, but, for a start, I need to go back to work".

"You'll go back to England?" Sarah was clearly disappointed, but she managed to hide it.

"Who knows? As I said, I'm not sure yet, it depends on what happens around here."

"Chris, do you remember everything that happened during your journey into the past?" Sarah continued asking and Chris nodded, adding,

"It's impossible to forget that passage through time."

"What was Sarah like, Chris?"

"Well, apart from being identical to you, she was brave, cheerful, amazingly interested in knowing everything. Her slavery could have turned her into someone full of hatred, but she had a strong inner power which prevented her from being defeated; she was ready to risk her life if necessary to defend her principles, her beliefs, her dreams..."

"Did you become very close friends? You must miss her." It seemed to Chris that Joana was trying to find out more, but not through direct questions.

"I'd say we did, yes, and yes to the second question as well. I do miss her and honestly, it feels *really* weird talking to you; being her and not being her, if you know what I mean."

"There's one way in which I really want to be like her."

"Which way's that?" Chris was very curious.

"I'd love to have her power of endurance."

"Well, maybe you can't feel it right now, but I believe you've got it, you've got Sarah's strength."

They talked for a long time, without noticing how the hours passed. By the time they went back to the house, Anne was on her own and gave them the news.

"Lucia's not here, but she told me it would happen tonight."

Chapter 41

*L*ater that day, when the sun was ready to set below the horizon and the sky began to lose its blue, people started to arrive and neither Chris nor Anne knew where they came from. Before they realized it, Joana's house was hosting more than twenty people and everyone had brought different gifts, which would be offered to Joana's *orisha*. Candles of every imaginable colour were lit around the room, together with incense sticks. Pots bursting with food appeared, some of them containing beef, others pork ribs or poultry or fish. Bowls filled up with black beans, yellow and white corn, eggs, potatoes and much more. There were bottles of whisky, cachaça, beer and other spirits; tobacco in all its shapes, flowers and baskets overloaded with bananas, pineapples, mangos, coconuts and other tropical fruits native to that region.

Lucia led Joana to her room, while Chris and Anne stayed in the lounge, respectfully silent, observing how the *bembé* was shaping up. They smiled shyly when a big woman with very dark skin and almost snow white hair approached them. She introduced herself as Mama Loisa and told the women she would stay with them to explain the development of the ritual.

Some of the young men, wearing traditional snow white trousers and shirts, walked through the room carrying their *batás;* percussion instruments made of hollow bamboo, the bottom open and the top end covered with a thin membrane of animal gut. The rest of them, women and men, waited patiently, some of them silent, some whispering amongst themselves. Unlike the musicians, all of them wore multicoloured dresses in order not to upset Joana's *orisha*, who could then see his favourite colours at the party.

The sound of the *batás* was filling the air, when Joana came out of her room, followed by Lucia. Their dresses were white as well. Chris's and Joana's eyes met and they smiled. In the meantime, the guests formed a circle around the two women and began to dance, following the rhythm of the *batás*, singing and clapping. Every now and then, in turn, they ceased the sensual movements of their graceful bodies to eat and drink.

To her own surprise, Anne was fascinated, wondering if the ritual that Patrick would need to undergo would be like this one. Chris, on the other hand, could not stop looking with awe at the two women in the centre of the circle, while she mentally repeated '*Everything will come out fine, Sarah, you'll see, everything will come out fine.*'

Joana was standing straight, her arms at her sides, and Lucia danced softly around her, touching her gently with her *elekes;* long necklaces used to purify the person whose *orisha* was going to be invited to join the party.

Little by little, Anne and Chris felt the spirit of the feast catching them, too, and their bodies began to dance, following the rhythm and the songs. The big black woman insisted they had a drink, the same as everybody else and kept passing them both a jar with some alcoholic drink. At the same time she was teaching them the words they had to repeat now and then for as long the ritual would last. '*Ayuba, tiwa okan ko lalafia pelu iwo wá,*' which meant 'We welcome you, our heart sings happy with your visit.'

Suddenly, the *batás* went silent and the chants stopped. Chris looked at Lucia and Joana and moved to approach them when she noticed Joana fainting. But the big woman's strong arms caught her.

"No, no, you must wait," she said.

Lucia was still waving her *elekes* over Joana, while reciting something that sounded like a plea. The *batás* started playing and the voices, singing once again, soared louder and louder.

"Lucia has welcomed Joana's *orisha*," the woman explained.

"But she's fainted!"

"Her *orisha* will possess her in order to enjoy the *bembé* held in his honour and Lucia will beg *Exú* to intercede, with the power only he has, before the only god." Every time the woman interrupted her explanation, she had a drink and made them drink as well.

Then Joana moaned and sat up with crossed legs. Lucia emulated her movements, as if following an instruction. They sat face to face and everybody was now dancing around them, passing the gifts they had brought.

"What are they doing now?" Chris wanted to know.

"They will eat, drink and negotiate."

"Negotiate? What will they *negotiate*?"

"*Mae Lucia* will ask Joana's *orisha* to give freedom to one of the minds."

"Does it mean that when her *orisha* goes and she comes back from this trance, she'll be one or the other?"

"That is right."

"And why would her *orisha* release one of the spirits, when he can have both?"

"That's why *Mae Lucia* has to negotiate something in exchange for the spirit to be freed."

Anne, who was right behind them, listening and watching everything carefully, noticed Chris's nervousness; she took her arm, squeezed it reassuringly and said, "If there really are spirits around, sweetheart, please don't draw their attention and go on dancing, ok?"

But whoever was in Joana's body, had already noticed their presence in the room and was staring at Chris. She got to her feet and walked towards her. Chris froze. Joana stretched out her arm, gave her a bottle and started dancing around her, clapping hands and laughing happily. Chris searched Lucia's eyes looking for help, but Lucia made a sign for her to go on dancing and drinking. Chris did so and from time to time, Lucia and the rest of the party joined them, whispering or praying to Joana's *orisha*, whose attention was only on Chris.

Very close to midnight, the spirit of the party began to ease. The candles were burning down and what had seemed a never ending feast had almost disappeared.

The guests started to display their tiredness and drunkenness, but they forced themselves to keep on celebrating. The tradition said nobody was to leave the party before the *orisha* put an end to the *bembé*, by giving thanks for it. That was exactly what happened next. Joana stopped in the middle of the room, catching everybody's attention. She looked at them one by one and said,

"*Aikú ati áyó lati gbogbo.*"

"Good health, long life and happiness to everyone," the woman translated.

The next minute Joana stared at Chris and added with a deep voice, "*Xangó ati Yansán gbó fun nigbágbogbo kan, lara na koja, lara na óre.*" She felt silent and her body sank gently to the floor, unconscious.

Chris looked at the woman, waiting for her to stop her going to Sarah this time too, but she did not. She did not translate Joana's words. She was just looking at Chris, not as she had during the night, but with a new and deep respect.

After two of the men helped carry Joana to her room, the guests picked up empty bottles, jars, bowls, instruments and even the leftovers and left the house as fast as they had arrived hours ago.

Chris went into the room to check on Joana and found her soundly asleep. She went back to the lounge to join Lucia and Anne. The room looked as if nothing had happened there.

"You must feel exhausted, Lucia." Lucia nodded, not trying to hide her tiredness, but she kept her eyes on Chris, smiling.

"Why are you looking at me like that?"

"He recognized you, Chris." Somehow Chris knew exactly what Lucia meant by that and she said,

"Is it because of what she said before fainting?"

"Yes."

"And is that good? I mean, if it weren't you wouldn't be smiling, would you? Does it mean I don't need to go through an initiation?"

"Aren't you interested in what he *said*?"

"Of course I am, I was just waiting for you to tell me!"

"*Xangó* and *Yansán* stay always one, in the past, in the present."

"Which means?"

"*Xangó* and *Yansán* are two of our *orishas*. *Yansán* reigns over the seas and rules the storms, *Xangó* reigns over the lightning and the fire and protects justice. Tradition says," Lucia took her time to speak, which made Anne impatient.

"Oh Lucia, come on, speak!"

"According to the Yoruba tradition, *Xangó* and *Yansán* are both bisexual and are many times seen as one." Chris remembered what she read in the magazine in Fortaleza.

"So?" Chris was not really sure what Lucia was saying.

"Joana's *orisha* recognized *your orisha*."

"Lucia, I still don't understand...wait, you're saying...so, who's my *orisha*, then?"

"*Yansán* is Joana's, *Xangó* is yours."

Chris did not even try to understand what she had possibly done in another life to have the spirit of a Yoruba god living inside of her. That understanding would probably take a very, very long time, if not a few lives; her belief in reincarnation having strengthened. What she did know, though, was that they would have to wait until the following morning to find out who was going to wake up; Joana or Sarah.

Before going to sleep, Anne asked Chris, "What are you finally going to do if it's Sarah who wakes up?"

"The same as if it's Joana who wakes up."

"What's that?"

"I'll think I'll stay here for a while."

"Here, in Bahia Esperanza? Aren't you coming back to London?"

"Not for the time being, my friend, and I don't mean to stay here in Bahia Esperanza, I mean Fortaleza."

"But who do you have here?" Anne asked. The sudden news made her briefly forget Chris' feelings for Sarah. "I'm sorry, I'm being really selfish."

"Oh, don't be sorry. We've met Lucia, she's a great woman. I'm sure we can develop this *Candomblé* friendship. Besides, nobody says we can't be friends with Joana too, if it's her who comes back, right? That means I've already got two potentially very good friends here. Besides, Anne, I just don't want to go back there, even if Sarah doesn't come back. Too much has happened."

"I can understand that, but do you really think it's going to be different here?"

"I don't know, but I can try to find out and if I don't feel that I can settle down, I can always look for other options, including London." She looked towards Joana's room and then she said:

"My life has changed dramatically, Anne, you know that, and I'd rather live my new life in a new place." Anne did not look very happy, knowing at some point they would part again.

"Come on, Anne, don't be sad. We can always spend the profit of the new business going to and fro!" She managed to make her friend laugh.

"I really miss Patrick, you know? But I don't feel he's in danger, only away for a while. I have no doubt that he'll be back. Can you explain that?"

"I'm not sure that needs to be explained. I'd rather believe that it's the power of the love you share, which makes you feel strong about him."

"Don't you feel the same for Sarah?"

"Maybe I do." Chris smiled.

CHAPTER 42

The following morning, Chris woke up very early and went down to the beach. It was so easy to enjoy every minute and feel at peace in that small paradise. She sat on the same rock she had been chatting on with Sarah the day before and let her memories flow to finally purge them.

Her homeland, her family, her job, Steve, everything belonged to the past now, as if one big door was closing, the same time a new one was opening, leading to a totally unknown world which she felt eager to live in and explore.

"Granddad, I know you're somewhere out there, listening," she said in a normal voice, "I also know things will happen as they have to, even if, sometimes, it won't happen the way we'd like it to. I just beg you, wherever you are, give me strength to accept whatever happens and to live and enjoy one day at a time, learning what there might be to learn."

"Hey," Chris felt the stab in her stomach, "talking to the sea again?"

"It... it can be very addictive, you know. How are you feeling?"

"I feel good, a bit weak, but good. How are you, *Stranger*?"

Chris jumped off the rock to stand in front of her and muttered, "Sarah?" She could not hide her joy, she did not want to.

"I thought you might be pleased to see me, after two hundred years..." Sarah teased her gently, even though it was obvious she was very tense as well.

"Of course I'm pleased, it's just that... I..." she stammered again, "I don't know what to say, can you remember... everything?"

"I do, every single detail and Chris, there's nothing to say. Not now, at least, things will happen as they have to..." saying which she moved forward and they clung to each other in a long, warm embrace.

The scream coming from the house chilled them both to the bone. Without giving it a second thought, they ran back, but stopped in their tracks before Patrick saw them. He was standing at the front door, holding Lucia from behind. Chris and Sarah hid in the bushes while he forced Lucia to go in.

"We've got to do something," Sarah said.

"Before trying anything silly, let's just think for a minute, okay? Maybe he'll come out again when he finds we're not there."

"I doubt it, Chris. He'll wait for us there, I'm sure."

"But we can't go in just like that. Did you see his hand? I don't know where he got it, but he had a gun!"

"Come!"

"But..." Sarah was already pulling her, almost dragging her through the bushes to the back of the house, from where they would have a good view of the main big window in the lounge. Once there, they saw him, walking around nervously. Anne and Lucia were sitting on the sofa. Chris's memory of Joseph and Elizabeth's cabin came back and made her feel terrified.

"Are you all right? You're white as a sheet!"

"Sorry, I was just remembering..."

"You never told me what really happened there with that man, when I was unconscious, Stranger," Chris wondered if Sarah could read her mind.

"Do you remember that as well?"

"I do remember getting to that cabin after leaving you." She lowered her head, as if apologizing for running away two centuries ago. "The hunter caught me and when I tried to escape he hit me and then you were there, next to me. Will you tell me what happened there?"

"Nothing nice, believe me. Maybe I'll tell you one of these days." She really did not want to remember that horrible experience. Then she added, "*Now* it's very different, Sarah. The hunter then was drunk and unarmed and I could take him by surprise. Patrick is far from being drunk, he's got a gun and he knows we're around. He just needs to wait for us. I can't see how we could take him by surprise."

"I know how," Sarah said and, surprising Chris with a quick movement, she stood up abandoning her hidden position.

"What are you doing?! He'll see you!" She tried to pull her down again, but Sarah let go of Chris's hand and said,

"Trust me, Stranger." Her eyes had a quirky and mysterious brightness. "And be prepared; at my call, walk with me. It's extremely important, though, that you keep your mind busy with the strongest and nicest memories of your friend. Think of all the moments he has been good and loving and go back to those moments over and over again, okay?" She waited for Chris to nod as a sign that she had understood and she closed her eyes. She was facing the lounge window now, fully in sight for any who looked out. Her lips began to move slowly and, a moment later, Chris realized Sarah was praying. She let her arms drop by her sides, her middle fingers touching her thumbs. Something was about to happen. After last night's experience, Chris was ready to see any demonstration of the power the *Candomblé* followers had. Sarah's voice became louder and clearer as she prayed in Yoruba dialect.

Chris did not understand the words but, for some strange reason, she knew exactly what was going on. Sarah was calling for Lucia to unite the strength of their prayers and intercede for Patrick's spirit in front of his *orisha* and their one God of the Universe.

"Mi abure Lucia, mi abure, didé ati gbó temi òrò, gbó temi òrò, Lucia mi abure, didé ati gbó temi òrò…"

Chris moved her eyes from Sarah to the house, where, after a while, she could see Lucia getting up. She could not see Patrick. Sarah repeated her chant and slowly stretched her hand out to Chris, who took it, trembling. She stood up as well, petrified, but Sarah's touch eased her anxiety and she began to remember every single moment of happiness and laughter she had shared with Patrick. She did not know then, but Lucia had asked Anne to do exactly the same.

They walked very slowly to the back door and went in, while both Sarah and Lucia continued their prayers:

"Oide! Oide" Forzas do ar, terra, mar e lume, oide! Santas Companhas, si e verdade que tendes mais poder que a humana xente, eiqui e agora facede cos corpo deste amigo deixe de queimarse no chamas de todo embruxamento e quede asi sua ialma libre dos males, aché gbó, aché gbó!"

Lucia took Chris's other hand and the four of them formed a semi-circle. They approached Patrick, who seemed to have entered a trance and was about to faint. Each second he lost more and more of his strength and his heavy body staggered, while he tried to keep his eyes fixed on the women. He still had the gun in his hand, but was not able to aim it. He was desperately fighting to keep upright, but some invisible power was overwhelming him. He fell on his knees, trying to recover and aim the gun again, but he failed. Finally he collapsed, writhing like an injured wild animal, groaning furiously and loudly, as if asking for help and, at the same time, challenging whatever it was that was attacking him. The gun flew out of his hand.

Anne, who was out of her mind staring at her lover suffering in front of her, tried to move towards him, but Chris prevented her from doing that. Whatever was happening there, they could not interfere. Lucia and Joana were still holding hands and began slowly to come closer to Patrick's body, repeating the same words, over and over again.

If Chris and Anne thought for one moment they had already

seen everything, they were wrong. Strong convulsions attacked Patrick. His head, his legs, his arms and hands were somehow lifted and pulled down again, like a puppet manipulated by clumsy and inexperienced hands. Suddenly his unconscious body was suspended in the air and remained there for a short while until it adopted the foetal position. With his legs and arms pressed to his stomach, he was thrown with ferocity against the wall. Anne screamed, horrified. They were pale and both their mouths fell open, while Lucia and Joana continued their prayers.

Suddenly the windows and door of the house flew open and instinctively the four women hugged each other in one corner of the room to protect themselves from the hurricane winds the gods seemed to be sending. At that point, nobody was able to do anything, they could only wait.

The power of the whirlwind picked up the small table and threw it towards them, hitting Chris. Anne felt her friend fall down, unconscious, but did not have the strength to help her, without getting caught in the stormy winds as well. Lucia and Joana were still praying, even more strongly now.

Time seemed to stop, until all of a sudden everything returned to normal. The wind stopped; the windows and door stopped rattling. Silence reigned again and finally Lucia and Joana seemed to return from their trance.

"Chris!" Sarah saw her lying on the floor and ran to her, trying to bring her round. Anne was already bending over Patrick. Lucia went to the sofa and sank onto it, speechless, her eyes closed.

"Patrick my love, please, please, wake up!" Anne was stroking his face while whispering loving and tender words in his ear. "Just tell me you're back and all right, please wake up, baby." She hugged him against her chest and kissed his forehead, his cheeks, over and over again. Then she kissed his lips, softly first, more desperately passionate afterwards, until she finally felt him kissing her back.

"Anne, sweetheart, what...?" he tried to get up but immediately felt his whole body aching and lay back resting in the arms of the woman he loved so much. "What's going on? Where are we?"

"Don't you remember, baby?" she asked, but he shook his head.

"But you're ok, are you? Are you sure it's you? Are you my Patrick?" she said concerned and he smiled, worried.

"What do you mean is it me? Who else could I be?"

Anne was smiling more relaxed now, "It's a long story, darling, a *very* long story! I'm so happy you're ok!" She kissed him again, almost taking his breath away, but he did not seem to mind.

On the other side of the room, Chris was recovering too. Sarah, holding her head on her lap, was looking at her silently, while resting one of her hands on Chris's chest. Finally Chris opened her eyes and met Sarah's.

"Hey, Stranger, welcome back."

"Hey..." Sarah brushed a loose hair off her forehead, smiling.

"How do you feel, can you stand up?" she asked Chris, stroking her cheek with trembling fingers.

"I'm fine, I've got a terrible headache, but apart from that, I'm fine. I don't want to get up, though," she said shyly, caught by the eyes which had captivated her from the beginning. Sarah smiled, happy.

CHAPTER 43

Anne's cheerful laughter brought them all back to reality. They stood up and came closer to Lucia, who was still resting on the sofa.

"Lucia, are you all right?" Sarah sat down next to her, holding her hand.

"Yes, I'm fine. Everything's over."

"Well, I'm happy that everything's over, but Anne told me something about my not being me for a couple of days. Could you explain what happened and where we are? She also told me," Patrick said, looking at Sarah, "who you are, but I don't remember meeting you, sorry."

"You don't need to apologize, Patrick. I'm sure you'll understand very soon."

"How do you feel, Patrick?"

"My whole body is sore and I feel funny. Yes, funny's the word. I feel as if..."

"As if losing a heavy load of nightmares off your back?"

"Actually yes, that's exactly what I feel." He frowned but smiled at the same time.

"What happened to you and to Jo... Sarah," Lucia had to get used to calling her friend Sarah now, "is that your minds were divided."

"Divided?"

"Yes, divided between the past and the present. We believe," she explained, "that all of us keep in our deep unconscious the memories of our previous lives, which we don't usually remember because we couldn't handle the emotional stress of so many memories. Only those who are strong enough, can remember events that happened to them in other lives."

"You said *were* divided, Lucia," Anne said hopefully.

"Yes, that's why I said as well that everything's over. You were divided. In a previous life, Patrick was that slave hunter, full of hatred and thirst for revenge. His joy and reason to live was to see any slave, any black person, suffer and punished to death. His mind fed these feelings so intensively that they followed him until today."

"Do you mean that while I was this "other" guy here, I could have killed Sarah? I hardly knew her!"

"When you met her at the agency that day you recognized her, Patrick. And she recognized you. The encounter was so shocking, that the hunter took over your mind. Fugitive and slave met again and you had to fulfil your purpose. Sarah flew to the only place where she thought she could feel safe; the place where she'd arrived two hundred years ago. You would have never found her here in Bahia Esperanza if you hadn't followed her in Fortaleza."

"Good God, I'm really sorry," he looked again to Sarah, who only smiled.

"Everything's fine now, Patrick. You must think now, that it was precisely your kindness which helped you."

"That was the reason for the nightmares and for what happened with Paul?" Lucia nodded. Even if she did not know Paul's story, she could guess it.

"What about Sarah, Lucia?" Chris wanted to know.

"Sarah's mind was divided too, but the feelings she carried all her life were not of hatred or rancour."

"Sarah," Anne said, looking at her admiringly but also very curious, "can you remember your life two hundred years ago, when you met Chris?" The only answer she received from Sarah to her question was a gentle nod. She also noticed how Sarah and Chris looked at each other.

Patrick missed it. He was still too worried about the hunter. "Lucia, what will happen to me? I mean the hunter, will he..."

"He's gone, Patrick. And your nightmares are gone as well. Your *orisha* and you are in peace now."

"My *orisha*?"

Lucia explained to him about the *orishas* and filled him in with the previous night's events. She also told him about Chris's and Sarah's *orishas*.

"Who is my orisha?" Patrick wanted to know.

"*Ogún* is your orisha."

"*Ogún*?"

"Yes, the god of war, guardian of the blacksmiths and of those who in one way or another use the iron transformed into tools or weapons."

"Like the hunters did," Patrick said in a whisper.

"That's right. Perhaps you'd like to know that, according to our beliefs, *Ogún* became a bitter enemy of *Xangó* when *Yansán* left him to go with the latter. When you started believing in your nightmares, you gave him the power to come back, you all brought your *orishas* back."

"What will happen now?" Chris was asking this time.

"There will be peace. Our prayers to *Aché*, Spiritual Power of the

203

Universe, god of gods, were heard and *Xangó's* and *Yansán's* strength dragged *Ogún* away, releasing their –your physical bodies. From now on only you are responsible for your acts. Only you decide if you keep your *orishas* as your guardians or give them the power to take over your minds again."

"Does it mean that I could bring the hunter back?"

"Yes, if you allow your thoughts to do so. Your *orisha* exists to give you free will, Patrick, and our thoughts can guide our actions. We all still have something to learn from this. In other words, our *orishas* respect our wishes, our true wishes. If we want peace, we get peace. If we want war, that's exactly what we get."

"My previous life, Lucia, was it part of my karma?" Patrick asked.

"You mean your life with men?" Lucia was so straightforward that she made him blush. He nodded.

"For us, that's just another teaching. Your *feelings* haven't really changed, you've just accepted others. And by accepting, we're given new experiences to learn from. Your experience is now with Anne and the future depends on you, sharing the feelings you have for each other. Our bodies, Patrick, are only useful in this material life."

Every word Lucia was saying, was being engraved on Chris's and Sarah's hearts, as they heard her adding, "What's really important, is what we feel inside and what we do with those feelings, if we use them in a good or a bad way. There're still millions of people who need to understand this, but don't you worry, there is time. There are enough lives for everybody to understand and accept."

Everybody went silent at that moment. Patrick and Anne because they were thinking of Lucia's words. Lucia, Chris and Sarah, because they had felt the same presence outside. Lucia winked at them without the others noticing and they received her message, as if she'd said, "You should go."

They walked down the path to the beach, responding to the call both had heard. When they got there, Chris saw a figure pacing slowly towards them and as he came closer, she recognized him, not looking exactly the same as when she last saw him just before he died. He looked healthy and happy.

"Granddad! But... how can it be?" Chris was startled.

"You're still asking those questions, child?"

"I'm sorry, I'm..." She could not move.

"Would you like to come and give me a hug?"

Chris's eyes were full of tears. She walked slowly and reached for the hands the old man was extending to her. Then, she clung to his neck like she had done so many times when she was a little girl and needed a cuddle from him.

"I've missed you so much!" she cried, "I've needed you so much since you left!"

"You should know by now that I never left you, dearest child and I never will. You should know it has only been my physical body that you've been missing. I came to see you one more time to make sure you know I am close and that it doesn't matter how much our bodies change or how much time passes, I love you and I always will."

"I think I do know it now, Grandfather, and I also know that you've come to say goodbye because you must follow the path you've chosen. I love you, Grandpa, and you'll always be..." she looked at Sarah, "with us."

"I will indeed, precious."

Chris closed her eyes and hugged him one more time. When she opened them again, she saw the beloved old man's silhouette moving away, floating towards the reef, until it grew faint and merged with the mist of the breaking waves.

Sarah, standing silently behind her, put her arms around Chris, who accepted the warm hug, all shyness gone now. Holding hands firmly, Chris allowed herself to lean back on Sarah, tilting her head enough to feel her breath and the warmth of the close contact with her lips.

With the sea as her witness, Chris welcomed into her heart the presence of this woman who, only by encountering her, had opened her eyes and her mind to new teachings, to new knowledge, to new experiences.

Both of them were entering this new path which they would share, following their free will and listening to their hearts. Each of them was eager to know about the experiences of the other: Chris's return to the future and Sarah's odyssey in pursuit of freedom and her new life two hundred years ago.

Neither Chris nor Sarah had ever embraced life as they were doing now, realizing they had been given the gift of understanding and acceptance, the understanding of our free will to choose our lives and the acceptance and endurance to confront the consequences of our acts.

They knew they could build their future by learning from the past whilst enjoying and being grateful for every day.

They knew they were starting another journey, this time in the present, together.